I0744366

DeadWare

Acknowledgements

I owe so much to those helping me. The editing group consists of some amazing authors. We help each other to be better. Thanks to Ted Dreisinger, Larry Jagnow, Chris Baird and Janet McCormick

I have to thank Alexis Powers for helping launch my writing career.

Steve Linebaugh continues to be an inspiration in both the cover design and promotion. Keep kicking my butt, Steve to push promotion. Visit him at www.artbygordon.com.

My editor DeeAnna Galbraith keeps me on track.

Thank you all. You make me better.

R. L. Clayton
www.rlclaytonbooks.com
email at rlclayton10@gmail.com

ISBN 978-1-948015-27-1

Introduction

Cybercrime is a hot topic and likely to get hotter. Millions are extorted through ransomware. Much is not reported. The federal government cyber section fights cybercrime, hacking and fake news against government, not businesses. At some point an international agreement must be achieved to deal with this. Hotbed activity for hacking, ransomware and fake news comes from Russia, N. Korea, Iran, Israel, China and of course, the United States. What would drive the world to meet and address this? Read on.

DEADWARE
by R.L. Clayton

Prologue

Premier sniper Kiki Russell sat well back from the boarded-up window in the Saint Petersburg, Russia flat studying a wide- screen monitor sitting on the bare wooden floor. It was connected to a remote-controlled, tripod-mounted camera with a twenty-power telescopic lens mounted on the roof disguised as a crumpled vent. Twelve blocks away, a man emerged onto the roof of a three-story apartment building. He was not remarkable to look at–thin, scraggly beard, shaggy brown hair, pasty white complexion from too many hours indoors.

She could clearly see his black tee shirt with the image of a dragon devouring the world on it. He shook a cigarette from a pack that had been rolled in his sleeve, crumpled the empty pack, tossed it on the ground and lit up using a Zippo style lighter pulled from his tight black jeans.

She shook her head. Everybody in Russia smoked. Leon Ivanov, nickname Dragon Boy, was her assignment, and it wouldn't be cigarettes that killed him. He didn't look like one of the top hackers in Russia, but then, what do they look like?

"We capture him for Nick?" Kiki nodded. "Doesn't look too hard," said Zyra, sitting in a straight-back chair to her left.

Zyra was a Russian-born ex-Mossad agent who had contracted with Kiki and Nick several times before. She was tall, very slender with hair cut close to her scalp, black skin and blacker eyes. Calling her deadly was like describing a Mac truck as a pickup. She liked close work with a knife, watching as the light of life faded from her victim's eyes.

Chapter 1

Kiki Russell and Dr. Nick Sabino sat in ex-CIA Director David Kennedy's living room watching the lights glitter across Lake of the Woods in Virginia as darkness pushed the western glow away. David's house was two-story, fronted on the lake with its own dock. The floor-to-ceiling window and sliding glass door was one wall of the large room. Dark paneling and book shelves lined the other walls. A large oriental area rug covered the oak flooring.

"I've always liked this place," said Kiki, raising the tumbler of McCallum as a salute. Her dark brown hair was cut below her ears, her tan skin the result of mixed heritage. Her face was pretty, until her penetrating gaze focused on you. It could be intimidating.

"Not as pleasant in the winter," responded David with a laugh. "I'd rather be in your house in

Arizona then. Refill?" he asked rising. Kiki watched his uneven gait as he took her glass to the bar.

"How's the leg?" Nick asked, brushing his dark hair from his eyes. David had lost his leg in a car bomb attack several years ago. Only because Nick knew this was it noticeable. "Looks like you've lost some weight."

"Always the doctor, aren't you?" David replied. "Yeah, pushing back from the training table, so to speak." He handed Nick and Kiki their glasses.

"Arizona's nice with wind-factor temps at seventy," Nick chuckled. "Not so good in July. Even though it's nearly October, it's still a little warm for you northerners. Thanks for the invite, but why did you ask us here?" asked Nick.

"As you know, cybercrime has hit America hard. If it's not ransomware, it's hacking to harvest personal information that's sold for identity theft. Hacking into business email accounts has been a disaster. Our government has embarked on a concentrated effort to stem those attacks."

"According to the media, there has been success," said Kiki.

DeadWare

The *Fantasmas* attack cybercrime, but not electronically. Brutal attacks on the cyber community spread from Saint Petersburg to Moscow, where the *Fantasmas* attack the Russian Cyber Command losing two of their members. After a harrowing escape, they return to the US.

Former president Ron Carson chairs a United Nations conference to establish international laws regarding cybercrime to prevent electronic warfare from becoming kinetic–a shooting war. Russia mounts retaliatory attacks against the NSA.

UN cybercrime meetings are halted when the Israeli Cyber center is bombed. Israeli air force attacks on Iran are a disaster. Arab forces mass near the Golan. Israel strikes first, but again, it's a trap. Ron Carson brokers a ceasefire, but Israel must relinquish the occupied lands. United Nations troops are stationed in Israel and Palestine to ensure the peace holds. Both the Arabs and the Israelis begin to dislike the UN more than each other.

Ron Carson's message is that squabbles, no matter how ancient, will not be allowed to foment war.

Also by R. L. Clayton

The Evolution River Series
Sea Species
The Envoy
The Genesis

The Dead Series
Dead & Dead For Real
Dead Reckoning
Dead Again
Risen from the Dead
Dead Prey
Dead but Not Gone
DeadWare

Historical Novel
Wings of the WASP

Children's Book
with Abby Pickering
Penelope the Pooting Spider

"Money paid into cyber accounts has been recovered, warrants issued, but not nearly to the degree portrayed. The truth is billions are lost to cybercrime. Banks do not report the magnitude because of the loss of confidence that would follow. Wall Street puts a lot of effort in covering up the extent. Companies hit by ransomware quietly pay. The cyber security branch can trace hacks and attacks. The federal Cyber guys want everything reported, but as you know, info doesn't leak out, it gushes. They can issue arrest warrants, but without cooperation from the governments of the countries where the criminals are, nothing happens. Government hands are tied by laws. You know that."

Kiki nodded, taking a big sip of her drink, as she stared at him. "Can't pressure be brought to bear?"

"The largest bastion of cybercrime is Russia, much of it government sponsored. Iran, Ukraine and China make up most of the rest. North Korea used to be big, but they haven't done much since we wiped out their center during the Bio-Cyber War. All have government agencies actively engaging in cyber-attacks on the United States. We do the same. The National Security Administration monitors the world's electronic communications, but the world is a huge place. It's the silent cold war going on around us."

Kiki and Nick met his eyes, the unasked question hanging in the air.

"I've been asked by a friend representing a consortium of some of the biggest names in American industry and business for help in coming up with a plan to combat this scourge."

Kiki's laughter echoed around the room. "And you thought of us."

"After your success in Mexico with the cartels, yes, I did. Your bosses got what they wanted in dealing with some of the nastiest people on Earth. You and your team did that while eluding cartels, the police and the Company's attempts to kill you."

"They very nearly succeeded," noted Nick.

"Someday I'd like to hear how you got well. Miracle doesn't begin to describe your recoveries."

Kiki's lips were pressed together. "Maybe someday we'll be able to tell you," said Nick.

David shrugged, being familiar with need-to-know. "We've worked together since the start of the Bio-Cyber War. Your skill got you the well-earned reputation as the best sniper in the world." He nodded at Kiki. "While acting as a consultant with my old cronies at the CIA, I personally observed the frustration you wreaked on their Mexican drug operations." He smiled at them. "Yeah, you came to mind. Any ideas?"

"You know my solution with most problems is to shoot. It saves a lot of worthless negotiations," said Kiki.

"It's on the table." There was no humor in David's face. "This is like the war on terror except it's electronic and economic. Fighters aren't crossing borders physically, but they are here."

Nick's mouth hung open. "Surely, more pressure can be brought on the governments to control this without killing anybody." He glanced at Kiki, noticing the eager look on her face.

"Like with terrorists, they can't hide behind friendly borders. It's time to go after these bastards," Kiki was bubbling at the prospect. "I can contact the other members of the *Fantasmas*. "We could put that team back together."

"I won't ask who makes up your team. I need deniability."

"Ron has to be kept out of it completely, I

suppose," murmured Nick, referring to ex-president Ron Carson while staring at David.

"Striving to become the first world leader, he cannot have any knowledge. We feel the opening theater of our operation should be Russia. It will send a message."

"Who's we?" asked Nick.

David stared at him silently.

"With Russia as the TO, you will face more sophisticated opposition than in Mexico. We will support you as best we can from behind the scenes. The Company has many fingers in the Bear's den, but direct support cannot happen. Equipment and intelligence will largely be the extent. The gangs are every bit as vicious as the Mexican cartels, but have stronger control over the police and the military. Their government-sponsored operations will have full protection."

"Are you trying to discourage us?" laughed Kiki.

"Other than patriotic loyalty, why would we do this?" asked Nick.

"Ask whatever fees you want. They will be paid."

"Who besides you knows about us?"

"My friend is the spokesman for the consortium. He only knows we are addressing the problem. You and I will observe all security protocols." David handed them two phones. "These have heavy encryption. You know the routine."

"Give us all the intelligence you have on the Russian operations. We'll go over everything, put our plan together and give you a list of what we need."

"Who's this unnamed man?" asked Nick.

"He's an officer in a large corporation, one of an even larger group. I met him years ago before I joined the Company. I've had him vetted. He checks out." David smiled at Kiki. "He was a Marine sniper. You'd like him. If you ever meet. It's best if you know nothing else about him."

"A brother! I like him already."

"We'll leave for Arizona tomorrow and get started," said Nick.

"You could work from here," offered David.

Nick shook his head. "Bob and Kath Meisenburg are there, and I know the security. We'll start from my house."

Chapter 2

"Did you have any success?" asked Frank Pickett as he raised his Sierra Nevada Torpedo to his lips. The music and noise in the bar assured their conversation was private. Frank was at least six-feet- four, slim and fit. His face was kind until it wasn't. He had intense focus as a result of sniper training. His face wasn't kind then.

"We'll see. I think so." David held up his hand to forestall any questions. "This will be our last face-to-face meeting until this is over. If we need something, I'll get in touch." He handed Pickett a slip of paper. "That's an account number for you to deposit payments. Nobody else can know."

"I just put money into this account?"

"How you come up with the money is up to you, but this will be incredibly dangerous. Those we're going up against will hunt you down and kill you, your wife, your family and anybody else they even think is involved.""""

"Somehow, I have to have some accounting for where this money's going. I have to know if there's any success."

David frowned. "That's not how this will work. You will know of any success when the cybercrime issues start to disappear. The Russian mob has tendrils everywhere. They will pull out all stops to find information and cut this off. You and I are the only ones I trust." He looked into Pickett's eyes.

"My team doesn't know your name in case they fall into mob hands. Do not even tell the others you are dealing with there is a program going.

Pickering nodded. "We need major misdirection. We'll set up a big program to go after the cyber currency end. We'll also form a cyber security network co-op, pool resources, hire several firms. We can bury your costs within that budget."

"Your military is showing," chuckled David. "Everything has to be face-to-face conversations if we meet again. No telephones, no email. I would also suggest you step up personal security for yourselves and families. Make plans where to go with your family if something goes wrong." Frank's mouth dropped open. "Yeah, this is serious. These people are without conscience. "

Frank sat still for a few moments. "There is no theater of operations for this, is there?"

David shook his head. "Be sure you want to do this. No Mulligans here. It will get very bloody."

"We have to keep the blood on their side." Frank frowned. "Never thought I'd be in this position. I pictured myself sitting behind my expansive desk and telling people what to do."

"It's not too late to pull out." noted David.

Pickett shook his head. "We have to do something."

David handed him a phone. "Burner phone. Use this to contact me, nothing else. If it rings, pick the son of a bitch up. It'll be me. If it's not, RUN!"

Chapter 3

Sol Ayub stood by the short wall looking west from Nick's patio near Casa Grande, Arizona. He was medium height and fit with curly brown hair and a tan complexion. The mountains in the distance were hazy purple in the early morning sun. He turned back to the *Fantasmas* group seated around the pool. "This countryside much like my home in Israel, desert, mountains, patches of green where crops grow. Since our contract in Mexico, I have been able to spend much time home. But the sedentary life is not for me. My wife does not understand." He glanced at Dawn Bordowitz Ayub.

"Hah," laughed Dawn. "You think you're the only one bored with family life." She had a model's slim body and her shoulder-length straight blonde hair moved as she shook her head. She could be on any fashion mag as the cover girl.

Sasha Belikova chuckled. She was Russian-born, blonde and well-built. She and her brother, Ilia, immigrated from Russia to Israel. Their language skills as native Russian speakers and familiarity with the country made them attractive as Mossad agents. As an Olympic skier for Israel and very pretty, Sasha had easy access to many places when she returned to Sochi to compete. She rose from the table to join Sol, carrying her coffee. "It is like much of Israel. We," she gestured toward her brother Ilia and her mate, Zyra, "were also getting bored, though Ilia has been to Russia for the last few months."

"I've never been to Russia," said Bob. "Not sure I want to go, but we," he glanced at his wife, Kathy, "will do it for you," he said, gracing Nick and Kiki with a smile.

"I appreciate your offer, but you are much more valuable here. Yesterday, Nick and I were approached by David Kennedy. He is a retired CIA director," she explained to Sol. "We worked with him during the Bio-Cyber War."

"You mentioned him during our mission in Mexico. I remember."

"He also fed us intel in Mexico that saved us

some grief," added Nick, "even though he was working for the Company as a contractor at the time. We trust him."

"He is offering us a contract similar to the job we had in Mexico, but instead of drug cartels, the targets are cyber criminals."

"Where?" asked Ilia, a frown on his face.

"Most of the cybercrime comes from Russia," said Nick. "We'll start in Saint Petersburg."

"I spend the last four months in Russia. A dangerous place, more than Mexico where the government hired us. In Russia, it is the government we oppose. Their agreements with cyber hackers are they don't attack any Russians, they are protected. Hackers have schools. There are many. Violators disappear."

"You sound familiar with the situation," said Kiki.

Ilia glanced at Sol. The shake of his head was almost imperceptible.

Nick held up a hand. "Don't tell us more. We don't want you to have to kill us." The joke fell flat.

"There are private companies and independents operating there," Ilia continued. "They pay a tax to operate, mostly in the ransom and ID theft area."

"That's extortion," noted Dawn.

"Such is business in that country," stated Ilia, shaking his head. "Russian government branches also initiate cyber-attacks, though more against other country's government operations–federal, state and local. Unlike the smaller hackers, they are not in it for the money."

Sol coughed and stared at Kiki. "Until you said Russia, I was okay to bring Dawn in. Not so now. Too dangerous."

"Not your decision," snapped Dawn glancing from Sol to Kiki. "I'm in whether Sol says so or not."

"How we convince major businesses to shut down?" asked Zyra. "Make dangerous to operate, of course." She laughed. "That I know how to do."

Kiki gazed at Ilia for a moment, considering what he'd said. "Each area must be addressed differently." He nodded. "Our plan is to go after the hackers," she continued. "Indies we do individually, corporate we do hackers, but then go after bosses, government…I'm not sure."

"We work up food chain of command," said Sol. "Mossad gives us experience in doing that."

Ilia, Sasha and Zyra agreed."

"Indies first," said Zyra. "Easy targets. We make them into messages to stop. Not attract same attention as corporate bosses or government."

"When we move against them, we will be hunted." Sol's expression was grim. "Best we are gone or have deep hiding place."

* * *

"It feels good to have the team back together," said Kiki as she undressed for bed and donned a robe.

"I know you're excited to be working as a sniper again," said Nick, "but you like it more than me. I'd be happy working with my medical practice, helping patients."

"Nick, you know we need you. I need you." She glanced at him as her mind began to prickle. He nodded back acknowledging he felt it too. It was the Director, an otherworldly being that fed on human emotions. They had first encountered it when fighting Arab terrorists years ago. Both Nick and Kiki despised the creature, but it had imparted useful information to them, even saving their lives.

"Hello, Katherine and Nicholas. I have missed you, my favorite humans, this last year."

"Your only human contacts," corrected Kiki in her mind. "We hoped you were gone."

"Ha ha. I do not go anywhere. I am everywhere. Your venture into Russia will bring me many tasty meals of fear and hatred. For that I thank you, but I must warn you. This is dangerous. I would not want to lose my only human friends."

"We're not your friends," said Nick.

"I think of you as such, at least as much as I can. The brutality of the Russians brings me much pleasure, so be careful. Ta ta."

It was gone. Nick and Kiki stared at each other. "What's different than before?" asked Kiki with a shrug. As she put her arms around Nick, she shrugged off the robe and pulled him toward the bed.

Chapter 4

The apartment house Ilia rented for them in Saint Petersburg was ready for the wrecking ball, but that cost money. The only tenants were homeless, and with no utilities and frosty winds blowing through the broken windows, they'd moved out for the winter. Boarding up doors and windows, repairing the roof and cleaning up the detritus left behind took two months. During that time, the inside was cleaned, solar panels and satellite dishes installed on the roof, the basement set up for generators and new wiring run everywhere. The peeling paint and wallpaper were left. They weren't really moving in.

The old coal tunnel in the basement from the

Neva River was cleared and used to move equipment in without being seen. It was secured by steel doors at each end. On the outside, the building looked much as it had before—a derelict.

"Are we ready to move against the Indies?" asked Sol.

Zyra smiled. "We capture Dragon Boy tonight. He goes to club on Friday. Many other hackers there. Today is Friday."

"Nick, are you set up to question him?"

"The Isolation Chamber is up and ready. Fresh chemicals stocked." He looked at Dawn. "What has your research shown in Ivanov's background?"

"Though his parents were Russian Orthodox, he has no attachment to the church."

"Is he agnostic?"

"More atheist from what I've found."

"Was he close to his parents?"

"Once he showed a talent for computers, the state whisked him away to a school. He visited his parents only a few times, though attended their funerals."

"Any women in his life?" asked Sasha.

"He does go to the club but doesn't seem to have a steady. Leaves with different girls. Likes his vodka, but all Russians do.”

“Are these working girls?”

“Sometimes. They go to hotels. Those are probably the working girls or they are married. Other times he takes them back to his apartment.”

“Any siblings?” asked Nick.

“He has a sister in Moscow. They don’t talk. There was some kind of spat between them. Nobody knows what it was about.”

“How’d you find all this out?” asked Sol.

“I’m a reporter for *Izvestia*. I did online Zoom interviews using Russian translator software. We’re doing a story on Dragon Boy. People love to talk about the local hero.”

“Shit!” exclaimed Sol. “You talked to people. They will remember you when he disappears.”

“How else was I supposed to get information? There was nothing online. Besides, there’s no link back to me.”

“Okay,” said Nick. “Dawn, you don’t go outside. Nobody can see you. We can’t take a chance. If you are recognized and captured, we’re blown.”

“What about Sasha and Zyra when they go out to nab him?”

"Enough of this! We have to move forward," said Kiki.

"We'll bring him here tonight," said Sol. "I'll drive the van so Nick can sedate Ivanov. Dawn, monitor calls. Block any reports of a kidnapping. Zyra, Sasha, don't kill anyone. We don't need cops sniffing around."

"We know Russia. We know what to do," said Sasha.

* * *

Zyra wore a backless red dress accentuating her slender form. With black stiletto heels, she towered over most of the men in the club. With Sasha in a low-cut silk turquoise dress, heads turned as they wove through the crowd to the bar. "Don Julio, neat," ordered Zyra.

The bartender stared at them and snickered. "We got beer and vodka. Some wine, red or white. What you want?"

Sasha laughed, reached into her bag and pulled out a bottle of the amber tequila. "Put this behind your bar. Save it for us."

The bartender chuckled as he placed two glasses on the bar and poured their drinks. "No charge."

They turned and surveyed the bar. Techno music blasted, lights flashed in a seemingly random pattern. People gyrated on the dance floor, some were couples. Two women in bikinis danced on raised platforms. Tables ringed the floor and booths were against the wall. Smoke was as dense as a London fog.

Zyra glided through the crowd, Sasha behind her. She stopped at a table where Ivanov sat with two friends. She regarded him. "We sit here."

The two friends glared at her as Ivanov shooed the men away, making room for the two head-turning women. "Haven't seen you before," he said.

"Nice emblem," Zyra said, pointing at the golden dragon hanging from a chain around his neck. His black silk shirt highlighted the golden jewelry as the ruby eyes sparkled in the flashing lights.

"We're new," said Sasha.

"You don't know who I am?"

"Asshole with dragon chain," said Zyra.

Ivanov stared at her and burst out laughing. "I like these girls. Where are you from?"

"South," stated Zyra. "Where you from?"

Again, he laughed. "Right here. I grew up here. What are you drinking?" He pointed at their glasses.

"Don Julio," said Zyra. "Want a taste?"

Ivanov reached across her and picked up the glass. He took a tentative sip. "That's tequila, really smooth tequila. I didn't know they served that here."

"They don't," said Sasha. "We brought our own. Want some?"

"Sure."

Sasha signaled to the barkeeper with three fingers and pointed at the glasses. He nodded back at her.

"Why are you here?"

"Tourist," replied Zyra.

"And maybe some work," said Sasha.

"What kind of work do you do?"

"Pest control," said Zyra, a thin smile on her lips.

"We take care of rats," added Sasha. "What kind of work do you do?"

"You really haven't heard of me?" Both women shook their heads. "I work with computers."

"I order stuff online." Sasha held her arms out to give him a view of her dress.

"And you," Ivanov looked at Zyra.

She held her arms out. "I buy at thrift store."

Ivanov laughed so hard his face turned red. "Where are you staying?" he finally gasped out.

"No place yet," answered Zyra. She held up her empty glass.

"Let's go back to my place. It's not far. We can walk."

"Another drink first," said Zyra. "We have car with toothbrush."

While Ivanov was again laughing, Sasha signaled the bartender for more drinks and the bottle.

Chapter 5

"Change of plans," said Ilia. "They're going to Ivanov's apartment. Might be an opportunity. Any problems, and we rush the place."

Kiki laughed. "Any trouble would be saving Ivanov's life."

Ilia chuckled. "There is that. I'll leave the van close so they can get it. I'm going to his apartment house to watch their arrival. Bob, are you up on this?"

"Yeah," he responded through the satellite link, "got tracking and video. This could be a great chance to see what he operates."

* * *

Sasha and Zyra held Ivanov up as they staggered from the club. Not being used to tequila, he was in trouble. "Here's my van," announced Sasha. "You ride in front. If you gotta puke, say so or I leave you on the street. Got it, Leon?"

"How did you know my name was Leon?"

Zyra laughed. "All Russians called Ivan or Leon, but I like Leon. What's your real name?"

"Leon." They laughed for several blocks.

"Where are we going?" asked Sasha.

"Turn right next block," slurred Leon. "I own building on corner. Parking in garage beside building." He held up a fob. "Door will open."

They parked between a red Ferrari and a Toyota Land Cruiser. "Nice cars," said Sasha. "Computer work must pay well."

"The work I do, yeah."

With help from both of them, they approached the elevator. Leon punched keys twice, leaning closer each time to see better. "God Dammit!" The third time the doors opened to a mahogany paneled elevator with brass, maybe gold, trim. Leon held his watch next to the controls and the doors closed.

"Magic watch?" asked Zyra.

"Can't be too careful," slurred Leon, his voice barely understandable. "What was that stuff you gave me?"

"Some of the best tequila in the world," responded Sasha. "It's a learned taste."

"Yeah, I learned–kicked my ass."

The elevator door opened into a spacious and well-furnished living room. Sasha stepped out first, looked around and turned to Leon. "This is nice. Who's your decorator?" The walls were paneled in oak, the furniture had an American southwestern flair, with heavy oak base and multicolored fabric. The floor was Saltillo tile. "You like American western?"

"Yeah, it's not sterile like most furnishings in Russia, you know chrome and vinyl. Bedroom is French." He leered at them through bloodshot eyes.

"Let's have another drink." Sasha held up the half-full bottle of Don Julio. She went to the bar and poured three glasses. "You got music here? Not that techno shit, hurts my ears, something we can dance to." She swayed back and forth to pretend music.

"Got link?" asked Zyra, holding up her phone. "I have some."

Leon went to his desk. The whole top tilted up becoming a computer screen. He typed in commands and nodded to her. She brought up some salsa on her phone. Music blared from hidden speakers. The two women danced across the floor toward him. Each took an arm and they moved to the music. "This goes with tequila," said Zyra. The song ended.

"More of the Don," cried Sasha. Zyra poured. By the end of the next song, Leon could barely stand. They helped him to the couch where he collapsed. His eyes closed.

"Hey," said Sasha. "You awake?" No movement.

Zyra put her hand to her ear. "You get anything?"

"I'm in," said Bob. "Everything's open. I'm going to clone his drive and make a connection. Anything he does will come to us."

"Good. Let's find this French bedroom," said Zyra as she hoisted the unconscious man over her shoulder in a fireman's carry. "He better not puke on me."

Chapter 6

"What did we get?" asked Sol.

There was a short pause as Bob was still in Arizona. "We got pretty much everything. His address book is full of other hackers including some in the government. I got his cryptocurrency account and password. Shit, this boy's way rich. He's obviously in it for the fun now. I have his records of who he's ransomed, who paid, who didn't pay and who he's waiting on."

"This is great! We can use his computer to find next targets. So, I tell girls not to harm him. We keep using him. Others not be so lucky."

Bob chuckled. "This also gives me a chance to introduce a new virus I've been working on. It will give us access to whoever he communicates with, and it will turn the computer into a weapon."

"What you mean?"

"We'll have the ability to turn on the sound system so that an ultrasonic tone is emitted. Can't be heard by human ears, but after time will result in migraine headaches for anyone near. Headphones can make it real bad."

"Nobody can hear it?"

"Way beyond the range of human hearing. Dogs, maybe. I haven't tested it with them. You going to have the girls bug the place?"

"Risky. If the place is swept, he could find the equipment."

"What about holo mics on his windows?"

"Have to be located within a few hundred meters. We put those in van and park near when something going to happen."

"Okay, keep me linked in. I don't speak Russian. The translator program isn't always accurate, so I'll need an interpreter."

"I tell Kiki. Maybe she can do something."

* * *

Leon Ivanov woke with a hangover. It wasn't the worst he'd ever had, but justified medication. Rolling over with great effort, he tried to sit up, only to groan and fall back. There was a knock on the door. When he was able to focus, a pretty blonde wearing one of his tee shirts was walking toward him. She was short, making it long, almost to her knees. In her hand was a cup of coffee.

"Thought you might need this. You were pretty good last night." She laughed. "Did you take a little blue pill or are you always that good?"

He put the cup to his lips cautiously sipping the hot liquid. *I should remember that, but.... I remember getting back here with two girls and Mexican music but after that everything's a blank.*

"Zyra's in the kitchen making some breakfast, eggs and kippers with black bread. It's all we could find. I had to borrow one of your shirts. Hope you don't mind." She swayed as she handed him two tablets. "Aspirin. I carry it with me. We should be ready to eat after you shower."

He watched her turn and walk away, his stare on her shapely butt moving his tee shirt in a way that stirred him. With a grunt he rose and headed for the bathroom.

* * *

"Hope you like scrambled eggs," said Zyra, her back to him as she stood at the stove. "Not much groceries. Don't you eat? Find lots of junk stuff. Not for growing boy for breakfast."

Leon gaped at the way another of his tee shirts wasn't quite long enough for the tall Zyra. "You sound like my mother."

"Not look like her, I bet. You good last night, for both of us. Maybe we do that again. More Don Julio in van."

Ouch. Though the food made his stomach turn over, he forced himself to eat. His head felt better from the shower and the aspirin. As he cleaned his plate he became his normal self–almost.

"You still have link?" asked Zyra holding up her phone. "Maybe more music. Not salsa. Something for throbbing head," she laughed.

He walked into his living room/work station. The desk and computer looked exactly as he would normally leave them though he remembered nothing about shutting it down. He brought up his management screen. Nothing seemed amiss. No messages, no contacts, no one had accessed it. A couple of clicks later and some soft moonwalk music came from the speakers.

"I have work to do, and I need to be alone." He looked at the two women.

"Da. Us too," said Sasha. "We'll change clothes and be out of your hair. Maybe see you at the club again."

"I only go there on Friday."

"Okay, if we still in town, maybe then," said Zyra with a shrug.

Shit, he couldn't let them go this easy. He needed another night, one he'd remember. "You got a phone number?"

"On computer," said Zyra, holding it up. "Remember?"

"Yeah, okay. I'll give you a call. Next time, I supply the booze."

"Better than vodka," said Zyra.

"Better groceries too," laughed Sasha. "We do know how to cook."

Chapter 7

"David," said Kiki, "we need a little help." She was in the apartment house basement they'd set up as a command center. The wide-screen mounted on the wall was blank. They only used video when necessary. Bob said it was easier to encrypt smaller data messages. "Only a few of the team are fluent in Russian." From the Saint Petersburg apartment building, the *Fantasmas"* signals were scrambled and satellite only. Very hard to detect and read.

"Not to worry. The Company has the latest interpreter software. I'll send you the program. You can load it onto a thumb drive and use it with your ear buds. How's everything going?"

"Better than we'd hoped. We have an *in* on one of the best indie hackers. We'll set up some targets later today."

"Be careful. I have my NSA contacts listening

for any indication of attacks on hackers."

"Thanks for that. You won't see any results in the business world for a while. There are a lot of hackers here."

"We know."

"I'm sure there will be talk after the first few hits, when the hacker community figures out they're targets. Their response and that of their protectors will be interesting. It's big business over here. At some point, they will wake up to the fact there is a war going on, and it's gone kinetic, not electronic. When that happens, the feces will hit the ventilator, and we'll have to spend time defending. It'll cut down on our activity, so tell your contact to be patient."

"He knows. The translator software is on the way. Be careful."

* * *

The large monitor on the wall in the basement showed a map of Saint Petersburg. Red dots and circles were scattered across it. Bob's voice came over the speaker. "The dots are indie hackers we've identified from Leon's address book and our IP address monitor. The largest circle is the Internet Research Association building. That's the headquarters for hacking. They do internet fake news, misinformation, business and government hacking. It the troll center for both mob and government. What's your plan?"

Sol looked at Ilia. "IRA building is interesting. Maybe we do something there, but we go after indies first. Hit on one far away from us first. Capture hacker bring back here and question. Make more plans from what we learn." Sol pointed at a red dot in the town of Tosno, outside of Saint Petersburg. "Here first. Good roads, only thirty-five kilometers away. Bob, need best satellite map of town."

The equivalent of Google Maps came up, but with better resolution. The dot became a house in a moderate neighborhood. "If you park the van within two kilometers, launch a vulture drone. We'll watch and listen for a while," said Bob.

"Good to know coming and going from house," said Sol, glancing at his watch. "Late afternoon now. Team of Zyra, Sasha, Ilia go into house when quiet and dark. Kiki set up cover. Nick as driver and doctor to sedate. Leave in one hour." Sol studied the map. "Launch and retrieve drone in forest area on highway going in. Park at Dixy store.

It is close and won't be noticed."

Two hours later, they had a real-time view. It was early evening. The neighborhood was upscale and could pass for any U.S. residential area with nice houses and yards. Few cars were parked on the street, probably in garages. The drone was high overhead, looking like a large erne or small eagle, common in this area. Two people left the house and drove away. They returned an hour later with bags. "Grocery day," said Zyra. "Maybe something yummy."

"I'm picking up cell phone conversation and an internet connection," said Bob. Russian voices came over the speaker.

"Talking about a big score," said Sasha. "Ransom was paid."

"Who are they talking to?" asked Nick.

"I can get the number," said Bob.

"It is boss demanding his share," said Sol.

"Can you track that phone?" asked Nick.

"I can ping off some towers to get close," answered Bob.

"We go into house in two hours. It will be dark." Sol looked at Nick. "We find out more with your questions."

Nick closed his eyes and sighed. His shoulders slumped at the thought of another interrogation.

Chapter 8

Zyra crept closer to the rear of the house. A bluish light shone around a window blind. The rest of the house looked dark. "What goes on inside?" she asked over her com.

"Our hacker is online at the moment," said Bob. "He's trying to break into the database of a hospital in Atlanta using Pegasus. It's only a matter of time before he's in."

"Any other stuff going on?"

"Nothing electronic. I have three other heat signatures in two rooms, unmoving."

"Da," Zyra's voice came over the com units. "Sasha, Ilia, ready at front?"

"Yes."

"Good. Kiki, anything on street?"

"Houses dark, streets empty."

"I take lit room. You two take other rooms."

"Remember, Zyra, we want him alive," said Kiki.

"Da. I got it. One, two, three. We go!" She smashed in the door and ran toward the room with the lights.

Standing in the doorway, she saw a figure wearing headphones sitting in front of a large monitor, the only light in the room. Zyra tapped her on the shoulder. The girl jumped up and spun. Her mouth dropped open at the sight of the tall black woman, silenced pistol in one hand, knife in the other. Zyra shook her head, knife at her lips as the young woman inhaled to scream. Her mouth snapped shut. She knelt, hands behind her head, at Zyra's gesture.

Ilia appeared at the door. "A pair in one-bedroom, single man in the other. Asleep."

Zyra held up a black bag, zip ties and a gag. "Take her to van." She watched, gun trained, as Ilia tied and gagged the girl. The black bag went over her head. As Ilia guided the girl past Zyra, she turned and walked down the hall.

Sasha stood outside one bedroom door. She held up two fingers and pointed at another. Zyra nodded and stepped to the door. Silently she entered the room, lit only by moonlight through the open window. The couple was naked. The man was on his back, his hand resting on her. She was on her side, back to him. Soft snores came from them. She approached the bed, leaned across the woman, grabbed the man's hair and slit his throat in a single movement. The woman sat up completely confused. Her eyes widened as the blood geysered from her lover. Her mouth opened to scream, but Zyra's knife flashed across her throat. She gurgled, as her hand tried to staunch the flood.

Zyra quickly rifled the man's pants, grabbing his wallet and IDs. She picked up the woman's purse and stepped back to see if there were anything else of value. Yes, the phones. Stuffing everything into a pillowcase, she turned to leave.

In the hallway, she joined Sasha as she exited from the other room. Together, they returned to the computer, gathered it and all the drives they could find. At the van, they stashed the equipment around the unconscious woman lying on the floor. Nick had sedated her.

"Wait," said Zyra. She returned to the house. After five minutes, she was back with two grocery bags. "Waste not," she said.

"Did you kill the others?" asked Nick.

"Send message," answered Zyra.

He let out a breath with a soft moan and shook his head.

* * *

They retrieved the drone on the drive back to St Petersburg. In the storage building next to the coal tunnel, Ilia helped Nick load the unconscious woman onto the gurney he'd left there. They pushed it toward the insulated room they'd built in one corner. Nick went inside, turned on lights and checked the monitors mounted on the walls. An easy chair with a laptop alongside a folding chair were the only pieces of furniture. In one corner was a black coffin-like box, hoses, tubes, and wires connecting it to the monitors and a laptop. The box seemed to suck the light out of the room. He shuddered as he glanced at it. *God, I hate these interrogations.*

"Ilia, I need help with her." They stripped her and put her on a scale. She was small, forty-two kilos. Her blonde hair was cut short and framed a pretty face. Nick removed the crucifix from her neck, stared at it in his hand for a few seconds and went to the computer to enter data.

"I never see you do this before," Ilia said. "Tell me about it."

Nick nodded toward the black box. "That's an Isolation Chamber. Once inside, she will have no sensory input." He opened the lid. "That brine is body temperature. She will float, not touching anything. There is no light, and it has sound suppressors so she will hear nothing, even if she screams. She will, in essence, have left this world."

"Why?" asked Ilia.

"Better if you see." He placed sensor pads on the girl and IVs in both arms. A bone microphone was taped to the side of her head. Together, they placed her in the Chamber. Nick checked one display showing the usual functions–pulse rate, blood pressure, body temperature, respiration. The other monitor showed brain activity.

"Let's go upstairs to see what Dawn has found out about her."

"It's okay to leave her here?"

"She won't go anywhere."

* * *

Dawn sat at the computer with the girl's ID on the table. "Her name is Kira Siderov, twenty-one, attended the local computer hacking school. Her home address is in Veliky Novgorod, about ninety miles away. The address is her parents, so guess she's single. Parents are Russian Orthodox, but I think she quit attending church when she moved out. A couple of receipts indicate she's been living in Tosno about a year."

"You find anything on her computer, Bob?" asked Sol.

"Her Bitcoin account is about $200,000 equivalent, most of that transferred over the last three months. Her latest hack was a trucking firm in Dallas. They paid the ransom. She has a file full of personal data from a medical insurance company, and sold credit card info to a Russian mobster. She actually listed him as that."

"What's in her address book?" asked Kiki.

"It's loaded, hundreds of addresses. Some personal information on those she's familiar with, though not many. She hasn't been in the game that long. Some of the addresses are a series of x's. Don't think she knew the names. Those could be really bad guys. She did have Leon Ivanov in there with stars. Think she had a relationship with him."

"I'm not sure what else I can find out in the

interrogation," said Nick, "but we'll do her."

"Maybe not much," said Sol, "but she is the message."

Chapter 9

Nick sat in the easy-chair, the laptop on a small table in front of him. Ilia sat next to him. "I need to use the Russian translation program David sent me. If something's wrong, tell me." He inserted an earbud holding the other out. Ilia nodded and inserted it.

"I'm going to bring her around and talk to her. If you have questions or comments, use that tablet to write them down. Say nothing. You may leave at any time."

Ilia gave him a strange look as if to say, "Why would I want to leave?"

Nick watched the monitors. "First, I have to give her some curarine to paralyze her. We don't want her thrashing around. She's unconscious, so I'm going to give her some adrenalin and amphetamine. That," he pointed at another monitor, with several bar charts, "is my meds monitor." He placed his cursor on one and moved the bar up slightly. "This is the tricky part. We have to give her enough curarine to paralyze her, but not so much she can't breathe." He watched the respiration trace as it slowed. On the meds monitor he raised another bar. "This is the amphetamine level. He placed the cursor over another bar. "This is the adrenalin." He raised it. Her pulse rate and breathing increased. A last tweak of the curarine. "Now I'm giving her LSD." He glanced at Ilia. "I have to bend her mind and make her believe." He turned back to the keyboard. "She's waking up."

"Where am I?" The girl's voice came over the speaker, weak and unsteady. "I can't see!" she screamed. "I can't hear myself. I can't move!" Her voice had risen in panic. A loud howl echoed around the room. "Where am I?" she wailed.

"You're not in your world anymore," Nick said.

"Who is that? Where am I?" her voice a shriek.

"Calm yourself. Do you remember being at your house?"

"Yes. Some people came in with knives and guns. They took me." Her respiration and heart rate increased. Nick tweaked the sedative bar. "Are you with them, the ones who took me?"

"No, Kira. I am with you here."

"What is this place? Why can't I see or hear or feel?"

"You are not in your world anymore."

Did…did they kill me? Who are you?" she repeated.

"Why did you stop going to church?"

She gasped. "I…I didn't think God was in my life. It hurt my mother and dad when I stopped. I still believe, I do."

"And yet you became a thief, stealing from others electronically. Do you think that makes you less of a thief?"

"It's not the same as robbing somebody. I only steal from companies."

"You think that is okay with me? What about the information you sell? That hurts people."

She groaned. "You? You are God? And now I have to go to Hell?" Her voice was soft, on the verge of a sob.

"What did you learn about forgiveness when you went to church?"

"If I confess, my sins are forgiven, but there is

no priest now."

"The priests are only my representatives. It is always me you confess to. But that is not enough. You must also repent in your heart."

"You are God." She was silent for a minute. "How do I start?"

"You are very young, so there is not a long list, but start with today."

Nick glanced at Ilia. His brows were knitted in concentration as if he were the one confessing. He touched Ilia's arm and felt it jerk. Ilia understood the level of betrayal that was to take place.

Kira started relating her online activities, her hacking. She talked about cheating in school, hacking into other students' files. When she came to the part about working with the Russian mob, both Nick and Ilia perked up.

"You were paying for protection?"

"They said it was a tax for doing business. They said they would protect me."

"Did you ever meet them?"

"They came to the house, beat me up, beat up my boyfriend, threatened to kill us if I didn't pay." She gasped. "What about my boyfriend? He wasn't a hacker. Is he okay?"

"No."

She sobbed. "And his sister and her boyfriend?"

"No."

"Who were those people? Why did they come to my house? I paid!" she cried. "I paid."

"They were the competition. Rest now. We may talk again later."

"Am I forgiven? Will I go to Hell?" Her voice rose. "Don't leave me!"

Nick increased the sedative and watched as she slipped into unconsciousness. He turned off the microphone.

"What did we learn?" asked Ilia.

"Not a lot we didn't already know except more about the training program and how the system is set up."

"This was not about learning," said Ilia, shaking his head. "She is merely a tool to make a point." Nick nodded. "What happens to her now?" Ilia stared at him.

Chapter 10

"The girl didn't give us much more than we got from her computer." said Nick, glancing from face to face. They were in the basement around a table with food steaming in bowls. It was simple fare, meat and potatoes, a large bowl of borscht in the middle.

"Was it worth bringing her back and questioning her?" asked Kiki.

Nick shook his head. "What is apparent is that the low-level hackers have little useful information."

"We did recover money." said Sol.

"Didn't need her for that." said Ilia. "Question now is what do we do with her?"

Zyra crossed her arms. "If we did not bring her back, we kill her at house. Ending is same."

"New plan. Look like we want money, go after

hackers. For information we move up ladder," said Sol.

"At this moment, this looks like a random hit," said Sasha. "One or two more and the hackers will demand protection from these *robbers*."

Zyra laughed. "I like idea of hitting protectors. More action."

"The protectors will have information for us," remarked Sol. "We bring them back for Nick."

Nick winced. "What do we do with the girl?"

"We take care of her," said Zyra. "Make it fast."

"I can bring her back to herself." Nick's voice was almost a plea. "I did it with Rose."

"And then what?" asked Kiki. "You picture her going off to Finland and starting anew? Get real."

Nick frowned at the callousness of her remark. She was right, though. Kira was always going to end up dead or insane. Releasing her would put them all at risk.

"If hacker a man you have same problem?" asked Sol. Nick shrugged. "Zyra, Sasha, take care of her. Send message. Make it look like Chechens. That confuse them for a while."

"Not many Chechens this far north," said Ilia.

"That add to puzzle," responded Sol.

"Okay, we need to plan the next target," said Kiki. "Bob, bring up the map."

"Whew, you guys got a little heavy for me there." His brittle voice came over the speaker. Bob had been an okay field agent, but he was more comfortable in the office. "I'm really glad I'm not there." The monitor on the wall showed the St Petersburg area with red dots representing the indie hackers' locations. The information from Kira's computer had only added a few. A red and yellow circle had been added. "That is the location of the phone the guy called from about the payment. No guarantees he's still there."

"Do we want to stay in the same area or widen it?" asked Sasha. She pointed at an area south and west of St P. "We have several hackers near Baltiyskaya Sloboda. It's a very upscale community about thirty minutes away."

"Double hit?" asked Zyra. "Good message. Don't need to bring anybody back."

"We wait a few days to see fallout," said Sol.

"I get message from Leon." Zyra held up her phone. "Maybe Sasha and I go there for night or two. See if anything happening."

"No news of Tosno on his computer," said Bob. "He hacked into a US gas utility with ransomware. They haven't paid yet. I'll slip a workaround to them."

"Da," said Zyra. "Frustration good for him. Make him want more tequila." She laughed.

Nick studied the map. "Bob, can we put a drone over the site of the mob guy?"

"Yeah, tapping into his phone could give us a lot of info. The house is huge, located on a couple of acres. I'll put a raven in a tree near the house and the vulture overhead."

Zyra looked at Sasha. "We take care of girl tonight." She walked to the map and pointed. "This good spot to leave her. Not much traffic but she be found."

"Party clothes!" said Sasha. They laughed as they went upstairs.

Chapter 12

Andrei Petrov was pissed. This drive to Tosno shouldn't have been necessary. Kira owed him and she hadn't paid. Worse, she refused to answer her phone. The longer he drove, the hotter he got. Kira was good, but not great at hacking. They got a steady income from her. He could have sent his two enforcers, but this called for the personal touch. His fingers tightened on the wheel.

He parked two houses down from Kira's and watched for a few minutes. It was a habit he'd learned from working the streets–assess the scene. Her car was parked in front but there was no sign of movement. Instead of walking to the front door, he circled the house to the back. He stopped, gaping at the broken lock on the back door. His head swiveled side to side as he again checked for trouble. Nothing.

Pulling out his Tokerov pistol, he looked through the glass before easing the door open. He waited, watching and listening. Everything was still. As he stepped inside the kitchen, the coppery smell of blood became apparent. It was an odor he was quite familiar with. In the hall, he looked toward Kira's computer room, then toward the bedrooms. He listened for a creak of the floor, the sound of air from somebody breathing. Dead silence.

He crept down the hall to the first bedroom, pushed the door open with his pistol and stepped back ready to leap to the side if somebody was inside. The sunlight streaming through the window highlighted the bodies of the roommates sprawled across the blood-soaked sheets. As he stepped through the doorway, he checked–the room seemed empty. He went to the closet–clear. At the bedside, the smell of blood brought up memories he didn't relish. Their throats had been slashed, one neat cut severing carotid and windpipe. Professional. He backed out.

The second bedroom had only the boyfriend in similar condition. No Kira. His worry began to grow. He hurried to the computer room. It had been cleaned out. This wasn't a simple robbery. Along with the computer, all of her files and storage drives were gone. So was she. Druggies? No, Chechens? maybe, slim chance, or another gang was trying to take territory. He eased out the back door, checking to see nothing in the house connected to him.

From the road, he called his number two. "Gregor, check your sources to see if somebody is trying to move into our territory." Next, he called his man in the police department with an "anonymous tip" about a murder. Their investigation would be his investigation. Slamming his hand on the steering wheel, he screamed. He hated waiting on someone else to make a move.

Chapter 13

"We're here!" Sasha's laughing voice came over the intercom. Leon buzzed them in. When the doors opened, Sasha ran up and threw her arms around him. "We brought more of the Don."

Zyra stepped in with the bottle in her left hand. "How was your day?"

"You still sound like my mom."

"Da, natural tendencies."

"One of my friends has been kidnapped, her boyfriend killed."

Zyra poured him a generous drink. He downed half of it. "I lived with her while at school." He buried his face in his hands as he sank into the couch.

Sasha sat beside him, taking his hand. Zyra knelt to the side. "What happen? Start at beginning."

"Our friendship at school became more." He stopped. "I finished first and started working as an independent. I stayed in contact with her, helping where I could, but there was little room in my new life for a serious girlfriend or wife." He stared at Sasha then Zyra. In a whisper, he said, "I put her in contact with Andrei for some work." He drank the rest of the tequila in his glass. Zyra refilled it.

"You think this Andrei did something?"

"She told me he slapped her around once after she was late paying him, but to kidnap her makes no sense."

"You think this is business thing, not old boyfriend thing?" asked Zyra.

He took another large gulp, then stared at the glass as he set it on the table.

"You eat anything?" asked Sasha. "Since you have this Southwestern decor, I brought American-style steaks." He glanced at her. "Baked potatoes with sour cream."

"What is American-style steaks?"

"New York cut." She took her bag to the kitchen. "I'll call when it's ready."

Zyra poured him more tequila.

Sasha returned with a glass of water. "Drink

some of this to go with that Don. The food will taste better."

"What kind of work she do for this Andrei?" asked Zyra, moving onto the couch beside him.

He looked at her for several seconds. "Computer work."

"We need to guard you?" asked Zyra.

Leon laughed. "Right. As if. I have good security."

Zyra shrugged. "And you don't work for Andrei."

After several minutes of silence, Sasha yelled "Come and get it" from the kitchen.

Leon's beautiful setting graced the table. "Nice plates, silverware and crystal." commented Zyra.

"It's part of the decor I paid for. First time it's been used."

"Don't eat in much, huh," said Sasha.

"I don't cook."

Sasha laughed. "We noticed." She placed a platter with the steaks on the table. The aroma filled the room. Another plate held the baked potatoes. She poured a nice burgundy into their glasses. "*Buen provencia*–that's Spanish for *bon appetit*. "They toasted.

They finished the second bottle of wine as the last bites of steak were eaten. "Who wants port?" asked Sasha. Leon looked at her, one eyebrow raised. "Dessert wine," she explained.

Leon watched her set the small port glasses on the table. "I wondered what those little things were for." Cautiously, he tasted one. "Ummm. Sweet like a dessert. Good." He drank it like a soda, and held out his glass for more.

Sasha glanced at Zyra and filled his glass again.

* * *

With Zyra under one arm, and Sasha under the other, they half-carried half-dragged Leon to the bedroom. He was not unconscious, but that darkness was approaching. Sasha stood beside the bed slowly stripping like a dancer, while Zyra undressed Leon. His bloodshot eyes were glued to the gyrating Sasha. The task done, Zyra laid him on the bed. Sasha climbed in and snuggled against him. His response was diminutive, as he fought the alcohol fog.

Zyra stripped and climbed in on his other side. It was like a sandwich, Leon in the middle. His movements slowed, his eyes rolled up in his head. "Shame to waste this great bed," said Sasha sweeping her hand across the satin sheets.

"Da," replied Zyra as she rolled across Leon and embraced Sasha with a long deep kiss.

It was a wonderful night, interrupted only by Leon's snores. "Don't know how he could be better," laughed Sasha, giving Zyra a hug.

Chapter 14

"The car that arrived at our target house earlier in the evening is still parked outside," Bob said over their com units. "The guy who went inside hasn't come out and there's another guy sitting in the car. Chain smoker, lights up every thirty minutes."

"Last night, Leon told Zyra some of of Andrei's hackers are worried, demanding security. Looks like he listened," said Sol.

"I'm going to have to pull the drone unless your team can charge it," said Bob.

"What do we have to do?" asked Nick.

"The infrared laser is in the van with you. Plug it into the power outlet, open the sunroof and aim the lens up. I'll fly the drone to your location. It will find the beam and charge up in about thirty minutes. You won't have a view of the house during that time."

"I've got the laser aimed up," said Nick.

I'm moving the drone overhead now.

"Kiki has eyes on the house from her hide in the park across the street. If the guy in the car moves, she'll see it. What did you pick up inside the house?"

"I saw four heat signatures. One is moving, one is stationary. There are two hackers, both online at the moment. One just sent ransomware to an electric utility company in Pennsylvania. The other is trying to break into a bank in Delaware. It has pretty good security, but with Pegasus it's only a matter of time."

"With the security guards here, we could go to another site," said Nick.

"Team can handle it," said Sol. "Kiki, can you take out guard in car?"

"Not a problem. I'm only one-hundred-fifty meters away. This Blackout will only make a snap when I fire." The heads-up display on her helmet showed her crosshairs centered on the silhouette of a man through the driver's side window, the tip of a cigarette glowing.

"Zyra, where are you?" asked Sol.

"Outside back door."

"Ilia, Sasha where are you?"

"In bushes in front of house."

"How much more time to charge the drone?" asked Nick.

"It's not full, but has enough charge," answered Bob. "I'm moving it back to the house."

Is clear outside?" asked Sol.

"Nobody on the street, no cars," answered Kiki.

"Okay, go, Kiki," Sol said.

Kiki fired. The driver's side window became a spider web of cracks, and the man fell from view. She looked around to see if anyone had noticed. It was still quiet. She watched as Sasha went to the car, opened the door and honked the horn twice. She ran back to the front of the house joining Ilia on either side. Within seconds, the door flew open and a man stepped out easily visible with the light behind him.

Kiki's second shot hit him in the head. "Go, Zyra," she ordered as he fell back, Sasha and Ilia stepped over the body, silenced pistols at the ready as they entered.

"Hackers were in separate rooms," said Bob. "One on the right, the other on the left ahead of you." He watched the heat signatures of his team move into the house.

"You want them alive?" asked Ilia.

"What is to learn?" asked Zyra.

"Won't know until we ask," said Kiki. "Bring 'em."

"Both?" disappointment in Zyra's voice. "Need to send message."

"Leave one. Move guards inside," said Sol. "Send message."

Bob watched as Ilia and Sasha dragged the guards inside. A few minutes later, Zyra emerged from the house with another figure, hands bound and a hood over its head. The van pulled up, and Kiki helped Zyra put the person inside. Sasha and Ilia came out with pillowcases loaded with stuff fifteen minutes later. They closed the door and walked to the van.

"What you find in house?" asked Sol.

"They had wall-safe. Before she die, woman gave us combination. Lots of money," answered Zyra.

"I'm moving the drone to the pick-up point,"

said Bob. The whole operation had taken less than thirty minutes. Glad I'm not there to see inside that house, he thought.

Chapter 15

Three days and no further attacks on his hackers, thought Andrei Petrov. Perhaps the attack in Tosno was bandits, an isolated incident. There was theft, including Kira's computer and files. As soon as his team was able to break into her Bitcoin account, they'd know if it had been hit. The bitch hadn't shared her account information with him, one of the reasons for his trip there.

In the meantime, he kept getting messages that his hackers wanted protection. PUSSIES! In response, he'd sent two teams out to placate the noise. One team was in Baltiyskaya Sloboda because his most successful hackers, including his brother were there. The other team was at his office building. Little chance of a hit there, but it quieted the greatest number of these whiners. He'd also increased the security. Can't be too careful.

When he bought the mansion, it had been in bad shape. Built after the war, it needed a lot of work. He'd had it rewired completely, put in central heating and air conditioning, gas heater instead of the old coal-fired boiler in the basement. He even had a huge gas log fireplace installed in the main room. His contractor insisted on insulation everywhere. It had cut his heating bill, as if that mattered.

He stood behind his desk and moved across his study. The decor was chrome and black leather. He looked through the large window. His house sat in the middle of twenty acres of well-tended grass and manicured shrubs. The trees were showing the oranges and reds of fall. Autumn came early in these northern latitudes. Morning temperatures dipped well below freezing.

He checked the security monitors that covered the entire estate. All was quiet except for a box truck parked on the road near his driveway. He watched two employees access the gas line to his house. "Vasily, what's going on with the Gazprom truck on the street?" he asked his chief of security over the intercom.

"I'll check, Boss."

Three minutes later his monitor showed one of his ATVs approach the gate. Vasily got out and walked toward the workers. After a few minutes of conversation, his phone rang.

"Gazprom is doing some maintenance on the line. They have to cut the service for a while but will send a technician to make sure all of the appliances are working properly. No big deal, Boss."

"Da, okay." He was a little jumpy after the scene at Kira's house.

"Boss, I think we got a communication problem with the guards you sent to Baltiyskaya Sloboda. They didn't check in this morning, and I haven't been able to reach them. They're new guys and maybe don't understand our protocol. I'm going down there to knock their heads together and make sure everything is okay."

A sliver of worry niggled at Andrei. That was where his brother lived. He and his wife had worked with Andrei to set up the hacking operations in the St Petersburg area. "Call me as soon as you get there."

"Right, Boss. Will do."

* * *

Vasily parked behind the car his guards had used. Nobody was inside. That was wrong. Cautiously, he approached the driver's door, pistol at his side. The window was open, glass shards sparkled on the seat. He glanced around nervously, saw nobody. The curtains in the house were closed. Leaning down to look in, he saw the passenger window splattered with congealed blood and meaty pieces stuck to the cracked glass. Again, he glanced around, looking for danger. The neighborhood was quiet, still as a tomb.

"Boss, it looks like they've been hit. I haven't gone into the house yet, but my guard stationed outside is probably dead. I don't know if anybody's still here, but the dried blood says it's been hours since this happened."

"God Dammit! Go inside."

Vasily inserted an ear bud and put the phone in his jacket pocket. He wanted his hands free. "I'm at the door. No sign of break in. It's unlocked. My guards are on the floor inside, both dead, head shots. Their throats are slit, but the lack of blood tells me it was after they were dead."

"Fuck. Whoever did this is sending us a message. Anyone alive in the house?"

Vasily stepped over the bodies, his pistol sweeping the hallway. Trying to be silent was difficult, the blood on his shoes making sticky sounds with each step. He cleared the living room and the kitchen. "No sign of anybody, Boss. The first office has been tossed–computer gone, the files dumped, desk drawers pulled out. I'm going into the second office now. The woman is on her back, the carpet blood-soaked. She has cuts on her face and her throat cut, not post-mortem. This room has also been tossed. Everything is gone, and the wall safe door is open."

"Shit, they must have tortured her for the combination. No sign of my brother?"

"The rest of the house is empty. I'll take another quick look around, but I need to get out of here before the cops arrive."

"They had security cameras, but the recordings went to the computers. Take a look to be sure there aren't backups."

"There's nothing in the house. Maybe in the basement."

Vasily crept down the stairs, the single bulb in the room pushing the darkness into the corners. "Boss, it looks like there was a recording unit here, but it's been ripped out. They must have seen the cameras and did a search."

"Okay, come back. We'll let the police do the rest. They will share whatever they find. Don't worry about your fingerprints. I'll see that you are cleared."

As Vasily closed the front door, worry began to grow. *Was this a war? If these raiders had taken Andrei's brother, they could learn about the whole operation.*

Chapter 16

"This guy," exclaimed Zyra, elbowing their prisoner, "is brother of Andrei Petrov." She held up his wallet. "He is guy who Leon say is leader of hacking mob. We hit jackpot!" Kirill was unconscious on the gurney.

Nick glanced up. Ilia and he were about to push it into the interrogation room. "Dawn, get everything you can about him. I'll need it to get into his head."

"This will get response," said Sol. "Zyra, Sasha, go to Leon house. Learn what happening in world of hackers." He turned to the speakerphone. "Bob, need design of equipment to remove ethyl mercaptan from natural gas."

"Don't believe I've ever had a request for something like that. It'll take me a day or so for research and design. I'll be back to you."

"Needs to fit inside one of our box trucks." said Sol.

* * *

Ilia helped Nick strip and weigh Kirill. He was not a big man like his brother, eighty-five kilos. Nick entered the data in his computer. Ilia studied the tattoos on his body. "He was in prison. Joined Russian mafia there, probably with his brother. Nothing religious. This skull mark here," Ilia pointed, "says he killed a man."

"Let's get him wired up and in the tank," said Nick. "We need to find out what else Dawn has learned."

* * *

Dawn looked up from her computer as they entered her room. "Colored history," she said. "He and his brother went to prison for extortion ten years ago. They were recruited by the mafia because of their bookkeeping *talents*." Dawn laughed at the comments. "While there, Kirill had a fight with another inmate and killed him. Charges were dismissed under a claim of self-defense, though the bank account of the warden took a small jump soon afterward."

"We saw the tats," said Ilia. "What about after they got out?"

They started a hacking business that expanded to include others. I think they forced the others to form a ring of hackers in St Petersburg. Those in the ring are independent but pay protection to Andrei, who's the head. Kirill has a talent for hacking and teaches recruits. He and his wife hack from their home, but you already know that. When the Petrov operation grew large enough to be noticed, the Internet Research Agency absorbed their operation."

"I took a look at their Bitcoin account." She laughed. "We're in the wrong business. They're worth millions."

"What is the name of the man he killed in prison?" asked Nick.

Dawn typed for a few minutes. "Boris Volkov." She continued typing. "He was in prison for beating up his wife, the daughter of the local GRU head." She brought up a picture of him. They all leaned close to study it. "Hmm. Bad scar on his face. This may have been a murder for hire."

"That's a good starting point," said Nick. He glanced at Ilia. "Let's get going. This could be a long interrogation." As they left, he said over his shoulder, "Keep looking. Let us know of anything else interesting."

* * *

Inside the interrogation room, Nick glanced at the monitors, then at Ilia. "Let's wake him up." He pushed keys and watched the monitors. Ilia stared intently, trying to comprehend everything.

"He's coming around." Nick pointed to the monitor showing pulse rate and respiration. Both traces were rising. The monitor showing brain activity indicated consciousness. "He's trying to move."

"Where am I?" screamed a voice from the speaker. Nick and Ilia sat quietly. "Where am I?" the voice repeated in a higher tone.

"What's disconcerting to him is he can't hear his own screams," pointed out Nick.

"Help!" another scream. "Why can't I see? Why can't I move?" A long wail echoed around the room. They let him rant for fifteen minutes.

Nick turned on the microphone and the translation software. *"Are you done screaming? You sound like a little baby."*

Kirill stopped mid-scream. "Who is that?"

"You don't recognize my voice? I am hurt, but then you did crush my throat in prison."

"Boris?" There was silence. "I killed you. Why does your voice sound mechanical?"

"You did kill me. I have had no one to talk to for all these years so I haven't used my voice much. Was it my father-in-law who paid you to kill me?"

"I had no choice. They were going to kill me if I didn't."

"Did you have to make it so painful?"

"It is what I was told to do. Her father was a bastard. I hated him. He didn't particularly love Misha, but she was family."

Nick paused then nodded as he picked a line to follow. *"She could be a real pain in the ass. I was never good enough for her. It was the vodka. When she drank, she got nasty, calling me names, threatening me. She attacked me with a kitchen knife, nearly cut my head off. I had no choice."*

"Boris, you're dead."

"You saw to that."

"Then I'm…am I dead too?"

"You're not in your world anymore. I'd say welcome, but there's nothing to welcome you to. I'm actually glad you're here. At last, I have

someone to talk to."

"I can't be dead. I'd remember that."

"What do you remember?"

"People crashed into my house with guns and knives. I heard my wife scream, but it was cut off as if…" He sobbed. "They came into my room. A tall Black woman grabbed me and tied my hands behind my back. A bag was put over my head, then she walked me out to a car. Something stabbed me in the arm."

"That was the end of you. Hah. How does it feel to be killed?"

"I felt nothing, still don't. I thought I'd face judgement and go to hell."

"The church lies. It's the greatest scam ever. They make you believe and hold your soul hostage. You obey and pay. All lies."

"What about my wife?" He sobbed. "We had a good life I wanted to live quietly with her. This can't be the end."

"You were expecting more drama? That isn't how it works. One second you are in one world and then in another second you have left it behind. Accept it. Wailing and crying won't change anything. I had to after you killed me. At least now

I have someone to talk to, even if it is you. What's happening in the world? Tell me what did you do after you got out of prison?"

"My brother and I started a computer business."

"You mean like selling and servicing? That doesn't sound like you."

"No. We got the Pegasus software from Israel. With that, we're able to break into any computer in the world. We hack in and steal money or install ransomware and force them to pay."

"I don't know much about that. Who do you steal from?"

"At first we were small, but our mistake was hacking into Russian companies. The IRA sent some guys to convince us not to do that, very persuasive."

"Sort of like the one who convinced you to kill me?"

"Exactly. The real money is in America anyway."

"You went to America?"

"No, stupid. With the internet, we can reach out anywhere in the world from our house.

"Oh," said Nick, feigning doubt in his voice.

"How do you get paid?"

"Bitcoin."

"What's that?"

"It's a new money–electronic. Much better than the ruble or even American dollars. Hard to trace."

"You and your brother did this?"

"At first, yeah. After a while we began to recruit others to work for us. I was good at hacking and teaching; Andrei was good at organizing. When it became a big network, the IRA gang from Moscow moved in. They took over." There was bitterness in Kirill's voice.

"What's the IRA?"

"Internet Research Agency. It's a troll center, the largest internet hacking group in the country. You either work for them or you don't work."

"Who's the boss now?"

"It's a consortium. We're a member. They're ex-KGB and GRU, control everything. Everybody's getting rich, though."

"How did you get here?"

"Somebody new wants in. Doesn't matter, the Consortium will deal with them."

"But in the meantime, you're here."

"Is this all there is to death?"

"It's bad being alone. Not so much now that you're here."

"But what do we do? Where's Hell?"

"I think the churches got it wrong. All there is to do is talk–for eternity."

Chapter 17

The call from Daniel Novikov broke into Andrei's funk. He and Daniel had been school chums and remained friends. With pleasure and a little help by way of information, Andrei had watched him rise from a mere patrolman to Detective Inspector. Andrei had pulled a few strings to get the local police to bring him on as lead in the cases of the murders.

"If the murders had not been so alike, they could be called random, but the same people did both. I can tell by the way they were killed. Are you aware of another organization trying to take over your territory?"

"I have heard nothing."

"These were not the hooligans. They targeted hackers working for you, and your brother."

"They were robbers. Both Kira Siderov's and

Kirill's accounts were emptied within hours of their abductions."

"Hi-tech robbers. But why murder the others and in such a gruesome way?" Daniel asked.

Andrei had been pondering the same thing. "They are sending a message."

"What is the message and who is it to?"

"Don't be a hacker is a very general threat," answered Andrei. "It has made my people very nervous. I'm adding security for them."

"That may bring you more people. Indies are on their own, paying you only a privilege tax. They may want your join you for protection"

"There are a few I'd like to add to my stable. Keep me informed of any progress on these cases."

"Of course. Be careful."

Andrei was furious at the world. The IRA Consortium was supposed to prevent things like this. It was suspicious he'd received no warning. Furiously, he'd demanded a Consortium meeting about security. Thus far, his operation was the only one hit. Was this a move by someone else in the group trying to take over? Or was it someone new? The meeting was in three days, and he was trying to get his house ready to host it. He had always been good at reading people. Soon he would know if it was a move against him from the Consortium.

In the meantime, he had stationed guards at his hackers' businesses. Most worked from home. He had doubled the security staff here, installing additional cameras, motion detectors and lights. Dogs patrolled continuously. And he had people searching for his brother, though he held little hope he be found, at least alive.

No doubt, whoever had taken him had questioned him, probably in the worst way. A moment of grief caused a sob–Kirill was his only family. When he found those who did this, it would take weeks for them to die. They'd beg for it in the end.

From the security office, he checked the coverage. From the front of house to the street was fully covered. A camera at the gate revealed two guards. The grassy expanse in the rear all the way to the river and the boathouse was in four of the camera views. Guards patrolled, some with dogs. All guards were armed.

"Vasily, who's handling the catering?" he called over the intercom.

"Boss, your house manager is making all the

arrangements. I'm handling security. You need to work on your pitch for help. It's needed, but we don't want to give up anything. Weakness attracts wolves."

Andrei nodded to himself. He had to sell this as the beginning of a takeover attempt, and they were all liable. If another attack succeeded now, he would appear weak.

Chapter 18

"Meat and potatoes, meat and potatoes! It's time for a change in your diet," exclaimed Sasha.

"I eat fish too," answered Leon, defensively.

"I'm making Thai green curry stir fry," said Sasha. "You like hot?"

"Yeah, some."

"I'll tone it down for Russian palettes, wimpy."

Zyra chuckled. "Beer goes good with Thai." She held up bottles of Singha.

"I can't get too drunk tonight. There's a meeting at Andrei's house in two days. Got to have a clear head."

"We help with that," said Zyra. "Hot Thai keeps head clear."

Leon stared at her.

"So, who's going to be at this great meeting?" asked Sasha.

"Boss and bosses from Moscow. Boss's brother was kidnapped. His wife and two guards killed."

"You got guards? We didn't see any," said Zyra.

"I'm independent, pay dues. Doesn't include protection."

Zyra laughed. "Don't worry. We protect you."

"I tried to check you out, but nothing comes up. You are clean or ghosts." He turned back to the monitors. "You and my steel doors will protect me." He went to a bookcase, pulled out a book and pushed a button. The bookcase swung open to reveal racks of weapons. "I have more protection."

"Ooh, toys!" exclaimed Sasha, moving forward for a closer look. "Zyra, come see. He has rifles and pistols and grenades. Oh my!"

"What do you two know about weapons?"

"It's part of rat killing business." Zyra looked at Sasha and laughed.

"Only big rats," said Sasha.

Leon looked from one to the other. He couldn't tell how serious they were. "Maybe I will hire you as guards. Better than those hairy louts."

With a grocery bag in hand, Sasha walked to

the kitchen. "I'll have dinner ready in an hour. You two play nice."

"So, is meeting all-day thing?"

"Maybe longer. Security is tight. Might be two days."

"We stay here or go somewhere else?"

"I might be able to get you in as part of my operation. If you want to go." He watched to see her reaction.

"Need fancy dresses." She posed in her jeans with a flannel shirt like a jacket covering her tee shirt. "Don't have more than dress you see in club."

He went to a wall safe, entered the combination and reached inside. "Here, go buy something," he said handing her a credit card. "It's good for whatever you want to spend."

Zyra tucked it into her jeans pocket. "Thanks, Boss." She walked to the racks displaying weapons. "What is this?" she asked, pointing at a large rifle with a huge telescopic sight.

"That's a sniper rifle, a Dragunov. One of the best in the world. Accurate up to 800 meters."

"Just the thing for home defense," chuckled Zyra holding it up to her shoulder. "Show me security system you like so much."

Leon punched in another code on a keypad beside a door. Inside was a large monitor with six views covering the entrances into the building, a view of each side and the street, and one for the garage. The scenes cycled to different views every ten seconds. "I've got alarms and motion detectors too."

"This good start. I go over it. Look for weakness." She stared at him, pointed at herself. "Security guards."

"Dinner," called Sasha from the kitchen.

* * *

Leon reached for his fork. Sasha slapped his hand "No No No. Spoon. This is like a rice stew." She pointed at the bowl. "First put rice in the bowl then spoon in the curry," she explained as she filled her own bowl.

They dug in.

"Great flavor but a little hot," said Leon, guzzling his beer. It was his third since they started eating.

"Leon showed me his security system," Zyra said. "Need to know if we are guards."

"And what do you think?" he asked.

"Good system to tell you somebody is coming.

Then what?"

"That's why the arsenal."

"You against world. Don't think so. When they breach door and get inside, goose cooked. You need emergency way out."

"What about ways to make it very expensive to get inside." Leon squinted at her.

"Cost lives," said Zyra. "We make doors booby traps. Only delay to someone determined. Will still need way out."

"And somewhere to go," added Sasha.

"Rat killing business dangerous," said Zyra in answer to Leon's next question.

Chapter 19

"I receive plans," said Sol over the sat phone connected to Bob. "Doesn't look hard. Need at least four room air conditioners, duct work, lots of tape and bottle of nitrogen. May be able to get those here. We already have valve cutouts installed on pipeline to house."

"Good," said Bob. "Inside the box truck, mount the air conditioners ducted in series so air from one feeds into the next. Bring the natural gas in from the pipeline through a duct cut in the truck floor. Cycle it through the AC units and exit through another duct in the floor connected to the house supply line. It's all low pressure, but minimize leaks with the tape. Seal the box of the truck. Use the bottle of nitrogen to fill it to remove oxygen. We don't want a premature explosion."

"Okay, we have remote control of all gas

appliances in the house. Installed those when we serviced them after the maintenance work. Can bypass safeties to keep gas flowing. Also have remote to light it off when enough in house."

"Why did you pick Andrei's house instead of the IRA headquarters?"

"Softer target. Savushkina house not off target list. Just delayed. We have plans for it."

"When's the party?"

"Two days. Keep drones on watch."

"This is going to make one hell of an explosion."

"Yah, both at house and in hacking group."

"Best if you get outta Dodge quick as possible. Going to Finland?"

"No. Got more work to do. We leave for Moscow after. You set off boom when we say. Pick up drones on way. Nine-hour drive straight through."

"I'll minimize broadcasts to ensure batteries are fully charged."

"Ilia has farmhouse rented east of Moscow, but not too far away. He knows area, did work in Moscow for Mossad."

* * *

Sasha held up the blue satin low-cut dress, gazing at the mirror. "What do you think?" she asked turning to face Leon.

"Beautiful. Matches your eyes."

She held up the gold four-inch spike heels and a small gold clutch. "Goes with these too. A girl has to have bling, so…." A gold necklace with an aquamarine pendant dangled from her fingers.

Zyra had chosen a brilliant purple backless dress with a thigh-high slit up one side. The bodice was crossed strips of green silk that wrapped around her waist. She also had four-inch spike heels in green that would make her tower over most men. "No bling for me. You wear tux?"

Leon looked sheepish. "I don't have one."

The girls looked at each other and laughed. "Time to shop," they yelled in unison.

"We don't go with frump," said Zyra, as she poked him playfully.

"We have reputations to maintain," quipped Sasha.

With his arms firmly in their grips, they headed out the door.

"We know a tailor who can fix you up today. Cost a lot of money, though," laughed Sasha.

Leon grinned, obviously pleased to be in the company of these two striking women.

"Why you so happy?" asked Zyra.

"Two beautiful women taking care of me, who happen to be my bodyguards. What could be better?"

"You don't take us seriously. Don't think we can do it?"

"I like your company."

"We keep you safe," said Zyra.

Chapter 20

Sol addressed his group in the basement. "Moving in three days. We pack everything not needed so we can leave quick. We park second box truck at river coal tunnel. Personal gear in truck and van. Whatever not fit we get rid of. Want no trace we here. Ilia and I put together other box truck for operation. Everything clean, no trace. Sasha, Zyra you return in van to take care of Leon." The two looked at each other. The usual enthusiasm they showed at dispatching bad guys wasn't in their faces. "What?" asked Sol.

"We want to bring him with us. He could be useful," said Sasha.

"Knows about cyber guys and computers," said Zyra.

Sol's face clouded. "Does he want to leave?"

Zyra stared at Sol. "He knows nothing about us. We explain after boom."

"With us or gone." said Sol moving his finger across his throat. "After you tell him, have no choice. In his hands."

Zyra looked at Sasha. "We take care of him."

"Don't go to meeting. House will blow up."

* * *

"Why don't you want me to go to this meeting?" whined Leon. "I will be missed. Andrei may offer security to the indies."

"You don't trust us?" said Sasha, frowning.

"I do, but this is a cyber-community."

"You trust us, but Andrei's track record not too good. Two hits in ten days," pointed out Zyra. "Meeting too dangerous."

"Six people killed, including Andrei's guards." added Sasha. "Two people missing."

"I have to go," insisted Leon. "Andrei will ensure it's safe."

"You want us to tie you up?" asked Zyra. "Might be fun."

"What about the clothes we bought?"

"We'll put them on for you," laughed Sasha. "And take them off."

* * *

On the monitors showing views of Andrei's

mansion from the drones, Sol watched the guests arrive in a line of limos, Ferraris, and even a Corvette. The indies came in cabs, the military in GAZ Tigrs, the Russian Humvee equivalents. He counted thirty people entering. "Big meeting," he grunted. He was relieved that Zyra and Sasha were not there. Getting them out would have been a problem. He didn't see Ivanov either. How would his recruitment go? He shrugged. Not his problem…yet.

By the time the last vehicle dropped off people, lazy snowflakes began to drift down as darkness fell. *Good. Cold weather means heaters will be on.*

"When do you want to set up?" asked Ilia.

"We park truck when house starts to get dark. Maybe hour later begin feeding in gas. Turn on our air conditioners and switch to our gas."

"The air conditioning units will make the gas odorless?" asked Kiki.

"Ethyl mercaptan is added to natural gas and propane to give it that smell we recognize," said Bob. "The boiling point is low enough it will condense out like water in a humid climate," he explained. "By running the four AC units in series, most of it will be removed, hopefully enough nobody will notice a smell."

"They be asleep anyway," said Sol. "Turn off appliances hour after that, set controls so not ignite and then we fill house. Bob blow house when we clear."

"We need to let Sasha and Zyra know what the schedule is," said Ilia. He picked up his phone and dialed Sasha's number, put it on speaker.

"Hey, Bro, what's happening?"

"We go in four hours. Need you and Zyra back here at midnight."

"Yeah, okay."

"You still want to bring Leon?"

"If he stays, he'll be suspected, probably interrogated and killed."

"This is a complication. You know how Sol feels about complications."

"He could be a great asset to our mission," Sasha persisted. "We'll talk to him now."

"He become problem, we take care of him," said Zyra.

* * *

With the three of them in Leon's huge bed, Sasha placed her hand on Leon's chest and stared into his face. "We have something to tell you."

Zyra lay on his other side on the bed. "We're going away and want you to come with us."

"Going away where?" His face registered his surprise. "Why are you going away?"

"Something will happen tonight that will make Saint Petersburg dangerous for us."

"Maybe dangerous for you too," added Zyra. "You come with us.?"

"This is my home. I can't leave." He looked from Sasha to Zyra. "What's going to happen?"

"We very sorry," said Zyra. "We tell you too much already. You must join us."

"Join you in what?"

"We are with a group that killed the hackers," said Sasha.

Leon's mouth fell open, his eyes as big as saucers. "Not possible," he laughed. "Ha ha. Big joke on me."

"Tonight, Andrei's house will blow up. Everyone there will be killed. It's why we wouldn't let you go."

"Why are you doing this? Many of my friends are there."

"We contractors hired to shut down Russian hacking." Zyra took his face in her hands. "You must join us."

"Please," pleaded Sasha.

"And if I don't?"

Tears formed in Sasha's eyes. "You will be suspected when they investigate. You will be questioned."

"We offer to save your life," said Zyra. Unsaid was the word "Or."

"What would I do? I can't kill anyone."

"Do what you already do, except hack the hackers," offered Sasha.

"I have to leave all of this behind." He shook his head.

"Can be replaced. Not bad swap for life," said Zyra,

Chapter 21

Through binoculars, Daniel Novikov watched the stream of bad guys enter Andrei's house. He didn't agree with their business. It was theft and extortion, but in Russia it was considered legitimate. He and Andrei had been in school together. As a small very pale, tow-headed weakling, Daniel had been an easy target for the bullies. Andrei stepped in to protect him. They had been long-time friends since. After becoming a Detective Inspector, they passed information of mutual benefit back and forth. He knew the independent hacking business was illegal on paper, but Russian authorities condoned it, the mob ran it. Moscow had their own bureau of cyber warfare used mostly against the governments of their enemies.

By the time the last guest entered, snowflakes

were dancing through the beams from the spotlights around the house. It was going to be a cold stakeout, but he felt protective of Andrei. Not sure what help he could be on top of the guards and dogs patrolling the grounds, he needed to do something.

The two murder sites he'd investigated were troubling. Yes, money and computers were stolen, the Bitcoin accounts emptied. That represented a huge haul for robbers. But why kidnap the hackers with no ransom demands? There were pieces to this puzzle he didn't have.

His phone rang. "Novikov here."

"Detective, we have found a body near the river. It's a young woman, and from the description circulated, she could be the one missing from the murder site in Tosno."

"Give me the location. I'm on my way."

He started the car, welcoming the heat as he drove from his vantage point of Andrei's house. The body had been found about twenty minutes away. The guards at Andrei's house could handle security until he was able to return, might not be tonight.

Three patrol cars had parked to light an area

just off the foot-path along the river. One uniform was keeping bystanders away, though at this hour and in this weather, none were to be seen. Three others searched the area surrounding the body, one was taking pictures with his phone.

The young woman was nude, her white skin glowing under the lights except for the red-brown rivulets of dried blood from the ear-to-ear slash across her throat. Her hair was blond, short. Leaves had been carelessly tossed over her, but not enough to hide her. "Is the coroner on the way?" he asked a patrolman.

"He has been called."

"No one has touched the body?"

"I checked to see if she was dead. No pulse."

He glanced at the patrolmen walking the perimeter, heads down, flashlights playing across the ground. "Anything like footprints or tire tracks?"

"This is a public place, but the snow is covering the ground quickly."

"No witnesses, of course." he muttered.

Headlights flashed across them. The coroner was here. They both watched as the chubby man, a polite description, waddled toward them. "Hell of a night for this. Anything obvious, gunshot, strangulation, knife wounds?"

"Yeah, her throat was opened up," answered Daniel.

The coroner walked around her, looking from different angles. He bent low to inspect. "Nothing but the cut on this side. No sign of being bound, no defensive wounds." He glanced at the cop taking pictures. "You got everything here?" He nodded. "Help me turn her." Together, they rolled her over. White skin, nothing else.

He turned to Daniel. "Think she's a working girl got on the wrong side of her client?"

"She matches the description of a woman who disappeared from a murder scene in Tosno. Hacker, not a hooker."

The coroner grunted. "Okay. I won't know more until I get her back to the lab." He signaled to the ambulance drivers waiting to the side. They approached with a stretcher.

"Let me know what you find," said Daniel.

"You do the same," said the coroner, watching the search going on.

* * *

Andrei woke with a splitting headache. He lay

still in the dark willing it to go away, but no. He glanced at this clock–2:00 AM. Throwing off the covers, he got up to get something for his throbbing head. *God damn it was cold in here. Is my heater not working?* He stumbled as he walked toward the bathroom. *Why am I so dizzy? I didn't drink more than usual.* He gulped down two tablets. *I have to see what's wrong with the heat. I have a lot of important guests.*

He held onto the banister to keep from falling as he went down the stairs. His breath was coming faster as if he couldn't get enough oxygen. The vapor hung in the air. The room spun around him. Glancing at the fireplace, he saw that it was out. *That's not right.* He stood in front of it for several seconds before bending down to push the sparker. Nothing happened at the first click. He pushed again. A blue flame appeared, then his world exploded in fire.

Chapter 22

The snowfall had increased. The chances of finding anything here were growing smaller by the minute. Thunder rolled across the sky. *Strange for this time of year.* Daniel looked up, but the snow was falling heavily. He stayed for another two hours watching, trying to put together what they were missing. His phone chimed.

"Novikov, Andrei Petrov's house, now."

Daniel raced toward his car. His captain would only be up this late in an emergency. With a sinking feeling, he raced back to Andrei's house.

As he pulled up, flames reached toward the sky from the rubble that had been Andrei's mansion. He sat still, unable to process what he was seeing. A fire truck passed him, siren wailing. Men piled out, hooked up hoses and began pouring water on the ruin. Others connected hoses to the hydrant on the street. *How had this happened?*

He got out and tried to approach the house, but the heat drove him back. Nobody could have survived that.

He looked around. Fifty meters away were the smoking remains of a truck that had been parked on the street. *What could that be? The explosion at the house couldn't have done that.*

Cautiously, he approached. The truck door had been blown off and landed against the wall around Andrei's property, a scorched Gazprom sign visible. This truck had exploded. Something inside had done this. Equipment was strewn about from the blast. A body was next to the sign fragment. He went over to check it. The man was naked. He must have been in the cab to not have been blown apart. Daniel rolled him over. Shit! It was Andrei's brother!

* * *

"You were supposed to wait for our signal," exclaimed Sol on the secure phone to Bob. "We wanted to be hour down the road to Moscow before blast."

"I didn't do it. Something inside sparked it. I'll go over the thermal footage to see what happened.

Are you all right?"

"We barely finished disconnecting truck from the gas lines when house blew. We set timer for bomb in truck. Ran for blocks before calling Sasha and Zyra to pick us up. Froze my fucking balls off."

"Sorry," said Bob. "I'm looking at the thermal images before the blast. Somebody came downstairs and tried to light the fireplace. That's what did it."

"No help for that now. Call Nick. Get the other truck started toward highway. Send them map so they pick up drones. We meet up. I ride with them. Need Russian speaker in case they are stopped. Besides, crowded in here with Leon and his gear."

"He's with you?"

"Girls made him deal he couldn't refuse."

Chapter 23

Detective Inspector Daniel Novikov sat in his car, his headlights on the wreckage of the truck and Kirill's body. The coroner would determine the official cause of death, but the battered condition said the shockwave of the truck explosion had killed him. His throat was not cut. The house was like the war zones he'd seen in Ukraine a few years ago–senseless destruction there. Something told him not this time. Someone had a purpose.

He sat up with the realization that war had been declared war on hackers, at least the ones in Saint Petersburg. Who? Why? What had destroyed the house? What was this truck doing here, and why was it bombed? How did Kirill and Kira figure into this mess? They were hackers, of course, but what else?

His head swam with all the questions swirling

around. The sound of his phone startled him. "Novikov."

"Are you still at Petrov's house?"

"Yes, Captain, though I can't do much here. The snow is covering the area around the truck wreckage and the house is too hot to approach. The coroner is here looking over the body of Kirill Petrov. We'll do better in the morning. I'm going back to the office to organize the teams to investigate this and the girl's murder. I'm sure they are connected."

"I'll meet you there."

* * *

"Go through the events of tonight," said Captain Stravos.

Daniel paused, pulling out his notebook, as he began to organize his memories. "As you know, I was sent to investigate the murders and kidnapping in Tosno last week. We received a tip about another attack in Baltiyskaya Sloboda two days ago. The scene was very similar to Tosno, except the guards were killed. The hacker who disappeared was Andrei's brother."

"That was the body you found outside of Andrei's house?"

Daniel let out a deep sigh. "I knew him. We grew up together. When I spoke to Andrei about his disappearance, he was shaken. Though he doubled up on his security, I wanted to help. I was parked on the street outside of his house as his guests were arriving early in the evening. I saw thirty enter. They were members of the hacking community and the government cyber division. The Internet Research Agency was well represented."

"Shit!" Stravos grunted. "The government too. That means we'll be up to our asses with their pompous help."

"Andrei's operation has been struck twice. In both cases, gruesome murders happened at the residences, and the principal hackers disappeared along with computers, files and money."

"I read the reports," said the captain. "The way they were killed sent a message."

Daniel frowned, scanning his notes. "It did. Andrei wanted the community to pull together to protect their operations. He didn't know if the attacks were from an outside group trying to take over or someone within the group moving on him. He believed he would learn more with everybody together."

"Do we have a guest list?"

"I'll look into getting what I can, but the invitations were sent out electronically. I videoed the guests entering, but it may not be everybody."

"No survivors at the house?"

Daniel handed the captain his phone with pictures he'd taken. "I don't see how."

The captain's office was silent for a few seconds.

"You left Andrei's when you got the call about the girl's body?"

Daniel nodded. "The park was about twenty minutes away. Not much in the way of clues. She was naked, her throat cut. The investigating team covered the area, but the snow was starting to come down pretty hard. I thought I heard thunder, but I now realize it was the explosion at Andrei's. I left after your call."

Daniel's phone rang. "Novikov." He listened for a minute. It was the coroner. He placed the phone on speaker.

"The girl's death was the result of her throat being slashed. Not so obvious were the needle sites on her arms. Do you know if she used drugs?" asked the coroner.

"I do not. What about the tox screen?"

"Results will take a few days unless you can jump the queue." Daniel glanced at the captain.

"We found evidence of some adhesive stuck to her skin, like I'd expect from tape. I'll mark the sites in my report."

"What about the explosion at Andrei Petrov's house?"

"Yeah. I'm going to be very busy."

"It'll take a while to get inside the house. It's a pile of rubble, but another body was outside on the street. We're interested in what you find with that one."

"Jump the queue," ordered the captain.

Chapter 24

Once outside the city, the streets were nearly deserted. Sol called Leon, who was riding with Zyra in the van, and asked him to keep them up-to-date on news about the explosion at Andrei's house. Leon was startled by the request. Kiki looked at Sol. That request was his test to see if Leon was going to fit in. It was also Leon's chance to assess himself.

Within ten minutes, he read the news flying in the ether. "The house of Andrei Petrov was leveled by a blast that destroyed it. A meeting of those in the cyber business was taking place. The search for survivors has been hampered as the structure is unsafe to enter and snow is covering the site." Leon stopped reading.

Sol had been translating for Kiki and Nick.

"Are you ok?" asked Kiki. Sol translated.

In a choked voice, Leon answered, "I knew many of those people. They were my friends."

"Take a few minutes. We can wait," said Sol. He glanced out the truck windshield as snowflakes danced through the headlight beams.

Ten minutes later, Leon spoke. "I can't do this. I need to stop. I need air."

"We'll stop in an hour," said Sol. "Zyra, you read for us."

The news reports were thin on detail which showed how little the police knew, or were releasing.

* * *

The snow had slowed when Sol pulled off the road at a wide spot, Leon jumped out and began to vomit. Sasha went to help him while Zyra watched.

Wiping his mouth, he glared at her. "You people murdered my friends." He swung his fist at her.

She easily sidestepped the pathetic blow and slapped him. "We did. Your hacking is a direct attack on the people who hired us to stop it. We're just doing our job."

"Your *job* is to murder my friends. We never hurt anyone."

She grabbed his shoulders and shook him. "I won't argue with you. Pull yourself together."

"Or what?" he snarled.

Sasha glanced at Zyra, who had been observing the exchange. Sasha put her arm around him. "Or you'll join your friends."

* * *

The farmhouse near Moscow Ilia had for them was one of several in Russia secretly owned by Mossad. It was remote but still near the city. Vehicles could be parked in the barn, and there were enough bedrooms to accommodate. Though it had a satellite dish, their group, the *Fantasmas*, needed their own secure communications. Within an hour they were up and running.

Sol called Bob to give him a status report. "We're here, sending drones up on surveillance mode. We're all pretty knackered from last few days, so keep eye out for us. Give alarm if anything happens."

"Got it. Get some rest."

Sol turned to Zyra. "I'm holding you to your word. If Leon becomes problem, he's your problem. You and Sasha will take care of him."

"Da. At least if we do it, we make it quick. Not happen with interrogators." She turned and left.

* * *

"You can't keep me here," whined Leon as the two women lay on either side of him on the bed. The bedroom was neat but small with a bed barely wide enough for them. A single worn chest of drawers was the only other piece of furniture.

Zyra laughed. "Relax. Enjoy company. Two beautiful naked women with you in bed."

"If you need to go to the bathroom, now is the time," said Sasha.

"I do."

Zyra sighed and rose, holding out her hand. "You're going with me?" Leon stammered.

"You might need help."

"I can't go if someone's watching."

"Then you will explode. If you wet bed, I will spank you."

Sasha laughed. "He might enjoy that."

"Not way I do it."

Chapter 25

Detective Inspector Daniel Novikov sat in his office slowly peering at his computer screen, reading through the coroner's autopsy reports of Kira Siderov and Kirill Petrov. Captain Stravos' knock on his door startled him from his study.

"I've gotten a lot of pressure from Moscow in the last week. What do you have?"

Daniel sat back in his chair and clasped his fingers together. "Siderov died from a knife cut that severed her carotid artery. It was expertly done, as were the murders of the others in her house and Kirill's wife. The two guards had been shot in the head. Ballistics on the bullets show 7.62 mm caliber but not high velocity. Their throats slashed post mortem, a message."

"Some message," murmured Stravos.

"Kirill died from the traumatic shock of the

explosion of the truck. Neither Kirill's or Kira's cause of death came as a surprise. It was obvious at the scenes." He pointed at his computer screen. "The tox screens indicate a spectrum of drugs in both bodies including sedatives, stimulants, hallucinogenic drugs and curarine. I had to look that one up. It causes paralysis."

"What the hell?" exclaimed Stravos. "Who did this? What were they after?"

Daniel shook his head. "That is the puzzle. I think somebody interrogated them using drugs.

Kira's body showed no injury other than her throat. She wasn't tortured, at least in the GRU way. It's hard to tell with Kirill because the explosion caused so much physical damage."

Stravos knitted his eyebrows in puzzlement. "Were the people who did this looking for information about Andrei's meeting?"

"Their computers were stolen, and their bank accounts emptied. I'm trying to find out about their Bitcoin accounts, but that's really hard to access. Leon Ivanov is an expert hacker I've used for technical assistance before, but he's disappeared."

The captain stood and paced a few steps. "Surely there is a tie-in between the murders and the explosion at Petrov's house. But why kill all the others at the hackers' houses?"

"To precipitate the meeting." He watched Stravos stop as he turned the idea over in his head. "It brought all those people together in one place."

"Huh," grunted the captain. "Do we know anything about what caused the explosion?"

"It's early in the investigation. They're still digging bodies out of the house. The experts are on site, but so far, they haven't found any trace of explosives. I'm seeking information from the military about any missile or drone tracks that showed up. But they're not very cooperative."

"I'll see what I can do. What about the truck that was blown up?"

"Stolen two months ago. The debris scattered around it was air conditioning equipment, but the truck was owned by a furniture company. Semtex was used to blow it up. One more interesting thing is that the gas line to Andrei's house had valves and a cutout. Not standard installation."

"Could the truck have pumped explosive gas in?"

"I'm talking to Gazprom about that. No foreign residue is in the pipelines. There was a nitrogen tank in the debris of the truck, but that's all."

The captain peered at Daniel. "Have you gotten any sleep?"

"Not in a while."

"Go home. This case isn't going anywhere fast. Get some rest."

"I know, sir. If the killers were after the hackers, they killed most of the important ones in the Saint Petersburg area."

"Maybe it will quiet down now."

Chapter 26

Sol pointed at the monitor mounted on the wall of the largest room at the farmhouse. "That huge building is Russian equivalent of Pentagon in DC. As new division, cyber headquarters is in smaller building to one side. That is target." The *Fantasmas* were seated around the room studying the screen. He circled the building with a laser pointer. Bob had put his bird drones around it. Combining that with Google Maps, he was able to zoom in and rotate the view using the 3-D mode.

"It is a concrete block, tight security. There are no windows, and two guards on each side of the few doors." His laser pointer circled items. "A loading dock at one end. Limited cars parked at the building. Workers come in by bus. Only higherups have cars," said Sol. "We suspect tunnels underneath, but have seen no sign of them yet."

"I haven't been able to pick up any electronic signals with my drones," said Bob, "which tells me it's heavily shielded."

"I suppose a missile strike is out of the question," said Kiki, smirking.

"With this construction, not sure it would work," said Sol, missing the sarcasm.

"Whatever we do has to be done from the inside," noted Ilia. "We have to get to someone on the staff. Follow the buses."

"I can track one with drones," said Bob.

"Graveyard shift might hold better potential," said Kiki. "It's probably made up of lower-ranked staff people, maintenance and service personnel."

"We can follow one from the gate using the van and the truck to trade off so they won't make us as we tail them," said Sasha.

"The buses may be faster than the drones. If we take a couple of days," said Bob, "we will know the route. Once we get the drop-off point, we'll set up to pick our target the next day."

Zyra glanced at Leon, sitting between her and Sasha. His face was expressionless, like it was made of stone. She leaned close to him. "You can help us or not."

"Help you attack my country!" he hissed. He stood to leave. Zyra took his arm and guided him from the room.

"Doesn't look too good for Leon," remarked Sol.

Dawn frowned. "What about the Chamber? Think we could get anything useful from him?"

"Better figure something out. Can't afford to have two people tied up on guard duty," said Sol.

* * *

Zyra pushed Leon down onto the bed. "You sign death warrant, boy. I am sorry. I like you."

"You are murdering innocent people, my friends and countrymen. Cybercrime is like pickpocketing, not serious. It's not a capital crime. I cannot go along with what you're doing."

She put her hands on her hips and leaned down, looming over him. "Let me give you education. Cyberwarfare is real and results in death. Many died in Ukraine because of misinformation and lies. People without water and food because of cyberwarfare. Want to see pictures of innocent dead people there? You not see them from Russian government or from free press. Just because bullets not used does not make you innocent. I understand loyalty to country, but country can be wrong."

"You're Russian. How can you say Russia is wrong?"

"I leave Russia years ago. Go to Israel. Sometimes they are wrong too, but I can see what is happening and decide for myself to support or oppose."

"By oppose you mean kill people?"

"Only those who deserve it."

"And you decide that?"

"Who better?"

"You'll kill me, won't you?"

"If you are a danger to us, yes."

"And if I say I won't be a danger?"

"You must make me believe you. Still, I can only try to convince Sol. He has final say."

"You'll carry out his orders."

"I am biased. He is not."

Leon stared at her, then turned away.

Chapter 27

Detective Inspector Daniel Novikov glanced from his computer screen to the government agent from Moscow. He had arrived this morning to "assist" in his investigation of the bombing at Andrei Petrov's house. The deaths of government cyber agents attending Andrei's meeting and the request of the IRA brought him in.

"You had other murders of cyber workers?" asked agent Solikov. He was a powerfully built man, bald with squinty eyes and a deep voice.

"There were two murder sites previously. In Tosno, three people were murdered and an independent hacker, Kira Siderov, was kidnapped. Her body was found here in Saint Petersburg the night of the bombing. All victims had their throats slashed in a professional manner. Computers and files were taken."

Solikov was scribbling notes. He looked up as Daniel paused. "And the other site?"

"Andrei Petrov's brother was kidnapped and his wife and two guards murdered. Their bodies were at Kirill's house in Baltiyskaya Sloboda, their throats slashed, though the guards were shot first. Kirill's body was found outside Andrei's house the night of the bombing. His death appears to be from an explosion of a vehicle parked on the street. His throat was not cut."

Solikov looked up. "Different killer?"

"Perhaps. We have not determined why the stolen truck was there or if it is connected to the explosion. Our investigators have not found traces of the explosive in the house. I'm leaning toward a gas explosion."

"Accidental? That is too great a coincidence."

Daniel nodded. "I agree, but the question then is why did a house full of people not smell the gas?"

"Different gas?"

"Perhaps, but we've found no tank that could have contained enough to fill the house. The appliances appear to have been tampered with, the safeties disconnected. This was no accident."

Solikov frowned. "Somebody is targeting the

cyber community."

"Successfully," said Daniel. "Cyber activity has dropped to near zero in Saint Petersburg. People are afraid. We're trying to find out who attended Andrei's meeting, but the guest list was on his computer, destroyed in the blast. I did video people entering. Not everybody would be shown if they entered before I got there. We're trying to identify the bodies, but some are not recognizable."

"Gather all your information. You will accompany me to Moscow. If this is an attack against the cyber community, Moscow may be the next site." As he left, he pulled out his phone.

And the government cyber section, thought Daniel. *If this is an attack against cybers, who's behind it? Most victims of cybercrime are in America. Would the US government send a team? That would escalate cyber-warfare to a whole new level.*

Chapter 28

Sasha followed the small man into the liquor store. She had been on his tail since he'd gotten off the bus from the Cyber Command building. His ratty hat was pulled low, almost covering his eyes, his well-worn coat covering his dirty overalls. He asked the clerk for the cheapest bottle of vodka he had.

When he reached into his pocket to pay, she stepped up. "I like that vodka there," she said, pointing at a much more expensive bottle.

The man turned his red-rimmed eyes on her. "Cannot afford that or you." He looked her up and down.

"I'm not for sale. Let me buy it for you." Surprise showed on his face. He shrugged. She paid.

As they walked out, she said, "I'm new in town.

Never been to Moscow before and have no place to stay. Can we share this bottle? My name is Sasha. What's yours?"

"Mikael."

The inside of the man's one-room flat was a small step above a wreck. The single light bulb hanging from the ceiling revealed yellowed paint peeling from the walls. It was impossible to tell what color the rug had once been. A hotplate was the only appliance. A grimy, stained mattress with stuffing emerging from several holes was on the floor. Atop a crate that served as a table sat a single dirty glass. She wrinkled her nose at the reek of sweat and urine.

Sasha immediately wanted to take a shower. As Mikael took off his overcoat, she opened the bottle, poured some into the glass and handed it to him. She took a swig from the bottle, as he watched with a wary stare.

"What do you want from me?"

"A place to drink and maybe to sleep."

"I have no money."

"I have no room," she replied. "What do you do?"

"I am a janitor at the government building,

night shift, basement."

"Must not pay well," she remarked, looking around the room.

"Pay is for shit." He finished off the glass of vodka. She refreshed it.

"You work every day?"

"Have Monday off." His words were slurred.

She pretended to drink from the bottle. "This is better than that rotgut you were about to buy. That stuff will kill you." She poured more into his glass.

After he passed out, she pressed her hand to her ear. "Okay, Nick, come on in."

Nick entered, strode to the snoring man, checked his pulse and pulled a hypodermic from his pocket. He squirted some of the clear liquid out. "Just want him unconscious, not dead," he explained. Ilia entered the room.

"It stinks in here." He and Nick striped the man, put the clothes in a bag and turned to go.

"Don't forget this," Sasha said, holding up the ID badge. "I'm getting out of here before I vomit."

Nick gave her another hypodermic. "Come back tonight. Give him this. It should keep him out until tomorrow morning."

* * *

Wearing the reeking clothes, Ilia kept his head down, the hat covering most of his face. The guards turned away as he passed through the service entrance into a long hallway.

A heavyset man stormed toward him. "Mikael, get your ass down to the basement. You didn't finish cleaning it yesterday. I'm not going to get my ass reamed because you don't do your job. You don't finish it tonight, I'll fire your ass after I get done kicking it."

Ilia hunched and waved acknowledgement as he started down the hall.

"Not that way you stupid shit. Down the stairs. Drunk again as usual, I see,"

Ilia peeked over his shoulder to see the man pointing to a doorway to the left.

The huge basement was filled cubicles, each with a desk and computer. About half had men typing, the only sound the clicking of their keys. Harsh overhead lighting and gray concrete walls ensured there was nothing cheery in the large room.

Ilia stumbled toward what he assumed was a janitor's closet. A large dust mop, rags and a wet mop and bucket rested beside the utility sink. He pulled out the dustmop and began making the rounds, sweeping the debris into piles. The computer operators ignored him. A tone rang after two hours, and the men filed out for a break.

In one deserted cubical he brought the monitor to life. A menu showed him the layout of the building. The basement was the ransomware division. It included the misinformation section. Bogus stories and fake news were created here. He paid particular attention to the method used to send them. Everything written went to a central office for review.

On the ground floor was cyber spying, hacking into systems to get information from government operations. The physical plant was also on the ground floor with a rollup door for access. Electrical, water, and HVAC distributed out into the building from there. The next level was for hacking into the control systems for utilities—electrical, water, gas and internet systems. The top floor was offices. In one corner was the security office, the department to prevent interference in Russia's cyber systems. It was defensive. A red dot on the computer screen indicated a meeting was going on.

Ilia finished the dry mopping and brought out

the bucket and began cleaning the floor. He worked his way over to the review office. As he entered, he heard the workers return. *Maybe next break.*

Chapter 29

In the meeting room of the Russian Cyber Security Division, Detective Inspector Daniel Novikov glanced at the faces of the men around the table. At Solikov's direction, he'd presented a summary of the events in Saint Petersburg that appeared directed against the cyber community. Novikov wasn't ready to say whether it was a political attack against them or a move to take over the that business.

"At the least," he said, "these could be a series of robberies, but the bombing of Andrei Petrov's house during the meeting of the cyber bosses appears to have targeted the community. We have no evidence of theft from Andrei's house or their Bitcoin accounts. It is particularly hard to trace those accounts. The robberies seem to be thefts of convenience, not the aim."

"What do you believe the objective was?" asked Solikov.

"It is my belief that someone wants to shut down the cybercrime. If so, who would that someone be?"

"It is the Americans, of course," said Colonel Zoloniski. He was short and thin with dark hair slicked back. His hatchet-like face gave him an air of someone deadly.

"Probably so," agreed Daniel, "but is it a government operation?"

"I will find out. We have our ways," said the colonel.

"Another question. Will this activity expand or is it limited to Saint Petersburg? That will tell us a lot," said Solikov.

"If we see attacks in other areas, we will call in the Wagner Group," said Colonel Zoloniski. "They can be trusted."

"Tell us about the bomb," said another man.

"We have found no chemical residue as would be expected from a bomb. Our conclusion is that it was a gas explosion. We found no large tank to supply enough gas to completely destroy the house. The source had to be from the line supplying the house. Supporting this is that the appliances had been tampered with so the safety devices wouldn't work." He glanced at Solikov.

"This raises two questions: How and when did this tampering happen? Why did no one smell the gas?

"Interviewing a surviving member of the security staff, he remembered a Gazprom truck performing maintenance a few weeks ago. Gazprom has no record of such. The gas supply line had a second shutoff valve and taps installed before and after one of these valves. Our suspicion is that the gas was deodorized and reintroduced in the line to the house. Gazprom is investigating how this could be done. During this maintenance operation, a technician could have entered the house and tampered with the appliances." Daniel glanced at the faces around him.

"I was at the scene shortly after the explosion, and the remains of a truck, which had been stolen a couple of months before, was on the street. It had been blown up, and the body of Andrei Petrov's brother was near it."

"It is your theory this truck contained equipment to deodorize the gas," said Zoloniski.

"It fits the evidence," confirmed Solikov.

"Have you identified who is responsible for this criminal act?"

"We have not," said Daniel. "We are reviewing the closed-circuit footage of all the cameras in the areas frequented by the cyber people. We have enlisted the help of hackers looking for those not familiar."

"Let me know when you come up with anything. The purpose of the Security Division is to protect our cyber operations."

Daniel chuckled to himself. Most cyber security was to protect against hacking.

Chapter 30

Sol walked around the farmhouse inspecting the construction. He called Ilia over. "Why is the bottom half of the wall made of stone stacked inside a wire mesh?"

"It stops bullets. But there's more. Between the inner and outer wall is explosive. The whole house is like a MON-50, the Russian version of the American Claymore mine. The kill zone is two-hundred meters and complete destruction inside. A company-sized assault would be destroyed."

"But you know Russia's love for tanks. An assault of hundreds would include tanks."

Ilia swept his hand around the countryside. "There are tank traps dug in the fields. It would not be easy for them to approach."

"They could use artillery."

"Yes, but they think they have us trapped. They

will want to capture those inside alive for questioning. Can't do that with artillery. It is a trap for them."

"Let's go have our meeting. We need to make plans for the Cyber Division."

The *Fantasmas* were gathered in the largest room at the farmhouse. It was not as rundown as the outside of the house would make one think. Ilia was standing to one side, a laser pointer directed at the big-screen mounted on the wall.

"In all, there about 1000 workers in the Cyber Division. On day shift 650 are inside. The rest are on night shift. Shifts are twelve hours. As an auxiliary building, it has independent utilities–gas, electrical with backup, water, sewage and heating/ air conditioning ventilation. As Bob noted, the shell of the building is a Faraday cage preventing outside electronic radiation from entering. Their connection to the internet is through a very sophisticated filtering system."

"What do you recommend?" asked Sol.

"This operation has to have long-term consequences. I believe we have to plan a physical attack. The security teams are too strong for us to overcome without high casualties. The vulnerabilities I see are the utilities. The building is too large for the type of gas attack we used in Saint Petersburg."

"What about an Electro-Magnetic Pulse to take out the computers?" asked Bob. "I have a unit powerful enough."

"We would have to get it inside the building. How big is it?"

"It would fit in the bed of a pickup truck."

"Can't get that in my lunchbox," laughed Ilia.

"Need to think longer time," said Sol. "Need to think after attack." He glanced around. "Where is Leon?"

"Handcuffed to the bed. He's blindfolded and wearing headphones playing techno music," said Sasha.

"Don't think he will make it," said Zyra.

"Keep him isolated but alive," said Sol. "May need him."

Both Zyra and Sasha stared at him.

"Bob, what is source of computer chips for Russian industry?"

"After things calmed down from the invasion and takeover of the Donbas region of Ukraine, Germany resumed the sale of chips to Russia.

China also supplies them. We know the Chinese chips have some imbedded circuitry that may give them a backdoor into the computers, but Russia considers them an ally. They prefer German chips."

"And the source of operating system software?"

"Russia writes their own."

"Is it possible to hack into the OS software?"

"Sure. Let me think of the best way. I'll get back to you."

"Ilia, you and I need to make a trip."

Chapter 31

Major Pushkin stared at the order he had just received. Not since the Ukraine operation had he shipped out Sarin. He had no doubt it was official. The signatures were right, as was the form. Three canisters, more than had been used against the Kurds. *Well, whatever the operation, I'm better off not knowing. When do I need to have this ready?* He read the form again. *Shit! A truck is scheduled to arrive today. These secret missions always take place with little notification.*

He called his lieutenant. "Growski, bring three canisters of Sarin to the loading dock for pickup."

Under international treaty, all stockpiles of Sarin were to be destroyed years ago, but everybody cheated. In this bunker was enough to kill every person on earth. It was the same with the weaponized Smallpox stores at Koltsovo until the

North Koreans had destroyed the site. They claimed their missile had been tampered with by the Americans. That was probably so. If this repository and the factory were known, the same might happen here.

Well, it's not my problem. I just follow orders.

* * *

Somewhere, Ilia had come up with two Russian uniforms, ID documents. and a copy of their orders for the three canisters of Sarin. Picking up the canisters had gone without a hitch. The bored guard smiled as Ilia gave him a bar of chocolate, a bottle of vodka and the copy of their orders. He'd loaded the pallet onto the truck and waved them on.

"We need to make a stop in Kirov," said Ilia as he turned off the highway. Sol nodded. It was late as they backed up to a warehouse loading dock. A muscular man with dark curly hair signaled for them to stop just as the back of the truck gently bumped the dock. Ilia got out and greeted him. They hugged and slapped each other on the back like old friends.

While Ilia opened the back of the truck, the man rolled a dolly with a pallet on it toward them.

Together, the two men lifted one of the canisters onto the pallet. The man disappeared back into the warehouse pushing the dolly.

Ilia climbed into the cab of the truck. "It's the price for the farmhouse we're using and the rest." He gestured toward the uniforms. Sol nodded as they pulled back onto the highway toward Moscow.

Six hours later they arrived at the farm, driving directly into the barn. "Long trip," said Sol walking toward the house. "I'm ready to sit on something that's not moving. What's going to happen to that canister?"

"Mossad will only use it appropriately."

Whatever that means, thought Sol. A lot of civilians somehow became appropriate targets.

* * *

"Bob's waiting to talk to you," said Dawn as they entered.

"First, I need a beer," said Sol. He pulled a Baltika #6 from the refrigerator. In the office he sat down and called Bob.

"Hey, Bob, what have you for me?"

"I did my research, and we can get my software

loaded as part of the operating system at the computer manufacturing plant. We need a good hacker to get into their system."

"Better than you?"

"Well, I could do it, but there are better people than me. We absolutely cannot leave tracks."

"If we got Leon to do it, could you ensure he doesn't fuck us over? He's bitter about Saint Petersburg."

"I can review what he does, but what if he thought he was hacking an American company?"

Sol was quiet for a few seconds. "That might work, but is it worth the effort if you can do it?"

"Let's try it. If I don't like what I'm seeing, I can always do it."

"I'll call you back."

* * *

Sol walked into the bedroom where Leon was sitting on the bed, Zyra beside him. "I've got a job we could use you for."

Leon glared at him. "I'm not doing anything against Russia."

"Actually, it's an American company we need help with. It's gone a bit rogue, and we want to install some software in its operating system."

"What's in it for me?"

You get to live another day. "I'm sure we can reach an agreement."

"I'll look at it."

"It won't be easy. This company is pretty sophisticated."

Leon shrugged, a bored look on his face. "Doesn't bother me."

Sol returned to the office. "We need to disguise this well, but I think he's in."

Chapter 32

Back in his office in Saint Petersburg, Daniel Novikov sat with another member of the cyber community reviewing video footage of places frequented by hackers. He had spoken with three so far with no hopeful results. They were reviewing the security cameras from a nightclub like many in the city–loud techno music, flashing lights, expensive drinks, cheap girls and boys. The tape was from three weeks ago, just before the first murders.

"Yeah, Friday nights rock," said Christian. "Everybody was there." He pointed at several figures. "I think that's Argoti. They really need to do something about the resolution. I can hardly make him out. He's not an indie, worked with Andrei Petrov. That big guy is a body guard. I think he's more for show."

Daniel leaned in, but the kid was right. The resolution was bad.

"There's Leon Ivanov. Some think he's the best hacker in Saint Petersburg, maybe the world."

Daniel recognized him. He hadn't seen the two women at the table in any of the previous videos. "What about them?" he pointed.

"Never saw them before. Man, that black one's hot. I'd remember her."

As they watched, Ivanov got up and left. The two women followed. "Seen them since?"

"Naw. Guess they were passing through. Maybe working girls. They come and go, know what I mean?"

"Anybody else a stranger?"

"I don't know everybody, so lots of strangers."

Daniel enlarged the picture of the three sitting at the table. There was a bottle on it. Not a vodka bottle. He tried to enlarge further, but the label blurred out. He captured the best shot to a photo, sent it to his phone. He and the kid watched other videos with nothing interesting.

* * *

Daniel walked into the club. When the

doorman asked for a cover, he flashed his badge. It was Friday night, but the place seemed dead. Since the explosion at Andrei's house, not many hackers felt like partying. At the bar, he showed the photo to several barkeepers. One remembered the women.

"Yah, they asked for some kind of tequila. When I said we didn't carry that, the blonde produced a bottle, had me pour for them. Later I sent the bottle to Ivanov's table."

"Did they leave together?"

"Don't know. It was pretty busy."

"Seen them since that night?"

"Nope. I'd remember."

"Thanks. If you think of anything, give me a call." He handed the man a card.

Time for a visit to Ivanov.

Fifteen minutes later he parked outside Leon's building. His rings at the door got no response. Nor did his calls. He called Stravos.

"Captain, sorry for the late hour. I might have a lead on the bombing. I need a warrant and an entry team for Leon Ivanov's building. I'm there. Nobody answers. He may have been in Petrov's house the night of the bombing, but I didn't see him."

"What's the connection?"

"He was at a nightclub three weeks ago with a couple of women nobody recognizes. I know it's thin, but we have nothing else."

The team arrived thirty minutes later. From the garage panel, they were able to activate the elevator. The team rushed in, guns ready. Daniel waited as they cleared the apartment. He waved them out.

Ivanov had some interesting decor, Southwestern American. The place was neat, not what he'd seen at other hacker houses. His computer and files were gone. Most of his clothes were in his closet. What caught his interest were the two evening gowns also in the closet. Briefly, he flashed on Ivanov wearing them, laughed at the image. One was too long, the other too small. These were new, price tags still attached, no store listed though. The women had stayed with him. Where were they?

A keypad located beside a locked door glowed red showing it was activated. "Captain, I need forensics and a lock expert to open an electronic lock. I'll send you a picture. Two women were staying with him. Everybody's gone. They must have left prints. He could have gone with them voluntarily or we have another kidnapping."

The forensics team and the lock expert showed up fifteen minutes later. While the team dusted for prints, the locksmith had the door open. It was a security setup. Monitors showed numerous views of the apartment and the outside of the building. The storage files were gone.

Downhearted at again finding nothing, he continued inspecting. Something was off in the area. He paced off the room dimensions. There was a hidden a room. Inch-by-inch, he went over the apartment again.

At the bookcase, he paused. Leon didn't seem the type to read, especially the classic books arrayed on the shelves. When he removed *War and Peace,* a button was behind it. He pushed it and the bookcase opened on another compartment. Weapons were displayed on the walls. "I need these checked for prints," he yelled.

Chapter 33

"Ivanov's apartment was cleaned by professionals," said Daniel. He was on a video call to Detective Solikov, who was with Colonel Zoloniski. "The surveillance tapes had been wiped. Not even Ivanov's prints were found."

"Shit!" exclaimed Solikov, a deep frown on his face.

"But from a rifle he had in a hidden cabinet, I got one partial print. From our records, we know it's not his."

"Did it look like he left or was taken?" asked Colonel Zoloniski.

"No signs of a struggle, but as I said, it was sanitized. I've been going over CCTV footage from security cameras of places members of the hacking community frequented. A couple of them are helping me look for strangers, but that's a long shot."

The knock on Daniel's door broke into the conversation. "Come!" he grunted, irked by the interruption. Daniel stared as his red-faced and overweight sergeant gasped for breath. "Did you run? I've never seen you run."

"I thought this was important enough you'd want to know right away. Sir, we got a hit on the partial print from Ivanov's apartment. The print is an eighty percent match to one we lifted from the murder scenes in Tosno and Baltiyskaya Sloboda."

Our first break. "Thank you, sergeant. Forward the prints to my computer. That will be all."

"Send those prints on to us," said Colonel Zoloniski. "We'll run them through our data-base."

"One of my hackers did pick out a couple of women he didn't know with Leon. They were at a club together. The outside CCTV showed them getting into a white van. The angle was wrong, so we didn't get a plate. It was probably stolen anyway."

"Do you have a shot we can use for facial recognition?" asked the colonel.

"Nothing clear, but I'll send everything to you."

"Perhaps we have something," said Detective

Solikov.

"I'm going to widen my search of the CCTV coverage to see if we can pick up these two women at other places. We may be able to get better photos."

"In your gut, Daniel, do you think they are involved in this?"

"The print at the murder scene cannot be ignored. I think they are."

"Call us with anything new. We'll see what we can find from our databases. Good work, detective." The colonel cut the connection.

* * *

Detective Novikov stared at the ceiling deep in thought. The women left the club with Ivanov. His apartment was sanitized. They might have been with him for more than one night. So…perhaps they shopped, at least for groceries. The dresses were new, but there was nothing telling what store.. If they weren't staying with him, then where? Where was Ivanov?

He sighed. A lot of legwork ahead. "Sergeant," he called, "Gather the group. We need a meeting. I have work assignments."

Chapter 34

From his office, Daniel Novikov was on a video conference with the Moscow office of Cyber Security. "We have made progress. By tracking the credit card use of Ivanov, we have video of the two women buying clothes. Our facial recognition database turned up nothing. Apparently the two have no police record. I am sending the files to you."

"With our national records, perhaps we can find something," said Colonel Zoloniski.

"You say they were buying clothes. What kind? Everyday or dress?" asked Solikov.

"Dress clothes like they were going to a party. A day later, Ivanov bought a tuxedo with a rush order for tailoring. The two women were with him. I believe they were planning to attend Andrei's party. I didn't see them go in, but they could have arrived before I started watching. Our forensics team has not found any remains matching the women. I don't think they were there."

"I have your files," said the colonel. "Give me a second to send them to our research division."

"Once I had the images, I widened my search for the two women. Our CCTV picked them up driving a white van near the river. They parked near the old access tunnels used to haul coal from the barges into buildings in the city. We followed one tunnel into an abandoned apartment building. From the outside, it looked ready for destruction, but the inside had been rehabbed. It was professionally sanitized–no prints, nothing left but empty space. This was where they stayed."

"How many others were involved?" asked Solikov?

"The CCTV showed a box truck, like the one that was blown up at Andrei's. parked near the entrance to the tunnel. Unfortunately, the camera angle and quality isn't great. Several men were recorded loading the truck with things from the building two days before the explosion. On the night of the blast, the van returned and parked beside the truck. In total, we counted eight people splitting up between the truck and the van before both vehicles departed. Nothing since that night."

"Do you believe they left Saint Petersburg?" asked Solikov.

"There have been no further incidents. We continue to monitor the CCTV footage but have not seen the two women or Ivanov. Nor has there been any activity on Ivanov's credit card. Since they cleaned out the building they were staying in, I think they are gone."

"Left Russia?" asked the colonel.

"We are watching the airports, the boat docks and the border crossings. If they already had transportation set up, we may have missed them."

"Good work, detective. We will distribute the pictures and vehicle descriptions."

"Also," added the colonel, "we will alert Finnish and Swedish authorities to be on the lookout. Perhaps if we ask nicely, they can review security footage since the night of the bombing. Nobody wants bombers roaming around."

"David, come to Moscow. Wherever they are,

I don't think it's in Saint Petersburg," said Solikov.

"I can hop on a flight and be there in the morning."

"We'll have more information about the two women by then."

Chapter 35

"Sol, David Kennedy called me," said Bob. "His buddies at NSA picked up chatter that your team may be compromised. Pictures of Zyra and Sasha have been distributed, along with their vehicle description. Somebody is hunting you and on the trail."

"This chatter was police?"

"A detective in Saint Petersburg is good. He found CCTV footage of the girls in the nightclub where they picked up Ivanov. Tracking credit card usage, he got pictures of them buying clothes. The van was also caught on video, so they have that description. By following it, they saw you leaving Saint Petersburg. Immigration authorities in Sweden and Finland are looking to see if you went there after the bombing."

"What is detective's name?"

"He didn't tell me, but he is communicating with Cyber Security in Moscow."

"They moving fast for Russians."

"Fast for anybody. This detective is good."

"We will finish in Moscow and get out. Plan is to go to Sochi and get boat there. Need that arranged."

"I'll talk to David. Any idea of your schedule?"

"We will move up schedule here. Sochi two days drive if we stop, one day straight through. So maybe less than one week. I will call."

"On another note, David's man has a company to use for Leon's hack. It is one of his companies so it will check out as legitimate. We will open a portal from that company into the chip manufacturer in Germany. To Leon, it will look like he's hacking into the American company."

"We do that tomorrow. Now, I must go paint vehicles."

"Keep the girls inside. No use taking any chances. Be careful. Things just got very dangerous. I'll talk to David to get the boat schedule moved up."

"Thank David for alert. Probably save lives."

* * *

"We must make hit tomorrow," said Sol to the group. "Pictures of Zyra and Sasha are on street. Also, description of truck and van. He stared at the two women. "So, you will not go outside until we go with plan."

"I wondered why you were buying all that spray paint," said Kiki. "Glad to hear you're not huffing it. What colors?"

"Black and gray. Will work for a while. We must be at exfil in Sochi in less than one week."

"When is the EMP device supposed to arrive?" asked Ilia.

According to tracking, is in FedEx warehouse. We pick up tomorrow on way to target."

"I can change my looks with a wig and some stuff," said Sasha.

"Not so easy for me," commented Zyra. "Not a lot of Africans here."

* * *

"Go get Leon. Time to see his skills."

Zyra removed the headphones and blindfold from Leon. "Time to go to work."

As she removed the handcuffs he whined, "Why did you lock me up? I said I'd help you."

She smiled at him. "Sol said to."

They walked into the kitchen. "Hey, this is my computer!" said Leon as he sat down at the table.

"Ya, we save it for you."

Sol came in and sat next to Leon. He placed his pistol on the table. "No funny business. You understand?"

"See you later," said Zyra as she left.

"Where's she going?" asked Leon.

"She have job to do." Sol inserted an earbud.

"Okay, I'm on," said Bob. "Anything he does, I'll see before it goes out. You sure about letting him use his own computer?"

"Ya, get going."

Leon looked at him and began typing.

"He's logging on, so his IP address will pop up if anybody is paying attention. They will know where you are."

Chapter 36

"We have information about the two women," said Colonel Zoloniski. "I will forward it to you."

Detective Novikov's phone rang. "What is it, Sergeant?" he asked. They were in Colonel Zoloniski's office at the Cyber Center.

"Sorry to interrupt you, sir, but Leon Ivanov's computer just popped up. Thought you'd like to know."

"Good work, sergeant. Do you have a location?"

"We're working on that now. It appears to be in the Moscow area. We'll be able to pinpoint it soon, maybe fifteen minutes."

"Call me as soon as you have it."

Daniel looked at Solikov and the colonel with a smile. "Leon's computer just came on line. My men should have the location soon."

"Do they know what he was doing?"

"I'll ask when they call back. They did say that he's close to Moscow but not in the city."

"Great work, Novikov." The colonel picked up his phone and issued orders to assemble a team. He reached for his coat as he stood. "You both will go with."

Daniel glanced at Solikov. "I hope Leon's with the bombers. I wouldn't miss this."

"Neither would I," said the detective, rising.

"We will be ready in thirty minutes. I'll muster the men from our security forces here. We'll bring in an armored troop carrier."

"No helicopter?" asked Daniel, half serious.

The colonel stared at him for a beat. "I want to keep this inhouse. That would require the Army."

* * *

It was a crisp morning and a clear day. From her hide atop a hotel 600 meters from the Cyber Command building, Kiki had an unobstructed view. Her hide was an inflatable box that looked like a piece of roof equipment. She watched the soldiers assemble in the parking lot outside. "Sol," she said into her com, "they're getting ready faster that we thought."

"Ya. Bob has drone watching."

Kiki glanced skyward to see a raven circling. "The vulture drone is overhead there?"

"Da. We'll know when they come. Dawn and I not finished packing gear. Truck deliver air conditioning package yet?"

Kiki had her AR-10 chambered in .25-06 with a suppressor and a high-tech sight. It made the slender rifle ungainly and heavy. She swung her rifle sight to the physical plant. "Nick and Sasha are unloading it now. Thank God she had that wig. Sol, there may not be enough time for them to come pick you up. You need to get out. Leave the equipment behind. Walk away. You can be a couple of miles down the road before anyone gets there."

"There will be time. What about Zyra and Ilia?"

"The van is pulled up at the loading dock. The crate with the EMP is on a dolly and they're pushing it inside."

* * *

Detectives Novikov and Solikov sat in their car

and watched the last of the men climb aboard the troop carrier, the snout of the heavy machinegun swinging as the man inside tested the controls. In addition, another troop truck was loaded. Thirty men had been pulled together in this short time. The colonel had stripped the security staff for this operation.

"They can move quickly with the proper motivation," noted Solikov.

Daniel grimaced as he watched the colonel haranguing them to hurry up. *Glad I don't work for Zoloniski.* As they pulled away from the building, he noted the gray delivery van with the sign COMPUTER COMPONENTS at the loading dock. Two people were pushing a dolly with a long crate inside the building. *Odd worker, the tall thin black man. Not usual in Moscow. Probably from Nigeria. We're getting a lot of refugees from there lately.*

* * *

"Sol, are you, Dawn, and Leon out? The troops just left."

"They send somebody ahead to watch until rest arrive. There is a Tigr parked on road. No way anybody can get here. Plan for truck to return is gone. Van and truck meet on highway south."

"Sol, you can run out the back! You have to get out!"

"If one in front, another in back. Open country all around. We buy time for you. This trap was always plan, just didn't know it was for us too. Go to Sochi, catch boat."

"He's right," said Bob. "There's another Tigr in back. They can't get out, you can't get in."

The feeling of helplessness froze, Kiki. "If I fire a few shots, the caravan will turn around. It'll give you time."

"Then everybody die or get friendly interrogation. Follow orders. Stay with plan."

Nick, Ilia, Sasha and Zyra had heard the exchange, but couldn't answer. With her vision blurred by tears, she sighted in on the single guard at the main entry door. *These bastards will pay.*

* * *

Sasha and Nick, wearing the uniforms of the air conditioning service company, wheeled the tank labeled freon up to the huge unit that pumped out the heat generated by the computers inside. In fifteen-minutes a hose from the large tank was attached to the main air duct. Inside the tank were the cylinders of Sarin. "Zyra, are you and Ilia clear?"

"Da. The crate is inside, the timer set. We leave now."

Nick opened the valve. He and Sasha hurried out to the truck. As he started it, a guard ran out. He went down, half his head gone from the high-velocity bullet. *Thank you, Kiki.* They drove out.

Chapter 37

Leading the column in his command car, Colonel Zoloniski passed the men in the Tigr guarding the entry to the farmhouse. It was like hundreds of others in the area: two story, frame and rock construction built on flat land. He stopped three-hundred meters away and signaled for the men to deploy, surrounding the structure. Once they were in place, he brought a bullhorn out.

"You are surrounded. Come out with your hands up." A single shot rang out, striking the windshield of the colonel's car. "Fire," he commanded. A fusillade of shots struck the building, shattering windows, knocking the door off its hinges and pocking the wood siding.

"Come out with your hands up. We won't shoot you." Another shot struck the colonel's windshield.

"Getting shot may be preferable to what you

have planned," Sol yelled back.

"Hold your fire," Zoloniski commanded. There was silence. A few minutes later, two figures stepped through the door, hands in the air. One was a man of average height, stockily built with dark curly hair. The other was a slender woman with straight blonde hair. "Anyone else in there?"

The man yelled, "Leon Ivanov is tied up inside. There's nobody else here."

"On your knees, feet crossed behind you, hands on your head."

Sol and Dawn complied. The colonel signaled and his men moved forward. Those in the back of the house stopped fifty meters away, maintaining the cordon in case there were more people inside who would try to escape out the back.

A team went inside. Colonel Zoloniski turned to the two detectives. "Remain here until we are sure everything is cleared." He strode forward, a dozen men accompanying him. They surrounded the two figures. Three men dragged Ivanov out.

"I wasn't part of this!" he screamed. "They kidnapped me."

Sol looked over his shoulder at Leon. "I am sorry. I would do same thing you did. Loyalty to your country is admirable."

The colonel stared at Sol. Suddenly his world exploded.

From their car, Daniel and Solikov watched in horror as the farmhouse disappeared in a ball of fire. The shockwave shook the ground. Rocks and steel balls mowed down everybody within two-hundred meters. "My God," screamed Daniel, "the whole house was a MON-50 mine!" He had seen the devastation those caused during his time in Ukraine. It was a horrible weapon.

He sank to the ground, not noticing the damage to their car. He turned to Solikov. There was blood running from one ear. "You're wounded."

"It's a scratch, nothing."

After a few minutes, Daniel looked at the sky. "Why? What was the purpose of this?" Solikov stared at him. "What did this accomplish? I mean beside killing a lot of people."

"You don't think that was the goal?"

"Always before they attacked the cyber people." Daniel stopped.

"My God! We have to get back to the Cyber Command Center. This was a diversion."

Solikov gawked at Daniel as he raced for the

car and jumped behind the wheel. Solikov climbed into the passenger seat as the car threw gravel and dirt from the spinning tires. They raced past the Tigr, the crew standing agape at the death scene.

* * *

Kiki watched the gray van pull away from the building. She'd already shot the guard at the front door and peppered the entry to keep everybody inside. They got the message. She switched her scope to the physical plant as the box truck started up. A guard ran toward the cab, but she cut him down. She looked at her watch. Ten seconds. Just in case, she placed her rifle and the electronic scope inside the special case with a copper mesh. She threw her watch inside. The electronic protection of the Cyber Center should protect her equipment, but she wanted to be sure.

Nothing electronic was working thanks to the Electro Magnetic Pulse bomb they'd delivered into the building. The Faraday cage that was a shield for the building kept the shockwave inside. It didn't matter, the Sarin gas had already doomed everybody.

Suddenly, a car that seemed familiar started to turn into the parking lot then swerved out and pulled in a couple of cars behind the box truck. "Nick, I think you have a tail. I think it's the one that went with the troops."

"What's it look like?"

"Black sedan, smashed windshield and dents. If you turn right at the next corner, then right again, I'll have a shot."

"Roger."

As Kiki hurried to the other side of the building, she uncased her rifle. Just as she peeked over the edge, she saw Nick and the truck pass. Behind another truck was the sedan. Her shot would be through the passenger window. To get the driver, she'd have to get the passenger out of the way. Her first shot hit the man's neck. He was flung to the side by the power of the bullet. The driver was trying to duck down amid the spray of blood. The car leapt forward. She fired again. He'd gone to the floor. Hit? It didn't matter, the car plowed into the back of the truck ahead of it. "You're clear."

"We'll pick you up at the corner."

"Kiki, I'm landing the raven on your roof by the fire-escape. If you have enough time, pick it up," said Bob.

"Nick, give me three minutes to clean up and get my gear." *Now to get out of town and grieve for Sol and Dawn.*

Chapter 38

Daniel was dazed by the shocks of the collision and the shooting, and he had a massive headache. Laying on the floor of the car, he inhaled sharply looking eye-to-eye at Solikov's blank stare from the passenger side. Cautiously, he tried to rise, reaching for the steering wheel to pull himself up, but his hand slipped on the blood and gore that covered the inside of the car. Solikov was dead, no doubt. The shooter had also tried to kill him, but his instinct to dive for the floor saved his life.

Through the spattered window, he looked up at the people crowding against his car asking if he was okay. Slowly his mind came back. The door was opened and he was pulled from the car and laid on the street. It was cold, so cold.

He looked into the face of a man leaning over him. "Take it easy. You've been shot. An ambulance is on the way."

He tried to rise, but was pushed back. "Not my blood."

"The gouge on your head says otherwise."

He tried to raise his hand, but blackness took him.

* * *

The first thing Daniel noticed was the hospital smell. After being wounded in Ukraine, he'd spent two weeks recuperating from a grenade explosion that blew shrapnel into his shoulder. He kept his eyes closed as that vision slowly faded. He knew that smell. He opened his eyes, seeing only the featureless white ceiling. The sound of shuffling feet was second thing that brought him back to this world. Someone was standing beside his bed.

"Detective, I'm glad you're back among the living," Captain Stravos said, smiling down at him. "Two millimeters more and you'd be dead."

"What happened?"

"A lot. The massacre at the farm house was a diversion to pull the security away from the Cyber Command Center." He shook his head. "Thirty-three people killed including Colonel Zoloniski.

The real tragedy is the attack on Cyber Command. These bastards used Sarin and murdered everyone inside. They also set off a device that destroyed all the electronics. This will set back the cyber warfare division of Russia by at least a year."

Like a series of still pictures, visions of the farmhouse and the people leaving the Cyber Command Center flashed. "I almost had them. Solikov and I were following their truck when he was killed and I was shot." The image of Solikov staring at nothing from his ruined face rose. He pushed it away.

"We're watching all roads from Moscow, but the horse is out of the barn. By the time we set up the roadblocks, they could have been a hundred kilometers away."

Daniel closed his eyes and sighed. "I failed."

The captain put his hand on Daniel's shoulder. "You need time off. Three brushes with death. Your guardian angel might be getting tired."

"Three?"

"Da." Stravos held up one finger. "If you had been closer to that farmhouse, you would have been killed." He held up another finger. "If you hadn't followed that truck, you'd have gone into the Cyber

Command building, and the nerve gas would have killed you." He held up a third finger. "If you hadn't fallen down in the car, the sniper would have gotten you." He waggled the three fingers. "Take some time off and reflect on how precious your life is."

"Perhaps I was saved for some reason."

"Perhaps you'll figure that out during your rest and recouperation. You'll be going back to Saint Petersburg in two days when you're well enough to travel. In the meantime, I've brought you some fishing magazines." He gestured at the stand on the table beside the bed. "I find fishing very relaxing."

Chapter 39

Memories and visions of Sol kept rising up as Kiki steered the van into a car park. They hadn't stopped driving and this was her third four-hour shift. They had six-hundred kilometers yet to go. This stop was a welcome break. Ilia set up the satellite dish so they could talk to Bob.

"Things are really hot in Moscow. Good you got out. They set up roadblocks mostly to the north and west, so I think you have pretty clear sailing all the way to Sochi. David spoke to your benefactor, and your ride out of the country is two days away."

"We're driving straight through, so we'll be there tomorrow," said Kiki.

"Do you have a place to stay?"

"I do." said Ilia. "We stayed there a few years ago. It's actually south and east of Sochi."

"I remember," said Zyra. "We will be safe."

"Too bad about your drone," said Nick. "We could probably use it there."

"As soon as I saw the troops deploy around the farmhouse, I programmed it to dive into the Moscow River. When the house blew up, I lost my link."

There was silence at the thought of the farmhouse and the loss of Dawn and Sol.

"I'm already building another with some improvements. It'll be better. In the meantime, you can use the raven Kiki saved."

"We will once we set up at the house," said Ilia.

"David says cyber activity out of Russia is nearly zero. Hackers are scared and the Cyber Command lost most of its people. All the equipment has to be replaced, and the German chip manufacturer will play a big part. Thanks to Leon, we'll have a surprise for the new generation of hackers. Call me before you get to Sochi for any alerts. David is on top of that."

"Nothing else here," said Ilia. "Time for us to get back on the road. Thanks for your help." The connection was cut and Ilia disassembled the satellite system.

* * *

They were on the road fifteen minutes later. "I feel a little bad about Leon," said Sasha as she guided the van back onto the highway with Zyra in the passenger seat. "He kinda got sucked into this."

"We could have stayed with original plan. He would be dead sooner. Not have the pleasure of our company," Zyra responded.

Sasha looked at the road, silent for a few minutes. "I like looking at that viewpoint better. Sure hope the Russians aren't watching the port at Sochi."

"You full of optimism."

Chapter 40

Rest and recuperation were not Detective Daniel Novikov's lifestyle. One day of fishing convinced him. At his desk in his office, he kept reviewing what they knew about these terrorists. They struck at cyber operations. Why? Were they contractors or government soldiers? They were clever, building tension within the community with terror tactics such that there would be a concentration of targets in one site. They had constructed one target of opportunity after another until the top goal was the government Cyber Division.

Were they done? He didn't think so. The cyber operations in Russia were damaged, perhaps for years. No reason to stay here. But first to escape.

If he were them, where would he go?

The whole country was searching for them, so

they had to get out of Russia. Traveling east from Moscow was not likely. There were thousands of kilometers of nothing and no access to a way out. Years ago, there had been an attack on the Koltsovo bio weapons storage facility. Those people had escaped by flying out to the east, but for now all planes except government flights were grounded.

West was a possibility. Those borders were being watched. Belarus was friendly to Russia. Ukraine was a possibility, especially since it claimed responsibility for the attacks. Mariupol, under Russian control, had been rebuilt, but after Putin was ousted, it was so loosely controlled that they were more closely aligned with the west. To get there by road they'd have to travel through the dangerous area around the Ukraine border. It was heavily patrolled after the counterattacks against the Russian refinery. The port of Taganrog was possible. From there they could sail to Mariupol.

North was the route he'd choose but Saint Petersburg was on the lookout. Boats, aircraft both commercial and private had been grounded. Anti-submarine patrols watched the coast constantly. The Finnish border was heavily patrolled, but this time of year, that was difficult. Heavy snowstorms could move in quickly.

South was nearly two-thousand kilometers to the Black Sea. Possible.

He idly flipped through his messages. Most had been read, but not one, the one the colonel had sent him that fateful day. With all that had happened, he'd forgotten about it.

The email had the files of the two women attached. He read.

The tall black woman was the daughter of immigrants from Cameroon, Africa. The family had sought refuge after helping the Wagner Group distribute arms to the al-Shebab Muslim terrorists trying to overthrow the government. Being African and very dark, the girl had been picked on in school by other kids. At age sixteen she had disappeared after stabbing one of her tormentors.

The blonde was a more interesting story. She and her brother were born in Russia but had immigrated to Israel. She had gone to America to attend the University of Utah where she took up skiing. Sasha had a talent. After several years, she made the Olympic team for Israel and competed in the slalom at the Sochi Olympics. Her name was Sasha Belikova. Her brother was Ilia Belikov. They both had been in Sochi a few years ago about the same time as the attack on Koltsovo. Daniel paused, as the event at Koltsovo and their presence in Sochi, only a few hours away, clicked. It was suspected that the brother worked for Mossad, though there was no clear proof. A security cam at a high-end hotel showed the African woman meeting with a major who disappeared soon after. South! It was a place they knew. They had been there, that's where they would go.

Chapter 41

Three hours away from Sochi, they pulled into a small park and called Bob.

"Really glad you called. An alert has gone out for Sochi. There's a roadblock set up and the patrols have been doubled at the airport and the seaport. You can't go there."

They all looked at Ilia. He closed his eyes as if picturing the area. "We'll backtrack past Novorossiysk and stay in Anapa. It's small, but tourists visit all the time. There are parks. They can pick us up off the beach. I'll send you the coordinates."

"How'd they figure out we'd be heading to Sochi?" asked Kiki.

"They're covering all borders, but I believe the detective in Saint Petersburg sent out the alert for Sochi. He's been on your tail the whole time. Smart guy."

"How'd we miss him at the farmhouse?"

"From what I saw, he and another man followed the convoy in a black car. They stayed out of the blast radius. When the house went, I lost my feed."

"I saw them," exclaimed Kiki. "They tried to follow Nick and Sasha from the Cyber Command Center. I got the passenger. Thought I got him too, but obviously I missed. I hate that."

"Not entirely," said Bob. "The report is he's in Saint Petersburg recuperating from wounds."

Kiki looked at Nick. He stared back at her, shaking his head. "We're not going back there," his voice was firm.

"Let's focus on getting out of Russia first," said Ilia. "If we don't do that, nothing matters."

"Thanks for the warning, Bob," said Nick." You definitely saved our asses.

"Sorry about Sol and Dawn. They meant a lot to me."

"Us too," said Sasha.

"We'll call you again when we get set," said Ilia. "Ciao."

Dead Ware

On the barbeques at their campsite, Nick and Kiki cooked chicken they bought at the park's convenience store. Ilia sat with them like friends enjoying an evening out. They waved greetings to other campers. Zyra and Sasha stayed in the box truck. They would use the showers and bathrooms after everyone had retired for the night.

Ilia, Nick and Kiki walked down to the beach. It was a clear night, stars twinkling, the full moon high overhead. A few other couples were sitting on the beach with wine and cheese enjoying the fall evening.

"What are we going to do with our gear?" asked Kiki.

"Yeah, what about the truck and the van?" Nick asked.

"We take what we can carry in one trip," answered Ilia. "I have a friend who runs drugs from Sochi to Moscow who will take the van. The truck and all evidence go to Ukraine where it will go up in a ball of fire. He has agreed, but it cost a lot of money. We can't leave anything that hints we were here. This detective is like a dog with a bone. If he suspects we came to Sochi, it's not much of a stretch to assume we left by boat. They will blockade and search everything."

"And you trust this guy, your friend?"

"He only gets half of the money until we confirm the truck is ashes."

"I hope it's more money than the truck is worth," said Kiki.

Chapter 42

Daniel's phone rang. He was supposed to be on leave.

"Detective Novikov, this is Colonel Dmitrev of Russian Security. I know you're recovering from your injures during the attack on the Cyber Division, but I need you in Moscow. As the only person with experience with these terrorists, you are to head up a taskforce to catch them."

"I'm flattered that you ask, sir, but I'm not sure I'm up to the job."

"It wasn't a request. I will see you tomorrow." He cut the call.

Daniel was stunned. With all the power of the Russian government, surely they didn't need him. He glanced at the piles of information in his den and smiled to himself. Perhaps he was the best person. He picked up the phone and called his boss.

"Captain Stravos, this is Detective Novikov."

"I already got the call. I hope you're well enough to face the Moscow bullies."

"I don't think I have any choice."

"I know. I'd hate to lose you, so when you need a break, take one. They need you, not the other way around–unless you get into the politics. I would advise you stay as far away as you can. It is poison. Many will try to use you. Stay neutral, do your job, document everything, confirm verbal orders in writing."

"Good advice, sir."

* * *

As Daniel deplaned, his head ached. The air pressure changes hadn't helped his recovery. Two uniformed men met him, one a major.

"Follow us, detective."

They walked at a brisk pace. Daniel did his own pace, his first sign of independence. With a grimace, the two soldiers slowed for him.

They escorted him to an office in the military headquarters. It had gray walls, a steel desk, and a window that overlooked the Cyber building. Guards at doors kept everyone away. He stood for a moment looking at it.

"It is contaminated," said a voice behind him. "We've teams doing the decon work, but it is slow going. All of the equipment will have to be replaced."

He turned to see a tall thin man wearing a pressed and clean uniform standing in the doorway. His gray hair was neatly barbered, his beard trimmed. He had entered so quietly Daniel hadn't heard him. "I'm Colonel Dmitrev. I assume your files are in that bag?" The man gestured at the attaché.

"Most of it, sir. I have more in my suitcase. Everything is backed up on my computer."

"Your captain said you were meticulous with your note taking. That is good. I've gone over the information we have, but I'd like you to go through everything. I want to hear the details, not read them in the reports. Follow me."

At the end of the hall, they entered another office, this one paneled with a large wooden desk and two chairs. The Colonel sat behind his desk and gestured Daniel toward one of the large leather-covered chairs. He pressed a button. "Bring in coffee for me." He glanced at Daniel, who nodded.

"And one for Detective Novikov."

He smiled. "I'm sorry to bring you down before you are fully recovered, but we feel time is of the essence. Start from the beginning, the murders and kidnapping in Tosno."

Daniel pulled out his notes, glanced at them for a few seconds and related his investigation to the colonel, who asked no questions, taking no notes.

Dmitrev placed his hands on the desk and stared at Daniel. "That's everything that was in your report. Now tell me what you felt, what you didn't put in there."

Daniel hesitated, gathering his thoughts. "The first thing that struck me was that the motive wasn't clear. Things were taken, so it could have been a robbery, but why murder the people? And why kidnap a low-level hacker? Sure, they got into her Bitcoin account and took that money, but robbery didn't seem to fit for me. Why the brutality of the murders? As you saw in the report, the scene was sanitized. No prints or other evidence of the murderers' identity."

"You assumed immediately that it was more than one person."

Daniel nodded. "I did, sir. One person could

not have murdered the three people and done the kidnapping. My guess is a team of at least four."

"That was my conclusion also. What about Baltiyskaya Sloboda?"

"It was very similar to the first except there were two guards killed. They were ex-soldiers, supposedly trained men."

"Trained for war, not urban murder."

"True, sir but they were armed. The one with the glass shards in his head never pulled his gun. The second never fired it. They were ambushed. With nobody in the neighborhood hearing shots, the gun was suppressed."

"A single gun?"

"Ballistics confirmed a single gun killed both men, a 7.62 mm bullet weighing two-hundred-twenty grains."

"That is consistent with a weapon used by American Special Forces," said Dmitrev.

"Yes, sir. Their throats were cut post mortem. That is a message. The wife's throat was slashed to kill her. She had signs of torture probably to get the safe combination. Within a day, their Bitcoin account was emptied."

"But you don't think robbery was the motive."

"No, sir, I don't. The money was to finance their operation. With the second murders, I now believe the message was to bring about a gathering of cyber personnel in one place. That was the objective all along."

"What about the autopsy results?"

Both the woman hacker and Andri's brother had an interesting combination of drugs. Neither was a user. We don't know why they were there.

"Killing the cyber people was not the end, was it?"

"I believe it was and remains so. The strike here at the Cyber Command Center is merely another phase in this operation with the same objective. These strikes have moved cyber warfare from electronic to physical."

The Colonel sat back in his chair and stared at the ceiling for a few seconds. "This is like the American's war on terror where national boundaries mean nothing."

"Yes, sir, it is."

"Our sources in the United States cannot find evidence this is a government-backed operation. The CIA, who one would suspect, seems to know nothing. That doesn't mean they object."

Daniel stared at his notes for a second. "Ukraine has the desire and perhaps the means after Russia attacked. They could be surrogates for the Americans."

Colonel Dmitrev nodded. "They could, and the viciousness shown wouldn't surprise me, but we have good sources within that regime. They do not back up that possibility."

"Contractors?"

"Almost certainly, but who's paying? Where would you send people to find them?"

"I believe the coast of the Black Sea holds the highest probability. There are many options. Sochi was my first choice as the two women and one of the men were there several years ago. They would be familiar with it."

"I agree." Dmitrev stood. "Pack your bags. You will lead the search in that area, answering only to me."

Daniel thought it best not to mention he hadn't even unpacked his bags.

Chapter 43

"Your ride will be there tonight," said Bob via the satellite phone. "As they get closer, I'll refine the time. Space and weight are limited, so take only what you need."

"We will be ready," said Ilia. "My man will be here after dark to take the vehicles. Our plan is to have him move the truck close to the Ukraine border to throw off any searchers. He'll burn it with everything we leave behind. He wants the van."

"According to David," said Bob, "the NSA picked up communications that the detective from Saint Petersburg is on his way to Sochi. He's been enlisted by the Military Security Command."

"Good thing we're not there," said Kiki.

"The action in Moscow has stirred up a hornet's nest. David seems quite concerned."

"Where are we going?"

"The plan is to transit out of the Black Sea at Istanbul into the Aegean Sea and then into the Med. David is working on a port where you can be dropped off and flown out."

"Good," said Nick. "We look forward to seeing you in Arizona."

* * *

The deep bong ringtone of Ilia's phone jarred everybody gathered in the box truck. He answered in Russian, spoke few words and broke the connection. "They will be here in five minutes."

Silently, they carried out the things to take with them. Sasha had a few clothes, a handgun and her rifle. Zyra had much the same but also her knives, Nick had a medical bag. Ilia had a laptop, the satellite radio and a handgun. Kiki had a change of clothes and her .25-06.

As they closed the back of the truck, Ilia set the thermite charges that would ensure the truck would become unidentifiable ash. A short dark-skinned man approached. His beard was black and full, his hair curly and wild. He and Ilia nodded at each other and moved away for privacy. They spoke in hushed tones. Ilia tapped a few keys on his phone and turned it so the man could see the screen. They shook hands and Ilia returned. The man walked to his car where other men waited.

"It is done. They will drive the truck to Zaporizhizhia where there will be a disastrous fire. I told them when the back of the truck is opened, there will be an explosion. They will have twenty seconds to clear the area."

"And you're sure they will follow the instructions?" asked Kiki.

"I paid $50,000 into their Bitcoin account. Another $50,000 will be paid when the truck is destroyed. It is incentive enough not to try to open the truck or sell it."

"He must suspect that we are a hot item," said Sasha.

"If he turns us in, he doesn't get paid. Any bounty offered would be peanuts in comparison."

The satellite phone rang. "This is David. Bob patched me into the line. NSA says forces are being directed along the coast of the Black Sea with orders to lock down the coast. In addition, the Black Sea Navy is directing ships to the area. I passed the information along to your ride, but they are about a hundred kilometers away. Their captain says they will speed things up.”

"Can you create a diversion east of Sochi?"

"I'll issue a notice of a sighting at a restaurant in Stavropol with pictures of the van and panel truck," said Bob. "That should slow them down for a few hours."

"The timing will be close before your ride arrives," said David.

"I can hack into the navy system and create a sonar track indicating a submarine is three-hundred kilometers west and south. That should pull the navy away."

"Thanks, Bob. Our fingers are crossed that it works," said Kiki. As the connection was broken, the *Fantasmas* looked at each other. If the ruses didn't work, they would be trapped.

An hour later the satellite phone rang again. Ilia spoke for only a few seconds.

He bent down to pick up his gear. "The boat is on the beach."

* * *

The inflatable Zodiac made the trip from the beach to the boat in ten minutes. It was a large pleasure craft, with lights glittering across the

201

water. It looked like a floating palace. Modern jazz echoed as they approached. It was white and sleek, with two decks, one was mostly glass and windows. The only thing missing to identify it as a party vessel was people dancing on the deck. They carried their things up the ramp while the Zodiac was hoisted aboard. A man in a navy sport coat with brass buttons awaited them.

"I'm Captain Rogers," he said with an Australian accent, holding out his hand. "Welcome aboard *Lightning of the Sea*." He turned to another man. "Take them below to their cabins. We sail immediately. Please remain in your cabins until someone comes to get you. We'll complete introductions once we are under way. You'll find clean clothes in the closets."

The sailor said nothing as he led them below. The cabins were luxurious. King-sized beds were covered with satin sheets, thick carpets across the floors, and a bathroom for each. As Kiki lay on the bed, she heard the highspeed whine of engines. Walking to the bathroom, the vibration of the floor could barely be felt.

"Nick, come look," exclaimed Kiki. He went to the bathroom. It was dominated by a large shower and spa tub. Kiki had already stripped off her clothes and eagerly reached for the buttons of his shirt. His arms encircled her as she opened his belt buckle. His hands slipped downward from her waist and pulled her against him.

An hour later they heard a light tap on the door. Nick answered. "Cocktails and a light snack are being served, sir. If you will follow me, please."

The man they'd met as they boarded greeted them in a high-end cocktail-like lounge. Kiki gazed at the opulence. Windows framed with polished teak looked out over the bow and to each side. In the light of the full moon, water flashed by. The cabinets and the bar were also teak, and the fixtures were gold. Two large cocktail tables were near the windows at each side with couches and chairs of dark leather. The lighting was from a series of lamps hung from the ceiling. The colored globes looked like huge raindrops and swayed gently from the motion of the boat. Quite a difference from our trimaran, thought Kiki.

In the light, they could see Rogers was over six feet tall, slim with sandy blond hair graying at the temples "As I said, I'm Captain Rogers." Again, he offered his hand. "I see you found the clothes."

"Yes, thank you. I'm…"

Rogers held up his hand. "No names, please." They shook.

Rogers looked at Kiki for a second, his brow furled. Ilia, Sasha and Zyra were already seated at the port couch, showered and dressed in smart casual clothes. "The bar is open, so help yourselves. We have crabcakes and prawns for a snack."

They each got scotch from the bar and moved toward the starboard couch. "To tell you a little about this boat," said Rogers, "it is very special." He nodded toward another uniformed man and circled a finger in the air. The man left the room. Kiki could hear the pride in his voice at being the captain. He obviously had been instructed to ask them no questions, instead choosing to tell them about the boat.

"Please sit for a few minutes. We are about to accelerate, and I wouldn't want anybody falling." After a series of thumps, there was a roar. The floor seemed to rise, and they took off like a rocket, acceleration pushing them back into their seats. "This boat is equipped with foils," he explained. "The roar is due to the two ducted fans that drive the boat." He glanced at his watch. "We're now doing sixty knots, but will slowly continue to accelerate to cruising speed, about eighty knots."

Nick glanced at Kiki. "The ride is so smooth," he commented.

"We're five meters above the water. Come, take a look."

They stepped toward the windows. Looking down, the moonlight glinted from the water as they flew over it. "I've never seen a boat like this," said Nick.

"Few people have, and we like to keep it that way," said Rogers. "It's one of only three in the world–the only one in private hands, those hands being a member of the Saudi royalty. Not many people are aware of its existence. When we get closer to other boats or land, especially during daylight, the foils will retract into the hull and fans will be hidden in compartments below deck."

"I saw foiling boats in the America's Cup yacht racing," said Nick. "But those boats were all carbon fiber."

"This one is all titanium, carbon fiber and honeycomb. It weighs less than one- third of any comparable boat." He laughed at their astonished looks.

He continued, "The America's Cup is where much of the foiling technology was developed. This boat is faster and more fuel efficient than any conventional boat. We have a single turbine powerplant that drives a hydraulic pump to power either the fans or the drive pumps. When it's in the water, it's a jet boat."

Nick was silent as he tried to fathom what this boat represented in maritime technology. This explained how the boat covered a hundred kilometers in an hour.

"We will approach the waterways near Istanbul in six hours. We'll go conventional at that time before sun-up. So, eat, rest and we'll breakfast in the morning.

Kiki watched the water whiz by. Imagine transitioning the Black Sea in six hours. *Only someone like Elon Musk, the Saudis or Russian oligarchs could afford this. Why is someone risking this for us? I wonder what they want in return?*

Chapter 44

Daniel and his two uniformed government *assistants* stepped off the plane in Sochi. Their silence during the flight continued as they escorted him to a car idling at the curb. One man held the door for him. At police headquarters, the door was held for him. *I don't want to get used to this. It's not me.*

A small conference room had been converted to his office. The computer on the desk already showed a map of the area. A red dot indicated the roadblock and inspection station that had been set up on the A-147, the main road into Sochi from Moscow. Other smaller dots indicated patrol units. His phone rang.

"I hope you find the accommodation satisfactory, detective," said Colonel Dmitrev.

"More than accommodating. Quite satisfactory."

"Good. What's your first order of business?"

"I'm going to inspect the roadblock and contact other units. I want to expand our area of concern. The sighting in Stavropol may have been wrong. It may have been a diversion to pull us away from Sochi. Somehow, they suspected we were looking in the region. Nonetheless, Sochi is hard to reach from the south or the west. We will continue to search that area."

"Are you sure you're up to this?"

"I'll take a break this afternoon. In the meantime, I want to circulate the photos of the two women and the brother."

"We have some news regarding the terrorists from the farmhouse. The bodies weren't completely destroyed. The man was Sol Ayub, an Israeli suspected of working with Mossad. Thus, he had skills. The woman has not turned up on any search. Her dental work and overall health suggest she is American, but we cannot be sure. We will continue trying to identify her."

"Is Mossad behind this?"

"They have no reason to attack us, other than the usual support we give their enemies. But that isn't new. Sol Ayub has been a mercenary for several years. Somebody paid him."

"Do you think they sacrificed themselves so the attack on the Cyber Headquarters could take place?"

"Sacrifice is not in the mercenary vocabulary. We believe the van was going to return to pick them up, but we were too fast. By the time the center was rigged, we were already at the farmhouse. They had no way to escape. It was always going to be a trap, they just got caught in it along with our people."

"Their first mistake," murmured Daniel.

"Yes, perhaps so," agreed the Colonel.

"Why did they stay at the farmhouse instead of being with the others?"

"We found satellite communications equipment. They were passing on messages to their hit team."

"Given the experience that the women and other man have, I believe they always intended to exit through Sochi," said Daniel. "So why haven't we seen them yet?"

"Perhaps they did take the eastern route and will come in from the south. I can check with units in Stavropol and Volgograd. Put them on alert. That route could add days."

"It would explain why nothing's happened. I will put roadblocks on the routes from the south."

"Good idea. I've alerted the air force and the Black Sea Navy. They had a possible indication of a submarine. The search is intense."

"Or," mused David, "they knew we were looking for them in Sochi. If we could figure that out, they could suspect we did." He didn't want to mention that there may be a leak.

There was silence on the line. "I'll look into that," said the Colonel.

"Colonel, a seaplane could pick them up from anywhere along the coast, so any unauthorized flights must be stopped. We have to make sure the inspection teams at the Bosporus understand the thoroughness needed in their searches of any vessels leaving the Black Sea. I will communicate these orders, but your name will add emphasis."

"I will make calls."

Chapter 45

"Here's to Sol and Dawn," said Sasha, raising her bottle of Sierra Nevada Torpedo, a strong IPA. Kiki, Nick, Ilia, Zyra, Bob and Kathy joined in clinking the necks together. They were at Nick's house in Casa Grande, sitting on the patio watching the quarter-moon set over the mountains to the west. It had been a typical fall day in Arizona, dry and pleasant, the temperature dropping since the sun had set.

"That trip through the Black Sea wasn't too bad," said Sasha, "but I have to say that the two hours in that minisub were getting to me."

"That was really the only hiccup," commented Kiki. Thank goodness Captain Rogers thought of putting us in there. The Russians didn't realize how close they were."

"Still, it was a little claustrophobic with five people in a four-person sub. I was really ready to get out of there when Rogers hoisted it aboard and let us out."

"Yeah, speaking of the ship, I've never seen such a display of luxury that boat represented," said Nick. "It makes our trimaran seem primitive in comparison."

"Smaller crew, though," laughed Kiki. "The jet that picked us up in Greece was pretty nice too."

"Though the private jet was luxurious, I was so beat I couldn't really enjoy it," said Ilia.

"Glad David had everything ready so we were able to clear customs and continue to Marana Regional."

The meals had been first rate, but they all slept most of the way. Nick's brother met them at the airport and drove them to Nick's house. They toasted whoever their host had been.

The doorbell rang. "You expecting anybody?" asked Kiki.

Bob rose to answer it. "Nope." His 1911 was tucked in the back of his pants. A few minutes later he appeared with David Kennedy. "Beer?" he asked.

"We've been expecting to hear from you," said Kiki, rising to give him a hug. "You remember

Sasha, Zyra and Ilia from the Russian operation in the Bio-Cyber War." They waved from their chairs.

David smiled. "Of course, I do. Welcome to the US. Sorry to hear about Sol and Dawn." Bob handed him a beer as he sat. "It's nice out here, much more pleasant than back east. Rain for the last three days, and we're well into fall."

"What's on the agenda?" asked Nick.

David's chuckle lacked humor. "The Russian operation has caused quite a stir. I've gotten calls from the alphabets– CIA, NSA, FBI and Homeland Security asking what the fuck was going on. I denied any knowledge, of course." He took a long sip of his beer. "So, you understand what happened, by moving cyber warfare from electronic to actual combat, we raised the stakes. There will be attacks on American soil."

"I wondered about that," said Bob.

"The agencies are out to get whoever did this to try to stave off the reprisals, so be careful."

"What about our sponsor?" asked Kiki.

"They want out."

"Not surprised," said Kathy. "It looked so good on paper but the reality was much tougher."

"I saw this coming." David glanced at them. "It

was inevitable, like the war on terrorism. Friendly countries can't hide terrorist anymore. It was demonstrated most pointedly when we got Usama Bin-Laden."

Sasha stared at him. "And even if it leads to attacks, you went ahead?"

David shrugged. "Somehow, we had to address the issue of cyber warfare and fake news attacks. What I'm hoping comes out of it is international agreements to curb or stop it. I'm meeting with Ron Carson next week to propose a police force to enforce those agreements."

"Russia not like that," said Zyra with a smirk.

"Sol always coordinated us," said Sasha, looking at Ilia. "You willing to run things?"

"Always worked alone. Not much of a leader but will give it a try."

"Nigeria or Iran were our next targets," said Nick, "though we have one more kick to deliver to Russia's balls." David stared at him for a few seconds. Nick shrugged. "It will dilute their hunt for us, a major diversion."

"Don't go back there."

"We can do it from here," said Bob.

"Big challenges in those other hacking

countries," said Zyra. "Except for me, we," she gestured at the *Fantasmas*, "don't blend in well."

"Hold off on that," said David. "Our sponsor is pulling out. I know you got a lot of money from the Bitcoin accounts, but as far as I'm concerned, that's yours. No money, no work is my philosophy."

"You want us to go on a hiatus for a while?" asked Kiki.

"Go ahead and make your plans, but stay here. We might use you for defense in the US. Kiki, you and Nick proved very useful during the terrorist attacks during the war in the Middle East. This would be the same but with a bigger team."

"And without any agency help, I presume," said Kiki.

"Black budget. We'll work on something to get you intelligence. Nobody will know about you."

Nick stared at David. "We wouldn't be the only team on the hunt, I suppose. Who's going to coordinate so we're not after each other?"

"Details have to be worked out, but I'm sure Ron will agree. When he becomes World Government President, he can push this forward."

Zyra was all smiles. "On the hunt for bad guys! Greatest sport ever."

Chapter 47

Daniel Novikov was despondent. He glanced from his notes to Colonel Dmitrev. They were in his office, nicely furnished in dark wood paneling, awards and pictures of the colonel with celebrities adorned the walls. "Sir, we searched every vessel leaving the Black Sea. They didn't get out that way. The air force spotted no unauthorized flights. In Zaporizhizhia, a truck-fire was reported. The truck burned completely. Whatever it was carrying burned very hot. Enough remained to identify it as similar to the truck outside Petrov's house. They could have escaped into Ukraine from there, but our border security searched every vehicle thoroughly. Escaping overland and evading our soldiers was the only route out."

"You think they've left Russia?"

"I'm not sure, sir. Either they have, or they want us to think so."

The colonel sat mulling this over. "If their mission was to shut down cyber-attacks and disinformation, it has succeeded, but only temporarily. We are already replacing the lost people and computers."

Daniel nodded. "Mother Russia always has a response to attacks. What's planned?"

"Detective, that is not in your *need-to-know*. Rest assured one is in the formative stages. We must identify those responsible to aim our attack at the right party. America denies any involvement, and our agents can find nothing to counter that."

"If not America, then who?"

"The big question. There are those who would attack America anyway, feeling they are ultimately responsible. I think that is foolhardy. Starting a shooting war on that basis would be bad and could escalate. Better if we go after the guilty."

"Are there European countries–Britain, France, Germany?"

"Each is possible, or maybe all of them–perhaps NATO."

"Too many involved, sir. Something would

leak."

"I agree with you, Detective. We're reaching out to contractors who might be involved, but so far nothing. It is particularly disturbing they used Sarin stolen from our own depot. That fact alone makes it hard to acknowledge we were attacked by a chemical agent."

"Do we have photos of the people who got the gas?"

"One was the man killed at the farmhouse. The other did not show his face to the camera, but he was below average height and slight in build. Phony orders were sent to the repository. They also carried forged orders. The counterfeits were well done, not by amateurs."

"Where do we go from here, sir?"

"I'll direct the search to the west, Ukraine, Romania, Bulgaria. You review everything going through the Black Sea."

"Our big assumption is they want to escape and went south or west."

"You are correct, detective. Until we hear differently, let's stick with that."

* * *

Daniel still wasn't satisfied the attackers had not gone through the Black Sea. It bothered him. The reports of all marine traffic transiting the Black Sea from the day of the attack ten days forward was on his computer. It was an imposing list–tankers, freighters, barges and pleasure craft. He narrowed the list to those near the northern coast in the four days after the attack. That helped. Next he filtered the list into separate categories–those stopping at Sochi, the details of the roadblocks and searches, those calling on other ports in the Black Sea, those exiting through the Bosporus, and those still in the Black Sea. He was looking for anomalies. The amount of data was huge. He reached for his phone.

"Colonel Dmitrev, do you have a contact who oversees the activities in the Black Sea? I'm not familiar enough to recognize when something's not right."

"I thought you were sure they didn't exit that way."

"I have to be positive."

"I will have him contact you. Glad you called. The truck found in Zaporizhizhia burned completely. Nothing but slag left, except a piece of the door frame that was blown clear and had the

VIN. It was reported stolen in Saint Petersburg three months ago. I think they escaped to the west."

"Or they wanted us to think so," said Daniel. There was silence before the line went dead.

Chapter 48

Major Petrovisky helped Daniel cull the maritime transport through the Black Sea. He found only one strange thing. "That private yacht," he pointed at a red dot on the map, "was in Sochi for a few days. When it left, it sailed west along the coast for a while before heading for the Bosporus. The transit takes two to three days for most shipping. A fast boat can do it in less. Twelve hours after it left the coast, we searched it before it entered the Bosporus. Such a trip is not possible."

"How do you track the ships?"

"Radar, patrol reports and satellite."

"Is it an error in the system?" asked Daniel.

"The only explanation. I have people checking now."

"May I see the registry for the ship."

The colonel typed a few commands and it came

up.

"Saudi owners. Oil money, of course." He tapped a few more keys.

"Who was on board when the vessel was searched?"

"Just crew, according to the report."

"Did they drop anybody off in Sochi?"

"Not according to the manifest."

What was such a boat doing cruising around the Black Sea with only crew? Daniel's phone rang. It was Colonel Dmitrev.

"Detective, they struck again in Saint Petersburg. The Internet Research Association building was destroyed."

"So, they didn't leave," murmured Daniel.

"Apparently not. Go see what you can find."

"Yes, sir."

* * *

Once again, Daniel was looking at rubble that had once been a building. Forty people died in this explosion, most of the bodies buried, at least parts of them. Rage was building within the detective's mind. This was murder on a mass scale. These killers were terrorists. He would find them.

"Sir, I have some information for you," said the chief inspector as he approached. Daniel turned to face the man. It was cold, and he was so tightly bundled in coat, hat, gloves, and scarf that it was hard to tell anything about him. His breath formed a cloud as he approached.

"We've found traces of plastique. It was the explosive used. From the way the building was destroyed, I believe the bomb was in the basement. The force of the blast was upward." He pointed. "That's why the debris is not so scattered."

"This building was the new headquarters for the IRA," noted Daniel. "How long ago did they move in?"

"Most of the construction was completed last month. IRA personnel moved in even though some parts weren't finished."

"I need to get an electronic forensic team in here to go through video and records stored on equipment that can't be easily removed. The rest we'll take back to headquarters."

"I'll direct my men to check the building integrity. We want it to be safe for them."

"Focus on the security office and the central mainframe computer office. I need to know who was accessing the building."

"The team removing remains will work around you."

Daniel flinched at the image of body parts scattered throughout the wreckage. *Not a job I would want.* "Let me know when you have access to the basement. I want to be with your investigators."

"Yes, sir."

Daniel shivered as he headed back to his car. It wasn't entirely from the cold.

* * *

"Colonel Dmitrev," came the terse answer to his call. "What do you have for me, detective?"

"The investigation is very preliminary. We find some evidence of an explosive, unlike Petrov's house. The investigating officer believes the bomb was in the basement. I'll be going down with them when it's safe."

"Was the bomb placed there during construction or after the IRA moved in?"

Daniel paused. "I'll go through the security footage. Whether it was before the move or after, how was it detonated?"

"Timer, cell phone or radio would be the usual ways. Call me as soon as you have anything. Needless to say, I've got people climbing up my ass for answers. I'm putting all police and military in the area on alert. The pressure to strike back at anyone is immense."

Chapter 49

"This patio should become a monument to freedom," said David. The warm Arizona autumn evening breeze wafted across the pool, creating small ripples. "That was a nice touch, blowing up the IRA building." He raised his margarita in salute. Ilia and Bob nodded thanks.

"Tasty," he said swirling the light green slush around the glass before taking a swig.

"Kiki makes the best margies in town," said Nick. "They'll go nicely with the Mexican food my brother is sending up from his restaurant."

"How is your brother?" asked David.

"He's had his ups and downs. When the economy went flat, so did the restaurant business. He started doing delivery to stay alive. It was hard on everyone. Luckily it's a family-run business. Everybody pitched in."

"He's okay now?"

"Yeah, expanding even."

David turned to Ilia. "That bomb did double duty–knocked out more hackers and drew the search back to St Petersburg."

"It was Sol's idea to put the bomb in while the building was under construction," answered Ilia. "Hardly any security. We built a false brick wall in the basement with half the bricks being C-4. Painted it to look like the other walls."

"How'd you detonate it?"

"I sent a focused signal to the detonator," said Bob. "They hadn't activated the Faraday cage protection yet."

"Weren't you worried about stray signals setting it off?"

Bob smiled. "It was triple encoded, a chance so remote as to be impossible."

"Well, it sure changed the direction of the search."

"Sol was good at planning for contingencies." Ilia looked at the floor. "I'm not that good."

"Depend on your people. Altogether you are."

Ilia shrugged. "If you say so."

David set his glass on the table. "NSA boys

contacted me. There's a Russian team heading for the US."

"FBI's job, right?" asked Zyra. "I think they need help." She placed her arm around Sasha.

"Normally, it would be their job, but the alphabet agencies can't coordinate well enough to tie their shoes. By the time they find out who's who and get their warrants, we'll have bodies. You," he looked at each of them, "set the rules in this conflict when you used Sarin."

"In other words, there are no rules," said Nick. "Do you know when and where they're coming in?"

"We thought it would be into DC under diplomatic protection, but they would be too easy to track. The thought now is through the southern border. They could land in Mexico easily. The cartels have many smuggling routes to cross the border. We've been watching some Russian cells here in the US collect arms and explosives. The arriving team will use them rather than try to bring them in."

"Ah, now I see why we help," said Zyra. "We know nothing about diplomats–just talking heads. But stealthy guys crossing borders, that I know."

"Before you separate the head from the body, we need to interrogate at least one," said David, as he stared at Nick.

Nick didn't flinch at the thought of this interrogation.

Chapter 50

David, Kiki, and Nick glanced around the atrium at the Atchley ranch. The soft roar of the waterfall and the aroma of the flowers almost made this Eden in the desert. "Thanks for inviting us in," said David. The ranch was about twenty-five miles from the Arizona border with Mexico. "We have a problem I believe you can help us with."

Tammy laughed. "I was pretty sure this wasn't a social call." She was a tall slender beauty with brown sun-streaked hair reaching to her waist. She ran the ranch while her husband Keith backed the Constitutional Advocates party running for seats in Congress. The Atchley ranch was a high-tech military training center. They contracted to domestic and foreign forces. The US military was among their clients.

"The US will be under attack very soon," said

David. "Our cartel people tell us they've been contracted to smuggle a group of people into the US. Our latest info says they're coming across the border near Sasabe within the next week. Their intent is to mount attacks against the NSA in reprisal for the attacks against hackers and the Cyber Division in Russia. That will be the start. They will go after the cyber divisions in our military, then individual hackers."

"Why are they attacking the US?" asked Tammy.

David chuckled. Tammy cut through bullshit like a hot knife through butter. He glanced at Kiki and Nick. "Somebody attacked the cyber community in Russia."

Keith laughed. He was tall, well built, with short blonde hair. "Of course, you had nothing to do with that." They all shrugged. "So why are you here?"

Kiki smiled. "We'd like to use the ranch as a base for a reception team."

"I can just imagine the type of reception you'd like to offer," snickered Tammy.

"Lucky for you, we're between contracts, so the facility is empty at the moment. What's the downside for us?" asked Keith. "Will we end up on somebody's radar?"

"We'll do everything we can to prevent that. Our main base will be my place in Casa Grande," said Nick. "You've been there."

"Impressive place," acknowledged Keith.

"We need something closer to the border first. We'd also like to use the eyes and ears of the militia groups you know to watch for them," said David.

As a hi-tech training center, the Atchley ranch network was widespread.

"The reservation has a lot of empty space," noted David. "They could help."

Keith nodded. "There are some smuggling tunnels on the rez that could be used. It's where I'd cross. What about this side of the border? Somebody has to pick them up."

"We'll intensify the drone and satellite coverage on both sides of the border to see who enters," said David.

Tammy frowned. "Natives won't like that. You willing to give 'em something to put up with y'all?"

"We're keeping this in a black budget, so we'll work with them for something."

"What's your plan?" asked Keith.

"Kiki and I will be here. We have three other people who will make up our team. I tried to get in touch with Rose Villas to recruit her. You remember her?"

Tammy nodded. "She's the sniper that set up with you on our hill to repel those assholes who tried to break in here. Knocked off a few, as I remember."

"So far, no luck finding her," said Kiki.

"We want to stop the terrorists at the border," said David. "It would be best if we captured the leader. Nick has some questions for him. We're sure this group isn't the one and only."

"Rumors of Nick's technique are floating around." Keith smiled. "I'm not too sure what that prophet fella did, but the radicals in our Constitutional Advocates movement calmed down. Sure, you can stay here. I assume you'll have Bob running the electronics for you? He has some fine toys."

"Bob will be monitoring radio and cell calls and operating his drones for surveillance," said David. "Everything will be tied into a system we'll set up here. We'll augment your solar farm to cover the increased power requirements."

Tammy stared at them. "Long as our names and the ranch never show up on anybody's list, we're fine with it. When's this kicking off?"

"The equipment is on the way," said David.

Both Tammy and Keith laughed. "Bit presumptuous, aren't we?"

"My equipment is in the van," said Kiki.

"Still using the .25-06?" asked Keith.

"Only when I need it. I sleep with it when Nick's away."

Chapter 51

Boris Popov was awakened by the jostling of the van. The day before had been long, and he needed to catch up on some sleep. The small Alpha Class submarine had rendezvoused with a shrimper in the Sea of Cortez a day ago. The trip from near the tip of the Baja to San Carlos had taken another day because the winds had whipped up rough seas. He hated the motion sickness he'd had since childhood.

He paid the captain in San Carlos, and by mid-afternoon they had boarded this van for the trip to the US border. The roads were good until this last leg, dirt tracks with choking dust roiling around them. He closed his eyes, but no matter how hard he tried, the visions of the mission kept him awake.

He and the four men with him had never been to the United States but had trained extensively for missions in any location. After crossing the border in a remote part of Arizona, another van would pick them up and take them to a safe house. Sleeper cells had accumulated the necessary guns, ammunition, and explosives they planned to use. They would spend a night at a Mexican ranch before the crossing the next night. He had been warned about dealing with the cartels in Mexico, but they had the best smuggling routes. With that thought, his hand strayed down to the Poloz nine-millimeter pistol tucked into his pants.

He glanced out the window as the van slid to a stop in front of an adobe ranch house. A thin wisp of smoke rose from the stovepipe atop the tin roof. The passenger hopped out and slid the door open. "Everybody out," he said in Spanish. Boris's crash course was enough for him to understand. He turned to the others.

"Set up a perimeter," he said in Russian, pointing to the flat open ground with few trees. "Ilya, you watch the house. Max, you watch these two. His head tilted toward the driver and his passenger. Let's get our gear unloaded."

Boris stood behind the driver instructing him to open the ranch house door. Showing no nervousness, the driver entered, Boris close behind. A man sat at a long table, his hands resting on top. His dark brown skin was wrinkled from the sun and age. With a smile he said, "Bienvenido, welcome. Store your things," his hand waved toward the rough beds lined up against the wall. "We will cross tomorrow night, so you and your men can get some rest. Maria is preparing dinner."

The smell of cooking wafted in from the kitchen.

The meal was simple, tortillas, beans and some tough stringy meat. The water had an earthy taste but seemed okay. Under the glow of a kerosene lamp, Boris unfolded a map showing the area. "Señor, where will we cross?"

The old man leaned over and studied the map for a few moments. "Aquí." His finger pointed at a spot. "We will drive here. It is a mile walk to the tunnel that crosses under the border. From here," his finger moved across the line marking the US-Mexico border to a point north, "you will walk for five miles to this road to be picked up. It is hilly land so you can evade the Border Patrol. This land belongs to the Tohono O'odom tribe. You must make the arrangements for your ride."

Boris studied the area. With everything clear, they should be able to make the road in two hours from the drop-off. He pulled out his phone and texted the GPS coordinates to the phone of the sleeper cell along with the message that he would contact them with the time to be there. It looked like the drive from the ranch house to the drop off point would take less than an hour– three hours from the time they left here–barring complications.

Chapter 52

Keith Atchley led Kiki and Nick toward the doublewide mobile. A native sat in an old easy chair beside the door, an AR-15 rifle resting on his lap. They had passed through San Miguel and continued south for another three miles before stopping here. Keith explained it was the headquarters for the native militia, the Cheoj.

The guard, a husky man with mahogany colored skin, black eyes and his black hair tied back in a pony tail rose and shook hands with Keith. His jeans were well-worn, as was his flannel shirt.

"I trained Joseph a year ago along with several other members," explained Keith, as they shook hands. He gestured toward Kiki and Nick. "I'd like to introduce you to Katherine Russell Sabino and Dr. Nick Sabino. This is Joseph Poteet." They stepped forward to shake hands.

Joseph held Kiki's hand for several seconds. "I

know you. You saved my life in the Sandbox when we were pinned down at a small village. Your shot taking out that machine gunner must have been over 800 yards. His next volley would have gotten both me and my brother." He smiled. "Never got the chance to thank you."

"We all fought together there," she said.

He opened the door to escort them in. "I thought you were dead. Reports had you killed in Casa Grande by that asshole, Captain Gallen. He was after the bounty the ragheads put on you. Glad to see he didn't get paid."

Kiki glanced around the sparsely-furnished living room. Native blankets covered the couch and easy chair. A wide-screen TV hung from one wall. "I know about Gallen now. Instead of killing me, the ragheads slaughtered my family." Her mouth was a thin line. "Gallen and his gang are gone now, and the world's a better place." She stepped to one side. "This is my husband, Nick. He saved my ass in the Sandbox. As a medic, he saved a lot of lives there."

Joseph shook Nick's hand. "Thanks, brother. Hey, Bro, look who's here for a visit.

"This is Kiki Russell." He smiled at her. "Jim

was the other guy whose life you saved that day."

A slender man rose from the couch. He was over six feet tall, skin the color of tanned leather. He wore his hair in braids. He too wore a flannel shirt of brilliant colors and worn jeans. His boots had a lot of miles on them. "I've wanted to meet you for a long time. Glad you're not dead."

"Me too," joked Kiki, looking up into his face.

"I'm sure this isn't a social visit. Keith, how's Tammy?"

"Feisty as ever."

Joseph chuckled at that. "We're a long way off the tourist track. What brings you here?"

"They need your help," said Keith. "A band of Russian terrorists is going to be coming across the border, and we believe it will be in this area."

"You with the government?" asked Jim as he peered at them.

"Nope," said Kiki. "Private contractors."

"Why the concern?"

She looked at Jim. "It's us they're after."

Jim chuckled. "You've been naughty. I read something about problems in cyber-land in Russia."

"That was you, huh?" said Joseph.

They said nothing.

"You know, we had people in New Mexico when the Chinese attacked last year. I wondered who the snipers were who supported us," said Jim.

"We also had some heavies come looking for trouble later," said Joseph. "Keith told us they were coming. You know anything about that?"

Again, they said nothing.

"If we help you, what's in it for us?" asked Joseph.

"What do you want?" asked Nick.

Jim looked at Joseph then at Nick. "How about a community solar power system for San Miguel. Every time there's a storm, we get blacked out."

"We'll have to check with that, but it's probably doable," said Nick.

Joseph stared at Kiki. "I want one of those new rifle scopes. You know the one I'm talking about."

"Make it two." added Jim.

"I'll see what I can do, but don't push it."

"Okay, so where would you think these guys will come across?" asked Keith.

"There's a tunnel south of here, about ten miles away," said Jim. "Belongs to the cartel. Mostly drugs but also people come through."

Keith opened a map on the table. "Show us."

Jim put his finger on a spot. "There. No roads directly to it. They use mules to move the drugs, you know illegals who want to come to the US. The road," he pointed again, "is about five miles away. It's the only way in unless they bushwhack the Baboquivaris. Rough terrain there. If that's the route they take, you'll need guides."

"You offering?" asked Keith.

"Scopes," said Jim, holding up two fingers.

Chapter 53

Detective Daniel Novikov sat back from his computer screen. Surveillance tapes from the IRA site during construction had been instructive, if he were in building construction. He wasn't. He saw the structure change from bare frame to a modern office building. The hint of something amiss came a month before the first murders in Tosno.

Two workers wheeled a pallet of bricks into the basement. That was not strange. They looked familiar, and that caught his attention. One of the workers looked like the man killed in Moscow, and who got the Sarin from the depot. The other looked like the small man who accompanied him.

They had placed the bomb in the building two months before detonating it.

In his gut he knew the small man was no longer in Russia. He called Colonel Dmitrev and relayed the news.

"We have already sent a team to the United States."

"We still don't know if they are responsible," stated Daniel.

"True, but attacks on the cyber community there will flush something out."

"Russians in America will create an international crisis, and they are sure to find out."

"These men are contractors, the Wagner group. Very tough and not Russian. We're using them in Africa. It's a small team, maybe four or five members. Their mission is to attack NSA offices first, then cyber security offices. They will work with sleeper cells we've had there for years."

"I will watch the results with interest. Did we learn anything more from the explosion at the farm house?"

"As we thought, it seems to have been a diversion for the attack on the Cyber Center. We're in the process of replacing the equipment and the personnel as quickly as possible."

"Did the security cameras catch anything in that attack?"

"These bastards knew where the cameras were.

Nothing clear can be used to identify the attackers. The people cleaning up the site are nervous about the Sarin."

"I don't blame them. Back to the original topic. I don't believe the attackers returned to Saint Petersburg. The bomb was set off remotely or by timer. If the attackers aren't here, how did they exit Russia? Where did they go? Who backed them? I have a new theory that fits the facts. I think they exited through the Bosporus on the boat, *Lightning of the Sea*. From there I do not know where they went, but I now believe they were not government backed. Our hackers have hurt businesses. I think they were hired by them."

"You are the detective. Find out which businesses."

"The truck fire in Zaporizhizhia seems to be very coincidental. The boat that seems to have crossed the Black Sea in mere hours could have been *Lightning of the Sea*."

"Keep me informed of progress."

"Yes, sir. I'd like to be kept in the information loop about the activities in America. They could have a bearing."

"I will do that, detective."

Chapter 54

"Okay, I've got my drone over the coordinates you gave me," said Bob over their comm. "I'm linking it to you."

Kiki, Nick, Ilia, and Keith looked at the monitor. They had set up a remote station in a van two miles from the tunnel exit Jim had indicated on a map of the area. Joseph was closer to the tunnel on horseback but wearing a comm unit. Jim was in his house watching the only road coming into the area with Zyra and Sasha.

When the sun set, the drone went to low light mode, the seemingly deserted area covered by the view changing from light-enhanced night vision green to black with glowing white spots of infrared every ten seconds. "Still not much moving there. Let the drone follow that road from the tunnel area for a while on the Mexican side," said Kiki.

"I can do it, but the drone will need a recharge

before dawn," answered Bob. "Or cut power usage by using either IR or NV. Your call."

"The smugglers usually come out about midnight," said Joseph. "Doesn't mean they will this time."

Kiki's earbud crackled. "Got an SUV on the road heading south," said Ilia. "Probably the pick-up. We will take it."

"Roger that," said Kiki. "Targets should be arriving soon. Joseph, we're moving closer to you. Let them exit and move away from the tunnel. You block access back into it. Remember, we want the leader alive."

"How will know who that is?"

"Easiest if we capture them all."

"There's a van heading for the tunnel entrance on the Mexican side," said Bob.

"We're five minutes away," answered Kiki.

"I'm circling the drone overhead," said Bob. "I see five men getting out. One man is handing something to the van driver."

"Probably paying him. Any way to identify that man?" asked Kiki.

"He's not the biggest or the smallest. It's the best I can do. They're climbing into a wrecked truck. The van is leaving."

"See any weapons?"

"Maybe handguns. No rifles."

"Doesn't mean there's not some in the tunnel," warned Kiki.

* * *

Jim moved his pickup until it was blocking the road going south. He raised the hood, stepped up on the bumper and leaned into the engine compartment. Within minutes, an SUV drove up and honked his horn.

"C'mon, move that crate," the driver yelled.

Jim stepped down, hands raised and moved toward the SUV. Sasha moved next to Jim, both lit up by the headlights.

"You want to help me push it off the road?" asked Jim.

"Yeah, okay."

As the driver got out, Zyra stepped behind him, her knife went to this throat. Sasha looked through the passenger window to make sure nobody else was in the car. She glanced at Zyra and the frozen man, sweat beading on this forehead.

"Don't kill him," said Sasha. "Nick will want to talk to him."

* * *

"They've moved past me heading for the mountains," said Joseph.

"Roger," answered Kiki. "Three two one. Freeze," she yelled. The well-trained men dropped to the ground. "You move, you're dead."

"They're pulling out guns," said Bob.

The men began firing toward Kiki's voice. The biggest man rose and ran toward her under the covering fire. They weren't even close with their shots. Her suppressed .300 Blackout round blew out the back of his head. They had certainly marked her muzzle flash now. She shifted position. More shots rang out. "Who's next?" she yelled. In a barrage of gunfire, the remaining four jumped up and ran in different directions. She dropped the smallest man. Clipped the legs of another who went down with a shout. "Joseph, can you take the one heading back to the tunnel?"

"You want him alive?"

"Yeah, at least for now. Bob, where's that last guy heading?"

"He's running for the mountains. Guess he still thinks his ride is coming."

"It is," said Ilia. "Different driver."

"He's about a three-hundred yards from you," said Bob. With the IR view, he watched as the SUV stopped. Two figures got out and moved to the side of the road.

"Joseph, you got your man?" asked Kiki.

"Yeah, won't go anywhere."

"Go after the one heading for the mountains. We'll pick up the one at the tunnel."

"Him alive too?"

"If possible. He may be the leader."

Nick was treating the wounded man. The injection he administered knocked him out. He checked the other two. Both were dead. He moved toward the tunnel and the man there. This medium-sized man was on the ground, a golf-ball sized lump on the side of his head. Nick checked his pulse, then gave him an injection. The conversations about the captured party meant he'd be busy with the Isolation Chamber for the next couple of days. Was he growing hardened? The usual trepidation at subjecting people to his interrogation was barely a whisper.

Chapter 55

Detective Novikov stared at the ship plans on his computer. To get them had been quite and ordeal. The Saudi prince who owned the boat had gone to great pains to keep the design secret. With the proper pressure on the boat builder, they had sent them to him. *Lightning of the Sea* was an amazing boat. Built of titanium and carbon fiber, it was exceptionally light and normally operated as a jet boat, powered by large pumps. As a jet boat, it had a shallow draft and could navigate close to shore.

It also had hydrofoils that would extend down five meters and lift the boat out of the water. Turbofan engines would then drive it at speeds greater than one-hundred kilometers per hour. Even though this boat had been searched, this was how the bombers had crossed the Black Sea in one night and escaped. He was sure of it. He reached for his phone.

"Colonel Dmitrev, I know how they got away."

"I need good news. Our team sent to America to attack the cybers has not been heard from. We assume they've been killed or captured. Another team is in the planning now."

"We sent a team without knowing the American government was involved?" Daniel asked incredulously.

"I argued for us to wait until we had a stronger case, but was overruled."

"I don't like where this is going, sir."

"I'm aware of the potential, but my opinion didn't carry the day. We need to bring in proof as soon as possible. How did the bombers do it?"

Daniel described the *Lightning of the Sea* and its capabilities.

"That sounds like an remarkable ship. Put pressure on the owner. Find out how and why he supported this string of murders. I want to go after the attackers and the source."

"That could prove delicate. The owner is a Saudi royal."

"Then be diplomatic, but do not be deterred."

"Yes, sir."

"Keep me informed of any progress. Forward those ship plans to me. This design sounds like something we would find useful."

"Yes, sir." Colonel Dmitrev hung up. With attacks imminent, it was imperative that a link be found, Daniel thought.

Chapter 56

The *Fantasmas* looked over the inert forms of the men they had stopped from crossing the border and potentially wreaking havoc with the cyber community in America. They were laid out on the ground behind Jim's house along with the SUV driver. Two were dead. The one Joseph had captured was scraped up from being dragged behind his horse back to the van. The other one Joseph had stopped had a huge lump on his head, and probably a concussion. The last one had a bullet wound in his leg. Their nationality wasn't obvious. The two dead were the huge black man and the small Asian. The other black man had the bullet wound. The SUV driver was unconscious from the injection Nick had given him.

"We'll take care of the bodies," said Jim. "Where are our rifle scopes?"

Kiki laughed. "Don't worry. They're on their way. We're working on the solar power system, but that's going to have to be a budgeted item. It'll take longer."

"What are you going to do with them?" asked Joseph, staring at the captives.

"Nick's going to interrogate them," answered Kiki.

"Does it involve pliers and hot knives?" asked Jim, a strange look on his face.

"Or honey and ants," snickered Joseph. "We Natives have that reputation."

"Joseph," Jim chuckled, "we didn't do that to those bad asses Keith sent down here a little over a year ago."

"What did happen to them?" asked Keith.

"They graciously gave us their weapons and SUVs before they went to the Happy Hunting grounds."

"No follow-up?"

"We moved the GPS locators and the bodies south of the border. Some people came around, but we knew nothing."

Nick pointed to the figures on the ground. "These men will be unharmed physically.

Psychologically not so good."

"Know anything about them?" asked Jim.

Kiki took their pictures and fingerprints with her phone.

"For your photo album?" asked Joseph, with a laugh.

"We're going to find out about them." She forwarded the photos to David Kennedy, then called. "We need to know who these guys are. We stopped them sneaking into the country. Any information would help Nick."

"From Mexico?"

"Yeah. They were using a smuggler's tunnel. Lightly armed. A SUV was enroute to pick them up. He's the one in a tee-shirt."

"I'll run them through facial recognition and fingerprint database."

"I'll forward some scrapings for DNA also. We'll be taking these guys to the Atchley ranch for Nick's interrogation."

"Call me when you arrive. Nice work. If they're Russians, could be another team coming."

"Soon as you have information about these guys, Nick will ask them."

"Let me know what you find out during your

questioning."

"We will." She hung up.

"Who he?" asked Joseph.

"A trusted friend with government contacts. We've worked with him for years," answered Nick.

Kiki emptied the pockets of the men. Nothing would identify them. One had a crumpled package of cigarettes, foreign. She took several from the pack and rolled them inside the mouth of the unconscious man before placing all of the items in a baggie. She glanced at James who was staring intently.

Tucking the baggie into her pack she said, "Never can tell when evidence becomes handy."

"These interrogations going to be at the Atchley ranch?" asked Jim. He glanced at Keith. "I wanna know more about this *non-physical interview*."

Nick looked at him. "I was planning to use Keith's ranch. It's secure and isolated. We dropped off our equipment on our way down here."

"We took training there," said Joseph.

"Yeah, it's isolated. Is that for the screams?" asked Jim with a smile.

Chapter 57

What's so magic about that?" exclaimed Joseph, pointing to the coffin-like black box. An underground storage room in the safe area behind the vault door had been converted to the new interrogation room. Hospital monitors hung from the walls and a lounge chair with a laptop and a microphone on a small table sat next to the Isolation Chamber. A folding chair was the only other piece of furniture.

"Help me and I'll show you," said Nick as he wheeled the unconscious figure in on the gurney. "First we have to weigh him." They stripped the man and placed him on a scale. "Ninety-eight kilos."

Nick sat in the lounge chair and gestured for Joseph to sit. "We'll be here for a short time while

I get him stabilized," Nick said, as he entered the figures into his laptop. "I already gave him a sedative." He typed some more. Nick attached sensor pads to the man's chest and head and inserted an IV. "I use a bone mike, and the chamber has a sound suppressor so he can't hear anything. Let's get him into the chamber." They lifted the man and placed him into the tepid brine.

On the wall, screens traced pulse rate, blood pressure, and respiration. Another monitor had traces on it. "That's brain activity. The curve is pretty flat because he's unconscious." Nick took a last look at the man, paused, and closed the chamber lid.

He brought up a file from David Kennedy. "His name is Boris Popov." There was a pause as Nick read more. "He's wanted in several countries for terrorism. Works for the Wagner Group in Nigeria aiding antigovernment movements." He glanced at Joseph. "Out of date information. He was raised Edo Aziomo in Lagos, Nigeria where he attended a Catholic boarding school. Had an incident with one of the nuns, Sister Magrite, who died of the injuries he inflicted on her. Sent to prison at age twelve. Escaped three years later and joined a resistance movement. Was recruited into the Wagner Group when he showed a talent for leadership and violence. He was sent to Russia for extensive training, where he became Boris Popov. Believed to be responsible for the bombing of a Catholic church and the kidnapping of fifty-three young girls. Eight staff were murdered during that event." Nick sat back in his chair. "Quite a piece of work."

Nick called David Kennedy.

"Hey, Nick. How's it going?"

"Hi, David. I need translation software for Nigerian."

"Huh! Haven't had that request before. Hold on." There was a pause. "It's on the way. I gather you're starting your interrogation."

"I am. Boris Popov is from Nigeria, so I need this to get into his head."

"Let me know what you learn."

"Thanks, David."

Nick turned to Joseph, who had been following the conversation.

"Let's wake him up." Joseph's face remained expressionless.

"First we have to paralyze him so he doesn't thrash about. Nick typed some commands and pulse rate and respiration curve began to fall. "Have to be careful he doesn't smother. Now we add some stimulant." He typed and the pulse rate quickened. "This is the tricky part–waking him up but keeping him unable to move. He's conscious now. See, he's trying to move." Nick pointed at the increasing pulse rate and respiration. He tweaked the curarine.

Joseph jumped as a scream rent the air. "He's awake now," said Nick. In Nigerian, then Russian Boris began shouting questions. The Russian translation software changed the shouts to English.

"Where am I? Why can't I move? Who did this?"

"We'll let him go on for a while. It's easier if he tires a bit." Nick stood. "I could use some coffee."

* * *

"How's it going?" asked Jim as they entered the atrium. Keith and Tammy looked up. The cascading waterfall created a soft roar that was almost hypnotizing in its serenity.

"Strangest interrogation I ever saw," said Joseph. "Remember in the Sandbox where we did everything we could think of?" Jim nodded. "We just gave this guy a bath. Didn't even waterboard him."

"What'd he tell you?"

Joseph shook his head. "Haven't started asking yet. Just left him yelling in there."

"What kind of interrogation is this?" asked Tammy. "You gotta clean up any blood or vomit or shit."

"None, I promise," said Nick. He walked over, checked blood pressure and pulse of the other unconscious men stretched out on the floor. He took the bandage off the wound of the one man, then stuck it back.

"He need that treated? Antibiotics or something?" asked Tammy.

"He won't live long enough for it to be a problem," said Nick.

Tammy's mouth snapped shut.

Chapter 58

"Sir, I have hit a dead-end regarding the ship *Lightning of the Sea*. The owner claims to have been unaware of the trip into the Black Sea. His captain took it on a shakedown cruise after modifications. The ship is presently at sea somewhere in the Mediterranean, and the captain and crew are unavailable," reported Daniel Novikov to Colonel Dmitrev.

"What is its destination?"

"The Saudi says it has several ports of call, but no fixed schedule. He claims he will fly to meet it during the next four months for pleasure trips."

"Direct him to have it call on the nearest port. Go there and meet with the crew. Interview them. We need information."

"Yes, sir."

Daniel knew better than describe how difficult it would be to get Saudi royalty to do anything they didn't want to. Rather than try over the phone, he booked a flight into Riyad. Face-to-face had a better chance. Next, he called his new assistant to schedule a meeting.

* * *

Joseph and Nick returned to the newly created interrogation room. Edo, or Boris, whichever name he'd respond better to, was quiet. Nick glanced at the monitors. He was conscious. "I'm giving him LSD and THC." He tweaked the controls while watching the monitors.

Nick adjusted the volume and tone before he spoke into the microphone. His words were translated into Nigerian with a higher pitch, sounding like a woman's voice. *"Edo, why did you beat me? I was only trying to teach you right from wrong."*

"Who is that?" His voice was raspy and hoarse from screaming.

"You killed me."

"Sister Magrite?" He moaned.

Nick pointed at the monitor showing pulse rate

and respiration. Both had spiked. Joseph stared.

"I lost my temper when you struck me."

"You were stealing, then you lied about it."

"How are you speaking to me? Where am I?"

"You're not in your world any longer."

"You mean I'm dead? I can't be dead!"

"Do you feel your body? Can you see?"

"No, but I hear you."

"Do you hear your own screams?"

Edo was silent. "If I'm dead, where's God to judge me?"

"You want to be judged? What did you learn about judgement and about hell? God will come, but you must ask forgiveness or spend eternity burning in hell. This you know."

"There is no God. He wouldn't let the things happen in the world that I saw." Edo stopped. "That I did."

"I'm here to remind you of your faith. You have strayed far. When you meet God, you must be ready to ask for forgiveness."

"Will you be with me?"

"You must meet God alone. Goodbye, Edo."

"Wait. Don't leave me."

Nick stared at Joseph. His mouth was open to

speak. Nick held up his hand to silence him.

"Do you want me to call you Edo?" Nick switched the translator to Russian. *"Or Boris?"*

"Boris. Who are you?" His voice had strengthened as if he wanted to draw on his Russian training.

"I will be judging you to see if you truly repent your sins. As Boris you committed grave sins. Those are the ones you must recant first. Start with the most recent."

"You are God?"

"I am."

"When did I die? I can't remember but I should."

"You came across the border with other men."

"It was my team. We are…were going to work with a local cell to attack an NSA facility as revenge for attacks made in Russia. What happened to them?"

"They and I will be speaking later.

"They're all dead too?"

"This facility you were going to attack was responsible for the assaults?"

"I don't know. I was only following orders."

"You follow orders. You don't question

whether they are right or wrong?"

"That was my training. After that attack, we had other targets."

"You were going to kill the people at these targets?"

"Yes and blow them up."

"But you had no explosives and only pistols."

"The local cell was to supply those. Since we didn't attack, are those sins?"

"What about other missions?"

"Before we came to America, we were in Nigeria where we fought against the government forces there. Russia wanted a government more favorable to them. We blew up buildings, killed people, kidnapped children for our soldiers, whatever was necessary to disrupt the government and weaken the public's faith in them."

"How many people have you killed?"

"Hundreds."

"Men, women, children. You have no remorse for those sins."

"I do. I regret them."

"I look into your soul and do not see it. We will go through everything. Perhaps then you will truly feel regret."

Nick clicked off the mic and turned to Joseph. "I'm going to get as much detail as I can on everything he has done. It will take hours. You needn't stay."

"I see why you don't like to do this." Joseph rose. "See ya in a while."

* * *

"David, there's another team coming into the US."

"Can't say I'm surprised, Katherine. Where and when?"

"All Nick found out was the landing is on the coast of the Gulf of Mexico. Our best guess is within two days."

"Is Nick done?"

"He's still working on the terrorists. We might find out more."

Chapter 59

Inspector Novikov was in total awe at the opulence of the jet as it winged its way toward Greece. The prince had been very accommodating about Daniel's request to meet with the crew of *Lightning of the Sea*, offering to fly him to its next port of call. He had spent two days as a guest before departure on the private jet. Never before had he seen such a display of wealth. The jet tilted down, and with the thump of the landing gear locking into place, Daniel reached for the seat belt.

"No need for that." Prince Sakuri bin Al Faisal smiled, flashing brilliantly white teeth below a thin mustache. "One of the advantages of a private jet."

"I have instructed the crew to be available for your questions as soon as we land. It was good you contacted me. *Lightning of the Sea* was starting on an extended cruise."

As they stepped off the plane, a black limousine followed by two black SUVs pulled up. Men wearing black suits and dark glasses got out. Obviously body guards, they surrounded Daniel and the prince scanning the area for threats. Another man opened the limo door for the prince to enter. Daniel followed. As the men got in, the doors closed with a solid thunk. *Armored.*

"The port is only a fifteen-minute drive," said the prince. "Would you like something to drink?" He pressed a button and a complete bar unfolded. "I don't imbibe myself, but no reason you shouldn't."

"Thank you. Perhaps after we meet the crew." Daniel watched the city flow by. When they stopped, the ritual with the men reversed, and he and Prince Faisal stepped out.

Lightning of the Sea was truly an awesome yacht. It took Daniel's breath away. Being from Saint Petersburg, he knew boats, and this was beyond anything he'd seen before.

At the head of the gangway in a dazzling white uniform stood a man ready to greet them. "Prince al Faisal, welcome aboard." He gave a slight bow of his head.

"I would like to introduce you to Detective Inspector Novikov of the Saint Petersburg police. This is Captain Rogers."

"G'day Inspector. Pleased ta meetcha." He held out his hand.

"Australian?" asked Daniel, taking his hand.

"Da," said Rogers with a laugh. "What can I do for ya?"

"I'd like to hear about your recent trip into the Black Sea."

"Let's go inside." He led them into a sumptuous dining room. "Adult beverages?" he asked. "Vodka?" He glanced at Daniel.

"Scotch," he answered.

Rogers' eyebrows rose. He chuckled. A man in a white jacket went to the bar to prepare two scotches and a strong tea for the prince.

"What was purpose of trip?"

"We made some improvements to *Lightning* and needed sea trials to check everything out. What are ya looking for, Inspector?"

"Did you pick up passengers?"

"We made a few stops. Nobody got on or off. Look, a team of inspectors came on board and searched." A belligerent tone crept into his voice.

"They found nothing."

Prince al Faisal held up a hand to forestall any animosity. "Perhaps if you took the Inspector on a tour so he could see for himself there is no place to smuggle people on this boat."

Properly admonished, Rogers apologized for his tone. "Let's finish our drinks and I'll show ya around."

"I will stay here. I have a few issues to deal with," said the prince.

* * *

Daniel was astounded by the engine room. It was spotless, with the turbine driven hydraulic pumps dominating the floorspace. "We normally run this as a jet boat, with a shallow draft allowing us to get to some great diving spots. In addition, we have hydrofoils that can lift the boat out of the water. We then use turbofans to power it forward. With little water resistance, we are capable of high speeds and great maneuverability. This works best in relatively calm water, like in the Black Sea. That's what we were testing."

"How fast can *Lightning of the Sea* go?"

"I'll let the prince tell you that."

"Why does he need a yacht like this?"

"What's need got to do with it?" laughed Rogers. "It is a pleasure boat, and the prince enjoys many pleasures including demonstrating his abilities."

"What is behind that hatch?" asked Daniel pointing.

"That's the diving pool. Would you like to see that?"

"Show me everything."

They entered a chamber with a pool in the center. Wet suits hung from the walls like deflated bodies. At one end was a compressor connected to a manifold capable of filling ten SCUBA tanks at a time. A mini-submarine the size of a car hung suspended above the pool. Daniel looked in all the lockers, even the sub. These were all the places a competent team would have searched, and he had spoken to the team. They were good. He had paid attention to the dimensions and spacing and was sure there were no hidden compartments.

"The prince is quite the diver. Been to many of the best spots in the world. Okay then, you've seen the entire boat. Is there anything else I can show you?"

Back in the dining room, the prince looked up from his laptop. "Ah I see your tour is complete." He looked at Rogers. "The trials went well?"

"Perfect, sir."

Turning back to Daniel, he asked, "With the trials a success, I'd like to experience this boat. Would you like to go for a sail, Detective?"

Daniel smiled. "I certainly would."

"Captain Rogers, the seas are calm. Make arrangements for us to take *Lightning of the Sea* out for a three-hour cruise. We'll make it a dinner cruise. Do you like Chilean sea bass, Detective?" Daniel nodded. "Tell the chef we eat in two hours."

A kilometer from the harbor, a thrum went through the ship as the speed picked up. It skipped across the water, then the deck seemed to rise. With a roar, the ride smoothed out. From the aft window of the dining room, Daniel marveled at the two jet-engine like turbines pushing the yacht smoothly forward at astonishing speed. He glanced down at his glass of scotch–not a ripple. What he wouldn't give for a boat like this.

Chapter 60

Completely exhausted, Nick fell into the couch in the atrium at the Atchley ranch. He tossed thumb drives to Kiki, Ilia and Sasha. "I've milked them dry. We now have more information about the Wagner Group than anybody in the world. David needs those." He waved at the thumb drives in their hands. "We also know about the other hit team coming into the US. It was a hurried operation, organization not well done. We can stop them."

"Nick, you look beat. Are you all right?" concern in Kiki's voice.

"Thirty-six hours of interrogation and I'm exhausted. I feel as drained as those poor fellows in there." He waved his hand toward the entrance to the Safe Room. "I'm going to bed."

"Want me to tuck you in?" asked Kiki with a smile.

"Rest, I need rest. I'll stumble in myself. Call David." Nick wobbled toward their bedroom.

* * *

"David, we're sending you the recordings of Nick's interrogation of the Russian terrorists we captured." Kiki had him on speakerphone. "You can set up operations for the sleeper cells indicated. We're sure there are more, but these are the only ones our captives knew about. You need to get a crew organized to intercept the other team coming into the country on the Gulf Coast."

"If they're entering on the Gulf Coast, then there's a boat involved. I'll alert the Coast Guard."

"From what Boris said, it's probably a small submarine, an Alpha Class. You might need the Navy in addition to the Coast Guard."

"Yeah, right. When and where's the landing to take place?"

"Boris said three days. That was a day ago."

"You didn't think to call me sooner?"

"We've been a little busy here."

Kiki heard David grunt dissatisfaction. "If I go to the FBI with this info, they'll want verification–same with Homeland Security. I can't blame them, but I'd have to tell them about you. I don't want to do that."

"I don't want you to. We'll take care of them, but we'll need a hop to Louisiana tonight that won't involve TSA inspections. We need our tools."

"I'll call the man backing this. He has that cute little fifteen passenger jet you returned from Europe on."

"What will you tell him?"

"As little as possible. He'll understand it's best if he knows nothing."

"Tell him we're intercepting killers sent for him. That should get you cooperation. Bring the jet to Marana Regional. We'll be there before six."

"Where are you going?"

"Boris wasn't completely clear. He said something about Holly Beach, Louisiana, so we're flying into Lake Charles. We'll need ground transportation."

"I'll arrange a couple of SUVs. Do you know anything about the sleeper cell?"

"We have enough info to find it. You could tip the Navy off and they can sink the sub before the team gets off."

"I could, but then the government will be

involved. That will open a whole load of shit I'm not ready for. Are you?"

"The image of all of us being questioned by our own government is ugly. I wouldn't want to deprive these guys of the fun of meeting the Isolation Chamber. We could learn more."

"What about the ones you have there in Arizona?"

The Cheoj militia wants our captives. Something about honor after they invaded sacred lands. I didn't ask any more."

"Is there anything else to get from them?"

"Nick says he milked them dry. The only thing left for them is institutions."

David sighed. "After seeing the others Nick questioned, I feel sorry for them, but not enough to put up a fight."

"David, I promised Jim and Joseph a couple of the newest rifle scopes and solar electrification for the village in exchange for their help in capturing these guys."

"You went out on a limb there. Those sights are the latest military issue. That will be difficult, but doable if I go to the manufacturer for some *samples*. I'll speak to the Secretary of Interior about the electrification. He can make that a publicity project to improve the plight of Native Americans."

"We'll keep you informed."

"Be careful. These guys are good. If they were supposed to communicate with Boris's team and couldn't, they may be expecting you."

"Yeah, we'll consider that."

* * *

"Jim and I need to go with you," said Joseph, crossing his arms and glancing at his brother. We helped you here." Jim smiled, "and we have friends in the native community in the Lake Charles area."

"Always best to have allies who know the land," chimed in Joseph.

"I can't offer you more stuff," said Kiki.

"We're not doing this for stuff," said Jim.

Chapter 61

Nick looked at the unconscious man stretched out on the floor. He was neither tall nor short, heavy nor thin. His brown hair was cut short. He had no distinguishing features and was as non-descript as any person Nick had ever seen.

The team had flown into Lake Charles on the private jet supplied by the businessman who'd financed them. The Isolation Chamber was with them. Two SUVs and a box truck were waiting at the general aviation airport. They'd installed the chamber in the box truck. Nick had prepped everything, anticipating another interrogation. Jim and Joseph had watched with great interest.

Just after midnight, they'd hit the address of the

sleeper cell that was to aid the commandos. They'd taken the sole survivor of that attack, the man now on the floor, to a RV park where he was being prepped for Nick. His introduction to the chamber awaited. They'd searched the house for anything to help them intercept the commandos. There was no information, but a cache of automatic weapons, a couple of mortars with rounds of ammunition and explosives. Ilia had Bob on the phone trying to help them break into the laptop but so far, no success.

* * *

Ilia and Joseph remained at the house awaiting any contact. Kiki and Zyra were in an SUV parked down the street. The three bodies of the residents were stashed in the garage. At two AM, the radio hand-set crackled. A voice spoke in Russian, asking for Vlad and a password. Ilia answered.

"Vlad is not able to talk right now. He's ill. Just a minute." Ilia held up the phone and yelled, "Vlad, what's the password?" Joseph retched into the phone. "Vlad, I need the password." Joseph retched again.

The Russian cut the connection. "Shit!" exclaimed Ilia. "They're suspicious. Bob, were you able to get a signal from the call?"

"Yeah. The call was made from offshore. I'm locked on. He's making another call. I'll patch you in."

Ilia listened to the Russian. "He thinks they've been compromised," translated Ilia. "He's being directed to an alternative site."

"Any idea where?" asked Joseph.

"They only said the secondary site," said Ilia. "Bob, stay locked on that phone. When he calls the contact at the secondary site let us know."

"Will do, but the signal is gone. The sub may have submerged. I'm using you guys as the relay. They could move out of range."

"Shit!" exclaimed Joseph.

"Maybe Nick will get something," said Ilia, "but that takes time."

* * *

Jim helped Nick strip and weigh the unconscious Vlad. After entering the data into his laptop, Nick attached the sensor pads and bone microphone. Together they hoisted him into the body-temperature brine in the Isolation Chamber. Nick checked the monitors to ensure everything was working. He glanced at Vlad then at Sasha. "Thus, he leaves this world." He closed the lid. "Glad you're here to translate for me. I don't like to depend on the software." She nodded at him.

Nick had almost no information about Vlad. He had no religious tats or jewelry. Nothing in the house indicated religious affiliation. They didn't know if he was a Russian immigrant or American born. They'd be flying blind until Nick had enough information to get into his head. "Kath, have you been able to find out anything about our guest?"

"Not much. Search is going on. Vlad Povich is Ukrainian born. Raised in Odesa. Family was Orthodox. He didn't join the church. Mother and father deceased. Fought with the ethnic Russian resistance until after Russia annexed eastern Ukraine. He joined the Wagner Group. The information gets really sketchy after that."

"Keep looking," said Nick. "Let me know anything else you find."

He looked at the monitors again. "Let's get this show on the road. I've never done this with so little information about the subject." Sasha's and Jim's faces showed their lack of understanding. "First, we'll wake him up. There'll be a lot of yelling. Sasha, listen to his words, but more importantly his tone. I need to know where his head is."

Nick keyed in commands to his laptop while watching the monitors. The traces changed. A scream rent the air as Vlad woke. The translation software, in a flat voice, spoke his queries of where he was, why he couldn't move or see or hear. Nick watched the monitors as Vlad struggled against the paralysis of the drugs. As the traces began to spike on the monitors, Nick keyed in instructions to increase the sedatives. He glanced at Sasha. "Is he panicking yet?"

She looked at him, organizing her thoughts. "He's on the verge." The screaming continued.

"That's okay. We'll let him tire a bit. Here's the scenario. You're going to speak to him like his mother. Use endearments. He has to believe he's talking with his dead mother and that he's dead." Nick glanced at Jim. His face showed confusion. "Once he buys into the idea he's dead, we're in his head. I'm giving him LSD and THC to help." Nick keyed in commands.

He pointed at Sasha and mouthed *Go*.

"Vladdie, is that you?"

There was silence as Vlad tried to comprehend the words directed into his skull via the bone mic. "Mom? Is that you?"

"It is me. What are you doing here?"

"Where is here?"

"Vlad, I died soon after your father. I didn't want to live."

"He was executed by the government as a Russian collaborator," Vlad snarled.

"He wasn't though." Sasha let out a sob. *"You know that."*

"It was me. I was the Russian collaborator." Vlad's voice broke. "I got papa killed."

"It's okay now. You're here with me. It's been very lonely. I'm glad you're here."

Nick glanced at Sasha. She was getting into the role.

"Where is here?"

"Vladdie, we're dead. What happened to you?"

He said nothing for a minute.

"It's easier once you accept it. Our fight is over."

Vlad gave out a soft cry. "I can't be dead. This can't be death."

"Vladdie, we are born, we live and we die. That is what we do. You were killed by someone. I died of a broken heart. Different, but we are the same now, dead."

"I had so much I wanted to do. I was supposed to make Russia great again. It was my dream."

"I had dreams too. I was lucky to live some of those with a wonderful man and raise a child. God decided I had done what was planned and it was time to go."

"I was part of a plan to destroy the great capitalist society that was crushing Russia."

"Those were the plans of men, not God. I am sorry you rejected the church. Your father and I tried to make you a member."

"Where is God now?"

"God will come to you according to God's plan, not yours."

"Is this heaven?"

"God put me here to greet you. Judgement will determine where you go from here. What was your plan?"

"I went to America years ago as a Ukrainian refugee and set up a sleeper cell. I was the leader. We were to join a team to attack the American cyber command. The Americans sent a team to Moscow and murdered hundreds of our soldiers with nerve gas. I was going to avenge them."

"But what got you here?"

Sasha was really getting into the program, Nick thought. She was good.

"Our house was attacked. We had no warning. They came in without a sound. I looked up when Misha's blood spattered around me. His throat had been cut by this black devil. She grabbed my hair before I could resist, yanked my head back and put her knife against my throat. But a voice stopped her. Someone shot me. It's all I remember."

"Oh, Vladdie, I'm so sorry. It was a brave thing you were doing. How were you going to meet with this team from Russia?"

"They were to call me. I give them a codeword and we'd meet them on the beach."

"And then?"

"They had the plans. We had weapons and explosives for our attack. We had two pickup trucks for the drive to Virginia. That's all I know."

"But if this didn't happen, what was the team to do?"

"There was a secondary cell to help them."

"Where was that?"

"I don't know. Since we were attacked, it's a good thing." There was silence for a few minutes. "Mama, what do we do now?"

Chapter 62

"I'm sorry, David," said Kiki. She and Nick were in their motel room in Lake Charles. "We just didn't have enough information to intercept the second team. Nick's interrogation didn't give us anything actionable except we think they're heading to Virginia. We're packing our gear into the jet so we can respond if we hear anything."

"I need to talk to Ron."

"What! You want to get the former president involved?"

"This was always going to be an international issue."

"So, you used us to force the *issue?*"

"Yup," he said unapologetically. "Now cybercrime can be addressed like terrorism.

Nobody wants a shooting war. Countries will work to prevent that."

"Coalitions and the UN enforce actions against terrorism."

"Not always," answered David. "I know first-hand of actions against terrorism solely by the United States. Obama's drone program is a glaring example of the United States taking action. The same with Osama bin Laden. Those were strictly US operations."

"You foresee the same thing with cybercrime? That drone program could never be used against major powers like Russia. Iran struck back after we nailed some leaders."

"Once we have the structure of an agreement, we have some basis for strikes."

"I'll believe it when I see it," snapped Kiki.

"As a former president, Ron can alert the FBI and Homeland Security of an imminent attack by Russian forces. We can let them take care of this."

"Are they up to the task?" Kiki asked, a bit of snark in her voice.

"Not in time for this strike. That is the reality. There will be a successful attack which will mollify the Russians so negotiations and an agreement can go ahead."

"You're going to sacrifice American lives?"

"There are causalities in war."

Kiki snarled. "Not if I can help it." She broke the connection and slammed the phone down.

Nick stared at her. "What are you going to do?"

"I'm going to find these Ruskie bastards and kill them, that's what." Her mind tingled. She looked at Nick. His expression said that the Director was here.

"Hello Katherine and Nicholas. It has been a while since we talked. I must thank you for the banquet in Moscow. Fear is a delicious flavor, and it still puddles in the minds of those seeking the new jobs at the Cyber Command in Moscow. The hatred you caused is the hot sauce to my meals."

"So glad you enjoyed that." Kiki's voice had a hard edge. "It was never our intent to feed you."

"I know, but you do it so well. Be cautious in your next endeavors. Instead of being an ally you could become an enemy of your own people."

"What do you mean?" asked Nick.

"You already know. Think carefully. Ta ta for now."

Kiki and Nick stared at each other. Tears of anger formed in Kiki's eyes. "Nick, I can't let Americans die when it can be prevented."

"K, we don't have enough information to do anything. Vlad had limited knowledge about this team of commandos, their targets, or other sleeper cells. We can only hope Bob can locate their phone when they contact the next cell."

Her sadness was a thin coating over the anger she felt.

Nick took her in his arms. "Let's get some sleep. He'll call with any news."

Chapter 63

David Kennedy sat in the den at Ron Carson's Idaho ranch. He had tried hard to keep any knowledge of the attacks in Russia away from him, but now with hit teams sent to America to attack the Cyber Division, this could be a publicity disaster, particularly if it led to a shooting war.

David had teamed with Ron Carson when he was Secretary of the Interior. They were ordered to respond to the attacks starting the Bio-Cyber War that crippled the economy of America. Half the population had perished as disease and a destroyed electrical grid struck.

Using the interrogation techniques of Nick Sabino, a taskforce was formed to track down the source and strike back. The success of the counter attacks vaulted Ron Carson into the public eye and eventually the office of president. He proved to be visionary by creating the Orbiting Power System, a string of satellites beaming solar energy to a world desperate for clean power. As the sole supplier, the United States maintained its status without selling weapons of war.

Ron also visualized a world government, similar to the United Nations, but with the authority to enforce peace and human rights. He continues to work for that.

He stared at David. "Let me see if I understand what you're saying. Since the United States government efforts to block cybercrime are exclusively applied to government operations, a group of businesses contracted hit teams to strike the source of these attacks, starting with Russia. Is that correct?"

"Yes, sir."

"Those were the events recently brought to light about an explosion in Saint Petersburg and a nerve gas attack in Moscow?"

"Yes, sir."

"And now Russia has sent teams to America to strike back in retaliation?"

"Yes, sir. We stopped one, but the other is somewhere in the US."

"Is anybody I know involved?"

"Do you want me to answer that?"

"Jesus H Christ!" He slammed his glass of scotch down on the table, spilling half of it. "What was a nice quiet little electronics war is going hot, threatening to expand into a world conflict. You're talking a kinetic war, the old-fashioned kind with bullets and bombs, maybe even nukes."

"Thought you oughta know, sir."

"And the parties involved are the same ones responsible for the mess in Mexico two years ago?"

David nodded.

"Shit! You truly have loosed the dogs of war. We both know what that group is capable of. It took every favor I owed to keep them from being the target of the hunt for those responsible for the murders of executives in the military industrial complex and several members of congress."

David raised his hands. "Sir, it is time we paid the same level of attention to cyber war as to terrorism. We need an international agreement regarding electronic attacks. As you well know, after the Bio-Cyber War, lives, even countries were destroyed. It continues today. This team took us from a purely defensive strategy to offensive. It's the same with terrorism. We have taken away the safe havens rather than just cowering behind supposedly safe walls."

Ron Carson stared at him. "What do you propose?"

"We start with an international meeting to discuss tactics to stop cybercrime."

"Sure, and everybody will nod and agree to curb it. But it will only be words. State sanctioned attacks will continue, Fake news will continue."

"Without consequences, that is true. With terrorism, forces attack terrorists wherever they are. It should be the same."

"Do you honestly believe we'll get agreements from Russia, North Korea, Iran and China? Hell, we're among the worst in cyber-attacks. The third world harbors for terrorists are easy to attack. Terrorism is their only real weapon against global powers. Sanctions can be imposed against violators, but…"

"They are long term and of questionable effectiveness. Russia still got what it wanted of Ukraine. Anybody knows that instant punishment is far more effective. The world is not the lawless wild west. It's time to do something about it."

Ex-president Carson drained his remaining scotch. "You want an international hit team to enforce anti-cybercrime like the one you sent into Russia?"

"After we get international agreements and laws, we'll need enforcers."

Ron sighed. "We'll need a big stick." He held up a finger. "And Russians don't forget. We'll have to deal with that too."

Chapter 64

Nikolai Presinkov viewed the building through his high-powered binoculars. Though it was pitch-black, he didn't need the night vision equipment they'd brought as the whole area was lit brighter than day. He and his team were in the woods near the perimeter fence surrounding the NSA facility. He had studied the satellite photos and knew there was no way his team could cover the five-hundred meters from the fence to the building before they'd be cut down.

The sleeper cell he'd met with in Florida had supplied them with a pair of one-hundred-twenty-millimeter mortars and antiaircraft shoulder-launched missiles. They'd mounted the mortars in the back of two pickup trucks so they could shoot and scoot. They'd be moving before the first mortar rounds hit. Helicopters were easy prey to the missiles. Using the maps, he'd laid out a route the trucks would follow in opposite directions around the perimeter. Firing from two directions would make it harder to find them. They would stop, set up and fire three rounds and move to the next spot. He anticipated being able to fire the forty mortar rounds in fifteen minutes. The trucks already were at the first firing points.

He would act as spotter. When the rounds were expended, the trucks would be abandoned and he'd pick up his men in the van, and they'd exfil the area. It looked good on paper. He knew better. This had all the earmarks of a suicide mission, which matched the final instruction he'd been given–no one gets taken alive. He reached for his phone to get the final okay.

* * *

Kiki watched her heads-up display showing the Russians as red dots moving into position for the attack. Bob had tracked the phone from the first night. They had followed. Anticipating the strike was to be against an NSA facility, they had projected it had to be this location. Bob had a drone up using the infrared viewer. She was in position to take out the spotter, probably the leader. He was a white silhouette in her scope. It was a four-hundred-yard shot. Piece of cake.

A voice came over her com unit. It was David Kennedy! How the hell did he do that? "Katherine, stand down. Let them attack. The building is abandoned. They won't kill anybody. After the attack, we want them alive."

"What the fuck are you doing in my op?"

"I'm doing what's best for the United States and the world. After this attack, the Russians will be ready to talk about what to do to control cybercrime. But we have to let them save face. We'll rub their nose in the shit when we prove it wasn't the US government who attacked them."

"How did you get on this com?"

"I talked to Bob. He agreed this was the best course of action."

"You threatened him, didn't you?"

"Only a little."

"How are you going to capture them? They'll certainly have suicide pills."

"Watch and learn."

The mortar barrage lasted less than fifteen

minutes. A scrambled fighter flew low overhead, but the fiery track of an antiaircraft missile drove him off. She could hear helicopters, but they didn't appear, probably due to the presence of the missiles.

With the explosion of the last rounds, the roof and top floors of the building collapsed. The underground facilities were probably safe. On her heads-up, Kiki watched four men climb into a waiting van. It sped down a road, one of only two possibilities to get out of the area quickly. It was obviously being driven by someone with night vision as there were no lights, not even brake lights.

She watched it careen around a corner where a Humvee had the road blocked. As the van screeched to a halt Kiki heard an earsplitting wail. She was almost a thousand yards away, and it hurt her ears.

"It's a sonic stunner," explained David. "Instantly incapacitates anyone it's aimed at. They won't have a chance to take their pills."

Soldiers flooded the area around the van, dragged the inert men out, bound their hands and feet, and shoved something into their mouths to prevent them from biting down. Hoods were thrown over their heads as they were strapped to stretchers and carried into two waiting vans. The whole operation took less than fifteen seconds.

"We'll need Nick now," said David.

Chapter 65

"Sir, I checked the ship's log after they left the Black Sea. They called on several ports," reported Daniel Novikov to Colonel Dmitrev. "I tried to get flight records from the airports, but the Greeks were particularly reluctant to release those. The private air strips made no records available. If they left the Black Sea aboard the *Lightning of the Sea*, their tracks have been covered well."

"One of our teams sent to America was intercepted. We haven't heard anything from them, nor are there any reports within the US government of their capture. They have disappeared, and we can't ask after them."

"Disappointing," said Daniel.

"All is not bad news. A second team scrubbed their landing when the leader became suspicious. They successfully landed at the secondary site and are proceeding to targets in Virginia. We will strike back."

"I'm sorry I was not able to supply evidence that it was the American government who was behind the attacks."

"After the strikes, we'll put our military on alert. I do not like to see this. There are those in our government who consider nuclear weapons acceptable. That is worrying."

"Neither will gain if we start attacking each other. Is there anything I can do?"

"Actually, there is. Make a statement that you have found no evidence of the American government involvement. In fact, you do not believe they were involved."

Daniel was stunned. Such a statement without permission could mean the end of his career. "Sir, I…"

"I understand what this could do to you," Dmitrev interrupted, "but it may prevent something much worse. I will back you up. So, we'll both be in the same boat. What's a couple of careers compared to nuclear war?"

"When do you want to make these statements?"

"We'll call a press conference tomorrow. Try

to not look like you've had a sleepless night, detective. That was a joke."

* * *

Daniel had never been so nervous. He looked out at the reporters, both foreign and domestic, and shuffled his notes. He began.

"I am Detective Inspector Daniel Novikov of the Saint Petersburg police. I was tasked with investigating the bombing and murders that occurred there several months ago. Due to the nature of the targets, the Cyber Command asked me to assist their own investigation.

"Near Moscow, we found a farmhouse used by these terrorists as headquarters. While attempting to arrest them, a bomb exploded killing the suspects and more than thirty of our soldiers." He shook his head. "It was a diversion. During that action, a nerve gas attack struck the Cyber Command headquarters, killing more than four-hundred of our citizens. The terrorists had a well-planned escape ready.

"Our efforts to track them has reached a dead end, though it is ongoing. One of the two terrorists at the farm house was identified as a mercenary.

Efforts to find out who hired him have proved fruitless so far. I do not believe the American government or any other government was behind these attacks. Colonel Dmitrev will speak more on this."

Daniel turned and stepped away as Dmitrev moved to the microphone.

"I am Colonel Dmitrev, Military Security. We have used all the tools at our disposal to find those ultimately responsible for these attacks. False trails were laid, indicating the Chechens or the Ukrainians were responsible. Not true. Our sources within the American government have strenuously denied any involvement. I believe them. Escalating electronic war to a shooting war benefits neither us nor them. It could potentially cost thousands of lives. Someone hired these terrorists. We will find out who and deal with them. There are those who would like to see two great powers at war. Perhaps among them are the culprits. We will find out. I will take questions."

Chapter 66

Daniel and the colonel stood at attention in the office of the President Kirov. The glares directed at them by him and his staff would whither most.

"Who gave you permission to hold a press conference?" snarled the president. Neither of them spoke. "Do you have any idea what you've done?" He rose and paced, his powerfully-built frame shaking in rage. They remained mute. "While you were telling the world that the United States government was not behind the attacks in our country, our commandos struck a major NSA facility in retaliation."

He spun to face his general in charge of military operations. "Have we heard anything from them?"

"No, sir," answered the portly man. "They

were under strict orders to not be taken alive. If they didn't escape, they are gone."

"Have there been any reports about the attack?"

Another man, his press secretary said, "The only report is of a disturbance at a secret facility in Virginia. The Americans seem to be keeping it quiet."

"Why would they do that?"

The silence was broken by his phone ringing. His red phone. "Da."

"President Kirov, this is the President of the United States." Kirov glanced at the others in the room. "We need to stop this madness before it escalates. The United States did not attack installations within Russia. I cannot emphasize that strongly enough. We have not released information about your attack on our facility because the public clamor would demand a retaliatory strike. I don't want to do that."

"If you didn't attack us, who did?"

"We're investigating and will share any information we get with you. In the meantime, let us both stand down. We both use cyber-attacks, but I am suspending those actions until we determine what has happened. As a measure of good faith, we'd like to see the same from you."

"There are many using those tools in the world."

"Yes, sir. If we both stop, perhaps it will be easier to trace the source of the attacks."

"I can halt the government attacks, but not the private. The same with you?"

"It is, Konstantin, but we will be much more active against those guilty of cybercrimes."

"Where do you see this going?"

"Former president Ron Carson has approached me about convening an international assembly to address rules for cybercrime. International accord is long overdue."

"I agree. I'm not admitting we had anything to do with the attack on your facility, but what is the fate of the attackers?"

"The attackers disappeared before we could capture them. We don't have them or any idea of where they would go. When they are captured, they will be interrogated and put on trial as terrorists."

"I await receiving the agenda."

"Nice speaking to you, Konstantin."

The Russian president spun to face the two men standing before his desk. "Is this what you wanted."

Colonel Dmitrev spoke for the first time. "Sir, we wanted to prevent war."

The president snorted.

"If I might suggest, Mr. President," said Daniel, "perhaps we might offer to assist the Americans in their hunt for who attacked us."

The president fixed him with a penetrating stare. "Detective Inspector Novikov, is it?"

"Yes, sir."

A pensive look came over the president's face. A brief smile graced his lips. "And I was about to have you executed. A good idea." He glanced at the others in the room. "You will report everything directly to me, of course. Colonel Dmitrev and I will closely follow any progress. You're not against the wall…for now."

Chapter 67

Under David's direction, Kiki and the team followed the vans to the Orange County airport. A waiting C-151, engines idling, squatted on the runway with its loading ramp down. The vans drove directly in. The box truck with Kiki and the team followed. The vehicles were secured to the deck, and as the last soldier left, the ramp began to close. The engines revved and the plane taxied to the end of the runway for takeoff.

Kiki, in the passenger seat of the van jumped as David rapped on the glass. "After takeoff, c'mon out," he yelled over the roar. "I have sandwiches and drinks up front."

They braced at the acceleration. With the clunk of the landing gear locking in place, the deck tilted in a steep climb. When it leveled, they made their way forward. David sat in a web seat holding a sandwich, a bottle of Gatorade clasped between his legs. He waved at two coolers tied against the bulkhead.

"What the fuck are you doing?" Kiki shouted.

"This is bigger than us," he responded around a mouthful of ham and cheese. He motioned for the others to gather around. "I spoke to Ron. We agreed this is our opportunity for international accord as to how to handle cybercrime. It is the new terrorism."

"We had it handled," said Kiki.

"What were you going to do, kill everyone? Sorry if we deprived you of that opportunity, but it's still available." He looked at Zyra. "After we're done, the prisoners are yours."

"Where are we going?" asked Jim.

"Your part of the country. We should be landing at the Pinal County Air Park in about five hours. We had to get out of the DC area. Too many eyes and ears, and we don't want government interference. The place leaks like a sieve."

David reached into his pocket and pulled out his phone, glanced at the caller and plugged it into a com system. "Use your coms," he instructed.

"Thank you for everything you've done," said former president Ron Carson. "We have a lot more to do, and the world will need your help. The only plan at the moment is to prevent a shooting war and get control of the cybercrime and abuse. I want you to understand how close we were to war, potentially nuclear war. This was as dire as the Cuban missile crisis. The danger isn't over, but we've bought time for heads to cool."

"What's next, Mr. President?" asked Kiki.

"It's Ron now, remember. With Nick's help we will interrogate our captives. The identities and backgrounds of the commandos is being checked. You'll have everything we can find out, Nick."

Nick nodded, a frown on his face. His abhorrence for the interrogations was well known.

"While you were in Virginia, we had an interesting development," said David. "Watch your heads-up. I'll play a news conference out of Russia."

They watched as Daniel Novikov and Colonel Dmitrev spoke. "Their heads will roll for that," commented David. "It was a brave thing to do to avert war. It was the right thing to do. We've checked into the backgrounds of those two. They are the chief investigators."

"I recognize one of them," blurted Kiki.

"We didn't hear that," said Ron.

Properly admonished at her gaff, Kiki's mouth snapped shut.

"Once we land, where are we going?" asked Ilia.

"We can stay at the old training facility on the National Guard grounds," said David. "We used it during the Bio-Cyber War, remember?"

"It's pretty austere," noted Nick. "There's my place in Casa Grande. With the underground area, there's room for all of us, and it's secure."

"I didn't want to prevail on you, but I'm glad you offered," said Ron. We'd thought about my ranch, but Idaho is far from everything. It's why I like it. You're better set up with Bob and Kathy there. By the way, welcome, Jim and Joseph. We're glad you're with us. Thank you for the help."

"Never thought I'd be speaking with the president," said Jim. "An honor to help."

"Ex-president. Call me Ron. I'll fly into Pinal and meet you there. I have to get out of DC. The situation here reminds me of the old saying, 'When in doubt, scream and shout, run and wave your arms about.'" That brought a chuckle. "Get some rest. Trying times ahead."

Chapter 68

The emergency commission meeting at the United Nations on cyber security was into its first day on Friday. Ron was chairing the meeting.

"Ladies and gentlemen, welcome to the international commission on Cybercrime. It is our aim to create the foundation for addressing international cybercrime, hacking, and fake news. To date, that battle has been mostly electronic. Recent events in Russia indicate that may no longer be the case. We are tasked with creating definitions and rules to counter cybercrimes and deter those from becoming a shooting war. I have placed a list of those attending here. We will start with an open discussion."

That something had to be done was quickly

agreed to. Ron's suggestion to model it after the accords regarding terrorism were met with mixed responses. Enforcement of any agreements would be a major sticking point. Sovereignty was always going to be an issue. Another was the definition of cybercrime. Near the end of the first session, Ron told each of the delegates to make up a list of what they considered to be cybercrime and what needed to be covered. Enforcement was tabled until they could decide what to enforce. They would meet again after the weekend.

Ron was happy to leave New York for the open skies of Arizona to enjoy the weekend.

Sitting on the patio at Nick's house, Ron felt the tension roll away as the sun was setting. Spring in Arizona was always a delightful season. Jim and Joseph had returned to the rez. Zyra, Ilia and Sasha were on vacation in Wyoming.

"How's it going?" asked Nick.

"As expected. Worse than herding cats. Our starting list of invitees was the G-20. We pared some down and added a couple depending on their involvement with cybercrime. Iran, and Israel were invited, but have withdrawn. As you know, both are major sponsors of cybercrime."

"I guess there's no surprise there. Until they are hit with a problem, no reason to change."

"We'll come up with some things and then present it to the United Nations for ratification."

"I don't envy you," said Nick. He held up his beer as a salute.

Ron took a big swig of his. "What happened to the commandos?"

"I spent a week on them. We got a lot of information about the Wagner Group, but as contractors, they knew little about the reason behind the attacks and who specifically hired them. Bob's trying to trace the money, but the Wagner Group is a well-known Russian contractor."

"Zyra took care of them," said Nick. "I think they're feeding pigs and fertilizing the garden plots of Jim and Joseph."

Ron winced as he heard this.

"I'm surprised Kiki didn't come back with you," said Nick.

"Russia sent an investigator looking for help in finding the attackers in Saint Petersburg and Moscow. The one guy, Inspector Daniel Novikov is good. I hope those responsible have covered their tracks well." He glanced at Nick quickly, then looked away.

"Kiki's keeping tabs on him with strict instructions to keep her distance and stay out of sight."

"I'm monitoring things," said Bob. "Kiki's set up across the street from Novikov's room to keep an eye on him. She can hear what goes on in his room. I'm working to intercept his phone and emails."

"What do you need?" asked Ron.

"Just hacking into the hotel's WIFI isn't enough. Russians will encrypt. If we can plant this," he held up a thumb drive sized box, "I'll get into the phones and computer. By getting his half of the conversation and the encrypted version, I should be able to break it."

"How are you going to plant that so it's not picked up on a sweep of the room?" asked Nick.

"It plugs into the smart TV."

Ron shook his head and held out his hand. If we're caught, things could go south."

"What is Kiki's cover?" asked Nick.

"She is my aide. She's using Sorvino as her last name so there's no record of her as a sniper or her activity in the Bio-Cyber War."

"That's pretty thin. We do have some Russian speakers on the team."

"Ilia, Sasha and Zyra are compromised," said Bob. "Their images were circulated. This detective is sharp, he'll recognize them."

"The biggest worry I have is keeping Novikov alive with Katherine around," said Ron.

The laughs at his joke were restrained.

David held up his hand. "You can't have Katherine at the sessions. It's a bad idea. Especially if Daniel Novikov is as good as we think. He will sense something about her. Even her watching from across the street could be a risk. Those who deal with killers can feel someone watching. It's a survival sensation. He will too. I can go in as your assistant and keep everybody informed."

"When you put it that way, I see the sense," said Ron. He clapped his hands. "I'm hungry for Mexican food. How about a trip to your brother's restaurant?"

"You're too recognizable," laughed Nick. "I can have it delivered. Besides, next to Kiki, I make the best margaritas in Arizona." He reached for his phone.

* * *

Kathy answered the doorbell. Following her back to the patio was the whole Sabino clan laden with food boxes. "I wanted my kids to meet one of the greatest presidents in the last fifty years," laughed Stephen.

"Only fifty?" laughed Nick. "Hey kids, how you doing?"

"Mr. President, this is Barb, my wife." She stepped forward and shook his hand. "This is my oldest, Jeff." The boy was tall but adolescent thin, He held out his hand. "And this is my youngest, Alan." The boy hadn't hit his growth spurt yet. He looked up at Ron as he held out his hand.

"You do stuff with my uncle Nick, huh?"

"Yeah, secret stuff we can't talk about. You won't tell anybody about my being here, right?"

"No sir. Your secret's good with me."

Ron glanced at Jeff, who also nodded.

"Margarita time," announced Nick, rising and going into the kitchen. "Barb, need some help." Within minutes, the growl of the blender echoed.

* * *

Kiki slowly undressed as she got ready for bed. She sat on the bed with her phone to her ear.

"Nick, what do you think about this setup?"

"David's reasoning is sound–*Keep your friends close, keep your enemies closer.*

"I'll stay out of sight."

"Don't take any chances."

"You already said it. I want to observe this David Novikov. I need to learn about him." She rose. "I'm going to watch Novikov's room until I hear snores. Talk to you tomorrow. Love you."

Chapter 69

Ron had broken the commission up and formed a team to help in the investigation of the attacks in Russia. It's what was promised. Detective Inspector Daniel Novikov looked at the investigating team gathered around the conference table. He carefully noted the names of the other six members as they introduced themselves. Taking notes was his detective norm.

Ron Carson rose. "Ladies and gentlemen, thank you for coming and volunteering to join this committee. This is a unique opportunity for us to work together in an international sign of cooperation. Cybercrime, fake news and vicious viruses have greatly dimmed the glow that computers and the internet brought. Cyber-attacks can be devastating. As many of you know, several years ago, the United States sustained cyber-attacks along with bio-attacks. Our economy was destroyed, more than half of our population died as a result. Today, attacks have escalated, and it's time to address this issue internationally. Most of the attacks remain electronic, but recently we believe cyber-attacks have given rise to kinetic attacks. That would be with explosives, bullets and recently nerve gas." He turned to Novikov.

"Russia has a strong cyber presence. Detective Novikov, you have been investigating the physical attacks in your country since they began. Could you please go through the cases for us?"

Daniel tapped on his tablet, sending the files to the others.

"If I may," said Ron Carson, "I can put the files up on the wide-screen TV as you talk."

Novikov nodded. "Please to excuse my English. It not so good. I summarize those files I send. Please to follow and review them in detail later. Ask any questions you have."

He began with the murders and kidnappings that took place near Saint Petersburg. File photos of the crime scenes appeared. Several members gasped. They were beyond brutal. He followed with his investigation into the bombing of Andrei

Petrov's house. "Thirty people died here." A scene of the heap of rubble that had been a mansion was on the screen.

"Common thread was involvement in cyber activities. At time, we still not ready to say this more than turf war, attempt to take over from existing organizations. Deaths of several national officials in this bombing brought Moscow investigators. Case moved from murders to terrorism. Moscow suspected cyber activity was target."

"You had no clues of the perps?" asked a detective from New York.

"Perps?" asked Daniel.

"Perpetrators," he explained.

Daniel chuckled then turned serious. "Did get clues. As you see, murders brutal and professional. First, thought robbery motive, but decapitations appear to be a message to frighten cyber community. Succeeded. Perps," he smiled at the NY detective, "sharp enough to empty Bitcoin accounts. After bombing, we sure of terrorist attacks on cyber community. I joined team in Moscow. Officials afraid terrorists move there."

"What kind of bomb was used?" asked David.

"No explosive residue found. Believe it was gas caused explosion, but gas without odor."

"How did they do that?" asked another detective.

Daniel shrugged. "Mystery," he answered. "Destroyed truck on street had some equipment." A photo of the wreckage of the box truck appeared. "Could not tie in, but Andrei Petrov's kidnapped brother's body near truck." A photo of the nude body sprawled against the wall came up, "I reach out to friends in cyber group for any information. Best friend not connect with me. Unusual. Found video of two women with him at local club." A blurry picture of Zyra and Sasha at Leon's table was on the screen. Their faces not clear. "Tracing Leon's credit card found closed circuit pictures of them using the card. First clue to identities."

David glanced at Ron, then turned back. "Were you able to put names to their faces?"

"Did not have good shot of faces. No. They showed again in video at river day later. Found location. No clues there. Disappeared after. My hacker friend never contact me. Not like him. Feared he was dead."

"The bombing was the last activity in Saint

Petersburg?" asked the NY detective.

"No. Internet Research Agency bombed later. I talk more of that after Moscow attack to keep timeline. In Moscow, get message from my friend. Follow IP address to farmhouse. Set up to assault, but was trap. Lose more than thirty soldiers. Two suspects killed, also my friend. I saw building explode. Everybody near killed. Terrible."

"Were you able to identify the suspects?" asked Ron.

"Only one. Mercenary, Israeli. Try to track movements, but nothing. Forged documents covered tracks. Other suspect unidentified. No records of fingerprints or DNA."

Daniel paused, took a deep breath, and continued. "I realize farmhouse a diversion for main attack on Cyber Commission headquarters. I rushed to get there. Sarin gas used. More than four-hundred killed. We were close. Perps," again he smiled at the NY detective, "still at building when I got there. I recognize one woman from Saint Petersburg nightclub. I give chase, but my driver killed by sniper. Actually, car wreck save my life. Had to go to hospital. I could not enter building. Would have died."

David felt Ron's gaze. He ignored it.

Ron looked at the detective who was obviously in need of rest. "Ladies and gentlemen, I would like to break for lunch. We'll continue this afternoon. If you have a chance, please study the files Detective Novikov supplied. Have ready any more questions for the detective about what we covered this morning ready."

Chapter 70

In Ron's hotel suite, David said, "I thought that went well this morning. I am impressed by Daniel Novikov. He seems to be very thorough, pays attention to detail, doesn't make assumptions without evidence."

"He'd be the envy of any law enforcement department in the country. It could be a worry."

David pulled out his phone and called Bob.

"Hey, David, how'd it go today?"

"This Russian detective is good. I know he's thought a lot about who would benefit from attacks on the cyber community, *and* who would benefit from war between the United States and Russia. Can you create a money trail to Sol's account?"

"Sure. Kathy's better, so we'll work together. We can move it through several countries. Where do you want it to originate?"

"China. They have the most to gain from war.

Bob, this trail has to be really good. No hint it's a plant. Make it difficult to find after I make the suggestion to follow the money. Some of our nation's best will be snooping, as will the Russians."

"We can put in false trails, dead ends and point suspicion at others."

David looked over at Ron, whose mouth was agape. "Be careful. I'd like nothing better than to bring some high-level Russian politicians under suspicion, but that's a risk. It may make them suspect false trails."

"Before you do anything, get back to us," said Ron. "I want to look it over. Thanks, talk to you tomorrow."

"David, great idea, but we need to discuss things before you make the suggestion. You do have a nefarious mind."

"The CIA trained me well, sir. Thank you, I think."

"This afternoon, we can get into their efforts to track the perps down. We should have Bob and Kathy's creation by tonight. That'll give us a chance to go through it with them. I know my knowledge of international monetary transfers is so small I won't understand what I'm seeing."

"Same with me, sir. One thing we need to do is wipe Dawn's records. Her DNA is in the system. It's best if she remains a Jane Doe with no ties to the United States."

"Good catch. You take care of it."

David reached for his phone.

"In the name of cooperation," said Ron, "we'll have to allow a search using their sample. I assume there is no trail of communications from the US to either Saint Petersburg or to Moscow,"

"I'll check with my NSA buddies."

"We need to be clean and open."

"Yes, sir. I'll limit contact. NSA's not as leaky as CIA, but we can't take chances."

"Right."

"Ron, if you need a break, my Lake of the Woods home is available. It's only a few hours away."

"We may take you up on that offer in a few days. I want to get as much done as we can while we're here."

"We could invite the detective. I'd like to get a better read."

"I'll ask him."

* * *

In her room, Kiki kicked off her shoes, pulled the spread back on the bed and flopped down. Keeping watch on the detective while not being seen had tired her out. Pulling out her phone, she dialed Nick.

"Hey, Babe, how'd it go today?"

"I'm pooped. I managed to find a spot where I can watch comings and goings from Novikov's room. The microphone of what's going on is good, but I'd sure like a camera in the meeting room."

It would be nice. I'll see what Bob can do.

"Is the Russian detective trouble?"

"Could be. We'll see. We got a few things in the works. Have you listened to the recording of the meeting?"

"I listened as the meeting was going on, but haven't gone through the recording again."

"This morning he took us through the attacks in Saint Petersburg and Moscow. They were closer to us than we knew. Leon Ivanov was a friend of the detective and source of info in the cyber community. When Novikov couldn't reach him, he went through thousands of CC videos and found

Sasha and Zyra using Leon's credit card."

"This guy is tenacious."

"He was the one who figured out the farmhouse was a diversion. He was there and rushed back to the Cyber Center. You know, I can count my misses on one hand. He is one. He arrived while we were packing up and I was covering from the roof of that building. I saw the car turn around to chase you. Shot his driver, but he ducked down before I got him. Then it was time to leave."

"If he truly becomes a danger, we could go sailing," Nick offered.

"Attractive, but we can't bail. In the afternoon. he covered the pursuit from Moscow. The diversion to Ukraine probably saved us. He inspected the boat we were on, but couldn't find any evidence we were there. He's still suspicious though."

"Lucky for the owner, whoever he is."

"I admire this detective, but he is a danger. I won't miss twice."

"K, you can't do anything without talking to Ron first."

"I know. I'll call you tomorrow. Love you."

"Love you best. Be careful."

Chapter 71

Kiki floated in blackness. In front of her glowed a box. Occasionally the lid would raise, emitting a red light. Shapes moved inside. As though struck by a cold draft, a chill went through her. She reached out to push the lid closed, trying to keep whatever was inside trapped. Something emerged and wrapped around her wrist. She jerked back, and the lid came off.

She recoiled as a thin stream of mist like smoke from a live butt in an ashtray wove its way up. It thickened and drifted toward her. She couldn't move away from it. The tendril swirled around her. An image of a firefight in the Sandbox pulled her back to that time. She was on a hill covering for her unit as it entered a village of mud huts and dusty streets. Like a machine, she picked off enemies, but instead of dying, specters rose from the bodies and floated toward her hands outstretched reaching. She screamed.

Her sheets were soaked with sweat. When the shaking subsided, she reached for her phone. She needed Nick's voice to reassure her.

"I was going to call you. What's going on, K?"

"I just had a nightmare from our time in the Sandbox. The visions of my targets are still hanging in the air and scaring the shit out of me."

"I was wondering how you kept PTSD at bay."

"I cram all those actions into a box and lock it up tight. Somehow, it opened."

"Are you going to be okay?"

"Just hearing your voice helps."

"Sometime, we're going to have to open that box and address the ghosts in there."

"It sounds easy when you say it, but I know better. As long as I see them as targets, I can handle it. If they become people…"

"Do you need me to come there?"

"I'm okay now. We'll make a date when this is over."

"When this interferes with your life, your time

is up."

"I'm locking that box. Call you tomorrow."

Kiki looked at the clock. Midnight. She lay back on the bed, stared at the ceiling and went through relaxation practice. She needed sleep, but the fear of her ghosts returning kept that away. *Focus*.

The tingling in Kiki's head woke her. She looked at the clock. Four AM. The Director had never done this before.

"Hello Katherine."

"You woke me. What's the idea?"

"That episode earlier was tasty for me, but good for you it was not."

"Yeah. It wasn't. I've got it under control now. I'm not sorry to interrupt your meal."

"A little thing is happening in another part of the world that will be a feast for me and problematic for you. It will be helpful in diverting attention from you, but intensify the pressure to achieve something in your commission."

"What happened?"

"Iran has attacked Israel with drones. They destroyed the Cyber Division building and everybody inside. Israel is hurriedly planning to

strike back. In their rush for vengeance, they will fall into Iran's ambush. It is a banquet for me. Your friends Ilia, Sasha and Zyra may be drawn in."

"Jesus! We're trying to prevent war and here it is.

"Be careful. Ta ta."

Kiki turned on the television and flipped through the news channels. There was nothing. The attack hadn't made it on the air yet. She called Sasha.

"What the fuck are you calling so late for?" Her voice was thick from sleep.

"Sasha, Israel has been attacked. They are at war!" She heard Zyra in the background asking what was going on.

"Z, turn on the television."

"It hasn't made the news yet," said Kiki.

"How do you know? Did Ron tell you?"

"He did not, but he's my next call. Don't grill me now. Someday I tell you how I know, but it isn't a conversation for the phone. I want you to understand. You, Ilia and Zyra may be tempted to go to Israel, but I would advise caution."

Again, she heard Zyra's voice. "Nothing on

TV. I call."

"The three of you should stay there for now. Your faces will become part of our investigation tomorrow. This detective has your pictures. He got yours and Zyra's from CCTV and Ilia's from security at the nerve gas depository. Let's see what shakes out."

"Call not going through," announced Zyra in the background.

"I'll call you back after I talk to Ron."

She dialed Ron's room. His sleepy voice answered. "Hello."

"Ron, this is Kiki. Iran attacked Israel, destroyed their Cyber Center. Israel is preparing retaliation."

"What!" She heard him searching the news channels. "There's nothing on television. How did you find out?"

"I'll tell you later. Do you have some sources faster than the news?"

"Yeah, sure."

"Zyra, Sasha and Ilia are in Wyoming. As you know from yesterday, Detective Novikov has pictures of them. They can't travel especially fly back to Israel. Can they go to your ranch in Idaho?"

"I'll let the staff know they're coming. Let me make a few calls and I'll ring you back. How do you know it was Iran?"

"The same source that told me of the attack. That it was Iran cannot be revealed. Pointing that finger has to come from evidence."

"Yeah, you're right."

Kiki called Sasha. "Ron says you can go to his ranch. Air travel is out of the question once those pictures are circulated. You'll be held for questioning. Russia will demand you be returned to them."

"We want to be in Israel to help." Her voice dropped. "But there's really nothing we could do. Who did this?"

"There's no evidence and nobody has claimed responsibility. Go to Ron's ranch and lay low."

"We see the sense of what you're saying," said Ilia. We'll go. Keep us informed about the commission."

"Those meetings will probably be delayed." Kiki saw the call waiting button flashing. "Ron's calling be back. I'll be in touch."

"Hi, Ron. What did you find out?"

"You will tell me how you knew about this

attack." It wasn't a suggestion. "The Whitehouse just found out. I'm going to have some explaining to do."

"Tell them your aide is psychic. That'll shut them up."

"Very funny–NOT! I need to call everybody on the commission to inform them today's meeting is postponed. I've been called to the Whitehouse."

"As your aide, I'll take care of those calls for you. We'll reschedule."

Next she called David Kennedy. "Hello, Katherine. Isn't this a little early for a social call?"

"Your CIA buddies haven't told you about the attack on Israel?"

"How the fuck did you know about that?"

"I told you a while back that I'm psychic."

"Your Director friend told you?"

"It did. It also warned me about fallout from this."

"Nice friend. This will probably scuttle the commission on cyber warfare."

"Or it will push new urgency. It was Israel's Cyber Center that was destroyed."

"Yeah, I see that on the satellite feed. I'm trying to get a picture of everything. Let me call you back."

"Thanks David. If the meetings get scrubbed, I may come visit you."

"You're always welcome. Where are you? No, don't answer that. Look forward to seeing you. Now I really want to hear more about your Director friend."

"David, I need background history on my identity as Katherine Sorvino, you know, without any reference to Russell. I'm acting as Ron's aide. This detective is thorough enough he'll probably run everybody through Russian intelligence. Don't want them to see I'm a sniper."

"Yeah, I thought about that, so it's in the works. I'll forward everything to you when I have it, maybe a couple of hours."

"Thanks, I may see you in a day or so."

Chapter 72

Former president Ron Carson looked around the situation room under the Whitehouse. President Taylor had invited him during this latest Middle East crisis. General Gerald Brown, Chief Military Advisor to the president described the attack. The wide screen showed the wreckage from enhanced satellite view. He clicked a button on the remote and the view switched to actual ground-level site footage.

"It appears two drone strikes hit the Israeli Cyber Center. The first hit at ground level and weakened the structure." He used the laser pointer to show where it had hit. "The second penetrated the top levels and detonated at midlevel, causing total building collapse. Much of the activity at this building was underground, so it was not directly hit, but it is now buried under tons of rubble. It will take days to remove and gain access to the lower levels. Those people are entombed."

"Israel is pretty good at defense. What happened that these drones got through?" asked the president.

"These drones must have been the latest stealth versions–very hard to detect. Since this was a stationary target, once it was programmed in, there was no radio communication. They flew with AI control."

"We have things like that?" asked Ron.

The general looked at him, not answering. He continued. "From the damage, we estimate five-hundred to one-thousand pounds of high explosive as a warhead."

"Who else has these drones?" asked Ron.

"These sophisticated designs have been under development by Iran, Russia, China, and us."

"Do we know where the drones were launched?" asked the president's chief of staff."

"We're going through satellite images, infrared and radar traces from our forces in the Mediterranean. Israel has accused Iran of attacking. We've seen no definite evidence yet, but we are looking especially hard at recordings of the air routes between Iran and Israel. With these drones, it will be very difficult to find anything. At most, they leave only a small heat trace, and being stealth, a very small radar signature. They can be programmed to fly a wayward route."

"I'm sure Israel is patiently waiting for evidence," remarked Ron, a wry look on his face.

The president turned toward Ron. "We are telling the Israelis to wait before striking."

General Brown's phone vibrated against the table. He picked it up and read the text. "Israel has launched a major air assault on Iran."

"Shit!" exclaimed Ron. "Pretentious bastards."

The president's phone chimed. He looked at the caller, sighed and answered, turning on speakerphone.

"As you already know, we've been attacked," said Moshe Ayub, the Israeli prime minister.

"We were looking at the first reports," answered the president. "Again, we urge patience before striking out. There is no proof who attacked."

"We all know it was Iran. They recently sold advanced technology drones to Russia, much more sophisticated than the ones they sold to Russia during the Ukraine war."

"Moshe, we're looking at records to find the launch site now. Thus far we've seen nothing from Iran."

"If they weren't launched from there, Iran supplied them to someone else. Ultimately, Iran is guilty."

"Recall your air force," said the president. "We will not support you in this."

"It's too late. They will be entering Iranian airspace in fifteen minutes. I want assurances that the United States remains our close ally."

"Yes, and as such, we are advising you to cease your attack and recall your planes."

"Not possible." The line went dead.

General Brown spoke to an aide who held up a remote and aimed it at the television. The image of the wreckage on the big screen was replaced by a satellite image of the coast of Iran. Icons indicated the Israeli planes' flight. As the planes crossed into Iran, hundreds of streaks representing antiaircraft missiles flared. Half of the planes disappeared. The rest scattered, but missiles were launched from other sites. Half of those disappeared. The survivors turned back to Israel. From the sea, more missiles struck.

"Jesus!" exclaimed the general. "It was a trap."

The president's phone chimed again. He looked at the caller.

"Wait to answer," said Ron. "Let's talk first. I'm not sure what we've seen is the end."

"What do you mean?"

"Israel's air force was the biggest tool in their military arsenal. We've just seen the loss of seventy-five percent." He turned to the general. "Do you have anything showing potential buildup of ground forces around Israel?"

The president paled as the general's aide again used the remote. A satellite map showing Israel came up.

"Where would you attack?" asked Ron, looking at the general.

"Golan, of course is prime." He circled it with a pointer. The view expanded around that area. He circled another area. "Shit! Ground forces are massing out of artillery range here." He zoomed in. "They have mobile ground-to-ground missiles." He studied the image and whispered to his aide who nodded. "Those are not crude Scud missiles. They are precision GPS directed and capable of eluding anti-missile defenses. They can pound Golan. Without air support it will be overrun within days."

"Check other strategic areas," said Ron. He looked at the president. "Are we prepared to go to war?"

Chapter 73

Kiki pressed the phone to her ear. "Detective Novikov, this is Katherine Sorvino, Ron Carson's aide. Due to a crisis in Israel, he has been called to the Whitehouse. Tomorrow's meeting has been postponed."

"What crisis?"

"Israel had been attacked; their Cyber Center destroyed. We're not sure when we'll be able to reschedule the commission on cybercrime. If the delay lasts any length of time, and you want a change of scenery, David Kennedy has invited you to his home."

"I must contact my government. If they want me to stay, I will see some of the sights of New York. My first visit. Please let me to know of scheduling for meetings. I consider them important."

"I will, sir."

From her hotel room window, she watched the detective's room through a spotter scope. She also had a holographic microphone that would pick up window vibrations when somebody spoke within the room. While he was sightseeing tomorrow, she'd check out his room. Bob was already working on tapping into his cell phone and internet connections.

Despite the warning from Ron, she wanted to keep close tabs on Novikov. While watching him, she called the other members of the investigating team and the other members of the commission to explain the postponement.

She saw Novikov pick up his cell phone. How she wished the taps were already in place. She turned on the Russian translator. At least she'd get half of the conversation.

Her phone rang. "David, what's going on?"

"I've sent your new history as Katherine Sorvino. You grew up in Casa Grande, went to school with Nick. No Army record. Nick's father got you a job with Ron Carson after his second term when he took over running the Orbiting Power System. You are not married, dedicated to a career with Carson."

"I'll forward copies of everything to Ron, but make sure he knows. An express package is in the lobby with all your documents."

"Thanks, David. I just finished calling everyone on the committee and the investigation team informing them of a reschedule."

"Let's give it a day and have the investigation team meet day after tomorrow. Ron doesn't have to be there. I'll chair. There will be a mic set up so you can hear everything."

"Bob is working on a tap of Novikov's phone. It should be ready later today. I want to meet the detective. Given my new history, I should be fine."

"I don't like it. Why would you dance around the dragon?"

"David, this is not a joy ride. I need a reading on him. I can only get that face-to-face."

"Risky. Your cover isn't that deep."

"Later today, I'll call the investigating team to let them know they'll meet on Thursday. Maybe Detective Novikov and I can come to your house for the weekend."

Chapter 74

In his room, Daniel Novikov studied the files on the members of the investigation committee. He'd received them electronically an hour ago. Ron Carson was well-known.

He'd risen from Secretary of the Interior to president in large part because of his response to the Bio-Cyber War twelve years ago. A team had invaded Russia and stolen smallpox vaccine from Koltsovo. They'd contaminated a shipment of vaccine destined for China, which proved fortunate for Russia when Chinese forces invading Russian territory were devastated by the contaminated vaccine. Russians died too.

Ron Carson was no friend to Russia. A couple of months later, a team posing as Cuban news reporters was suspected of blinding the president during his May Day speech to the country. That attack could not be tied to the US or Carson, but there were suspicions.

As president, he had admirably pulled his country back from the economic collapse. During his terms, he had worked tepidly to reestablish relations with Russia and China. Today, he was a trusted confidant to the current president.

David Kennedy was a former director of the CIA. His file could have applied to any director. Daniel felt that Kennedy knew more about these attacks. It was a feeling he got on previous cases. He would watch him closely.

The New York detectives were not remarkable, though they seemed competent. The European representative was there for show with little to offer.

Kennedy's suggestion to follow the money was good. Daniel had people trying to track that in Russia. Kennedy had brought in a consultant from the NSA.

The terrorist's bank account consisted of numerous block deposits as one would expect from a mercenary taking occasional contracts. His background was veiled by Israel. More information would be forthcoming, but it would take time.

The Jane Doe woman was a dead end so far, but her DNA was being run through data-bases. They'd find something.

More than once, Daniel thought about who would benefit from a war between Russia and the United States. Both countries would be weakened, creating opportunities. The European Union and China both came to mind.

The invasion of Ukraine had been expensive both in money and in international prestige. It had not resulted in raising the position of Russia as a world power. It had not deterred other neighbors from joining NATO. Instead, Europe had found alternate sources for gas and oil. If China hadn't stepped up and bought Russian oil and gas, the economic pressure would have been devastating. Could China again be contemplating taking over the oil-rich areas?

The Orbiting Power System had cut further into Russia's energy sales, another Ron Carson attack. Was it possible these attacks against the cyber community were his effort to destroy Russia? Daniel shook his head. Possible, but Carson starting a shooting war? Didn't ring true in his detective mind.

But David Kennedy? Perhaps, that invite to David Kennedy's house for the weekend would prove fruitful. He reached for the phone to call Carson's assistant.

Lightning of the Sea was a key, but he couldn't find the lock it fit. He mentally went through the search he'd conducted. His team at the Bosporus had been thorough. The "perps" had not been onboard. He laughed to himself at the term. If not there, where had they been? Like an explosion, an idea popped into his head. He called the leader of the search team.

He answered after the third ring, his voice thick with sleep. Novikov got right to the point. "Captain, when you searched shipping leaving the Bosporus, *Lightning of the Sea* was in your report. Did you search the minisub?"

Silence on the phone. "Captain, are you there?"

"Just trying to remember. There was no minisub on that boat. We would have searched it."

"Thank you, captain. Go back to sleep."

Novikov's mind leapt from idea to idea. If the operation was government run, they wouldn't have used a privately-owned boat for transport. This whole thing was privately funded. By who and why? Cybercrime targeted the private sector mostly. The latest victims had been several Chinese companies, but American companies had been hit hard. It had cost millions for those that paid. Those that didn't, paid a price in lost information and operations also millions. Follow the money.

Chapter 75

"Ron, I don't know how to address this attack against Israel," said President Taylor. Putting US troops in another conflict will rile the country. They've had enough war."

"Let me talk to Prime Minister Ayub."

"What will you say?"

"You can be assured it won't be rosy."

"We may not follow what you say, but okay. You are well-respected."

The phone rang. "Mister President, I have the Israeli Prime Minister on the line for you."

"Pass it through." He put the phone on speaker.

"Hello, Moshe. Looks like you've gotten yourself into a mess," said President Taylor.

"We need help. Our intelligence indicates a ground attack is imminent. With the loss of so much of our air force, our ground forces are vulnerable."

"Moshe, I've appointed former president Ron Carson to oversee this crisis. I'll let him speak."

"I remember Mr. Carson. A progressive as I recall."

"Mr. Prime Minister, what do you want the United States to do?" asked Ron.

"We need fighter planes and munitions."

"And you have the pilots and soldiers to use these?" Ron glanced at General Gerald Brown, who shook his head.

"No, we need those also."

"What you're asking is for the United States to go to war for you, is that correct?" Ron's voice had an edge to it. He felt General Brown's eyes on him.

"To save us from destruction, yes."

"You ignored our advice and got yourself into this mess."

"We had to respond. It's what these people understand."

"Without waiting for evidence, you attacked. Waiting would have given us time to assess the military situation. Intelligence could well have told us about the ambush of your air force. We could have planned a response."

The president and General Brown both nodded in agreement.

"Here's what we're prepared to offer. We will negotiate with you and your opposing forces for peace."

"Negotiate! We're about to be annihilated."

"I believe we can get a ceasefire. It will give us time to strike a bargain, but you're not in a position of strength. The bottom line is Israel will move ahead with the two-party agreement with the Palestinians. Jerusalem will be shared under United Nations control. You will grant equal citizenship to all Arabs living in Israel. You will abide by the United Nations resolutions as to Israel's position. The United States will not veto any of those."

"Mr. President, Richard," the Prime Minister's voice quavered. "We cannot do this. These demands are outrageous. How could you appoint this man?"

The president started to speak, but Ron held up his hand to stop him. "Mr. Prime Minister, the only peace I see between Israel and the Palestinians is occupation by United Nations forces. Your conflicts have embroiled us for decades. It's time to stop."

"That's outrageous. We will never agree to be occupied. Without your help. Israel could be destroyed."

"I do not want to see Israel destroyed," bellowed Ron. "I want to see peace."

"President Taylor," snarled Moshe, "we will ruin you in the press. You can kiss your political career goodbye."

"I'm in my second term. Ron is not into politics anymore. That's not much of a threat, but it does show your true nature."

"We will not give up Jerusalem."

"You take our proposal back and discuss it, but I wouldn't waste any time," said Ron. "We estimate the first attacks will happen within the next two days. Call us with your agreement. Goodbye, Mr. Prime Minister." Ron broke the connection.

"Boy! you started a shitstorm," said the president, shaking his head. "I think the Situation Room is now for our protection. I am certain we'll have rioting in the streets before the end of the day."

"Better prepare. Luckily, like the Six Day War, this will be over quickly one way or the other. I'm going to call in my expert."

"Who's that?" asked the president. "I thought I had the experts here already." He looked at those around the table.

"Mohammed al Jar, the Prophet will be of immense help, I think."

Chapter 76

Daniel placed his overnight bag in the open trunk of David's Tesla and stepped into the passenger side. A young woman was in the back seat. He turned to introduce himself. "I am Daniel Novikov." he held out his hand.

"Katherine Sorvino." She took his hand. "We've spoken on the phone."

"Ah yes. You are Ron Carson's assistant." He turned to David. "Thank you for invitation. The only homecooked meals I get are when I cook."

"Your wife doesn't cook?"

"Alas, I have no wife. Our marriage sacrificed on alter of job."

"Same thing happened to me," said David.

"And you?" asked Daniel turning to the back.

"Right guy hasn't been better than the job." She laughed. "Guess we're all job widowers and widows."

The drive down the I-95 was mostly silent as Kiki pretended to look at files while studying Daniel who watched the countryside roll by.

"Beautiful country," he remarked, "like Saint Petersburg–green."

"You miss it?" asked Kiki.

"I travel much lately. See wonderful places, but none are Saint Petersburg. How long is trip?"

"In this traffic, a little more than five hours. We'll stop for dinner along the way," said David.

"How long you work with Ron Carson?"

"The president assigned me to work with him during the Bio-Cyber War. I've been his adviser since then, though sometimes I do some contract work on the side."

"And you?" Daniel asked turning to face Kiki.

"I've been his assistant since his presidency ended."

"He must be good boss."

"He is," said David. "Rarely do you find someone with honesty and integrity, especially in politics."

"He became hero during Bio-Cyber War. Sent team to Russia to steal smallpox vaccine."

"He did," agreed David, "but that was the source of the virus used to attack the United States. It was what our country needed at the time."

"I hold no grudge." said Daniel with a shrug. "It was dark episode. We were controlled by China which became our enemy. Smallpox killed many thousands Chinese and Russians."

"Americans too." said David. "It was a black period; one we don't want to repeat."

To prevent more killing over cyber stuff, we must have agreement. Russia demands those who attacked us pay. You would do same."

"We would," agreed David. "It took us years to kill those who attacked us on 911, but we did." They pulled into a restaurant parking lot. "Italian food okay?"

The dining room was crowded, the noise level making conversation difficult. Seated at the table, a bottle of wine was ordered. As they looked over the menu, the wine arrived. "I ordered red," said David. "Hope that's okay."

The waitress took their orders and left.

"Time to cheer up," said Kiki. "Let's toast to solving the world's problems." She laughed as she held up her glass. "Daniel, you mentioned the yacht you suspected of getting the attackers out of Russia. Tell us about that."

Daniel took a sip. "Nice wine." He held up the glass as a salute. He smiled. "It was luxurious almost beyond description. I know boats being from Saint Petersburg. This boat was magnificent. Everything was carbon fiber, honeycomb or titanium to reduce weight, yet the trim was gold. It was a jet boat, with huge pumps to push it through water. Captain Rogers said it could cruise at thirty knots, but what was most amazing was that it had hydrofoils that would lift it from water. Turbofans like on jet airplanes would push it to very high speeds. I felt as if I was flying. A most amazing toy for a very rich man."

"You found no evidence it was used to transport those who attacked you?"

"Nothing. Gave me complete tour. Team that searched when boat was exiting the Black Sea found no sign nor did I. Still, no other alternatives looked good. I just have feeling."

David noticed the use of the present tense. He glanced at Kiki. Her eyes flicked toward him. She noticed it too.

"They finished their meal and resumed the

drive. Daniel seemed to nap until they stopped at the gate into Lake of the Woods.

"Nice house," commented Daniel as they approached the front door. "How long you live here?"

"I bought the place fifteen years ago."

In the living room, David opened the curtains to the sparkling lights dancing across the lake from the houses on the opposite shore.

"This is really nice."

"Would you like a nightcap?"

"Head not cold."

David and Kiki laughed.

"It's a last drink before bed," explained Kiki.

"I developed taste for your American bourbon. Do you have?"

"But of course." David poured three fingers of Makers Mark into three tumblers. "Here's to a relaxing few days. Perhaps, we can let the world take care of itself." He held up his glass.

Chapter 77

"What did you think of this detective?" asked Nick.

Kiki sat on her bed at David's house. She'd called Nick to chat and hear his voice. "I made a point of not talking. He is sharp with instinctive suspicion. One wrong word, and he'll wonder about me."

"You shouldn't have gone."

"No, I need to assess his threat level. I have to look into his eyes and watch his face."

"What are you going to do if he represents a threat?"

"I can't think about that. He would sense being hunted, being prey. I can't explain it, but that comes from the battlefield."

"Okay, just be careful. With the uproar in Israel, the world is now much more dangerous."

"Ron's in the middle of that. The commission to submit recommendations for international control of cybercrime has suspended meeting for now. David's heading up the investigation of the attacks in Russia. We felt we needed to continue that."

Nick chuckled. "I'm sure he'll do a good job. If Israel's suspicions are correct, and Iran is behind the attack, they're doing what the attackers did in Russia. Iran got tired of continuous cyber-attacks by Israel."

"Yeah, if anything, this will intensify efforts to come up with an international agreement. Have you had any contact with Ilia, Zyra, or Sasha?"

"No, but I'll do that. Neither you or David should attempt to contact them. We don't know who's listening."

"David thinks Israel will become a very dangerous place in the next couple of days. Our friends should be glad not to be there."

"Bob is reinforcing our security. As you suspected, Detective Novikov received Russian files on everyone. It's what we did on him. I'm forwarding Novikov's bio to you."

"Thanks. Can you give me a quick summary."

"Native of Saint Petersburg, he served in the Ukraine invasion as an intelligence officer. After discharge, he rapidly rose through the ranks in the Saint Petersburg police department. He had a close relationship with Andrei Petrov. Suspicions are Andrei used his considerable influence to get Novikov advanced, but the detective has proven to be very good."

"That's what I believe also. He misses little and reads people very well. Can we use his relationship with Petrov against him?"

"In many other countries we could. Not Russia. Collaboration between organized crime and law enforcement is the norm. He's very honorable, even by our standards."

"It'd be great if he were on our side."

"His loyalty to Russia makes that impossible," said Nick.

"I get the feeling he doesn't agree with the cybercrime programs, but he follows the law and his orders."

"That makes him a valuable asset to the commission on international cybercrime. If the law changes, I think he'll enforce it."

"What about the other people he's been

working with on this case?"

"We're looking into them. Influencing them may be possible, and they do give the orders."

"Be careful, K. I'm not sure what the detective would do if he suspected you. At the least, he'd report it and somebody else would make a decision."

Chapter 78

"Prime Minister," said Ron answering the call to President Taylor, "have you agreed to let us negotiate a settlement before this becomes a full-blown war?"

"I want to talk to President Taylor."

"I'm here," said the president. "you're on speakerphone."

"I'm letting you know we're sending a column of tanks against the mobile missile installations poised to attack Golan."

"Why are you telling us?" asked Ron.

"We need intelligence. We're not willing to risk any of the few planes we have left in a recon patrol."

"Intelligence we can give. I'll let General Brown fill you in on what we know."

"Mr. Prime Minister, we strongly oppose this

action. These Arab forces have been a step ahead of you since the drone strike. Our preliminary assessment is they have laid another trap to take out your tanks."

"What trap could they have?"

"The weapons used so far have been advanced technology. The drones used to attack the Cyber Center were Artificial Intelligence controlled. There was no communication between them and the ground. It made them nearly impossible to detect. An integrated battlefield would employ these measures also."

"What do you have to counter these?"

"Without battlefield air support, you are essentially blind."

"We have recon drones."

"Yes, but they communicate via radio. That makes them detectable, makes them targets. We could offer recon drones with upward directed antennas for satellite connection along with satellite recon." He glanced at the president who nodded agreement.

"Yes, we need those."

"You could have them along with operation personnel in a week."

"We're sending a column out tomorrow. A week is not acceptable."

"Then don't send them," bellowed Ron. "Your arrogance in the belief that Israeli military superiority will carry you is what will lead to your downfall. We will not be drawn into your war."

"The column is on its way. We will prevail."

"Moshe," said the president, "these are not the same people you faced in the Six Day War. They have counted on your impulsive behavior and planned to use your predictability against you."

"You want us to give up lands we have now, lands Israelis died for. We cannot do that. Our enemies want our destruction."

"And you continue to give them reasons for that," accused Ron.

"Send whatever you can. Our attack is going ahead." The line went dead.

There was silence in the Situation Room. The general picked up the remote and brought up a satellite view of the column churning through a valley toward the missile installations set to attack Golan. Troop carriers trailed the armored attack.

"The Israelis have this satellite view?" asked the president.

"Yes, sir. We're forwarding it to them," answered the general.

Several explosions blossomed on the screen. "So it begins," murmured Ron.

"What they've done is hit the mobile command center," the general circled the flaring hotspots, "knocking out their radar and drone control. I'm sure the airwaves are blanketed, making communication difficult. Now they're hitting the trailing vehicles," he circled more hotspots at the end of the column. "This is what we refer to as a killing box."

"Those hits seem extremely accurate." remarked Ron.

"As I warned the Prime Minister, this has all the hallmarks of a fully integrated battlefield. There are stealth targeting drones overhead controlled by AI. They are programmed to find the targets with passive sensors, infrared and magnetometer readings. They can recognize the shape of tanks, troop carriers, even facial recognition is possible. Nothing indicates where the drone is. It focuses on the target and follows it. A flash signal tells ground operators they have a target. The signal is so brief it can't be used to locate the drone. A missile is fired. At that point, the drone lights up the target with a laser to guide the missile to the target. It's all done without ground control. No wasted missiles. It can also be done with short range rockets or smart artillery, even cheaper than missiles. The drones are operating at an altitude making visual recognition very difficult. This is the new AI warfare."

"How do you know this is what we're seeing?" asked the president.

"It's what we would use. Notice, gentlemen, not a single enemy foot has stepped inside Israeli territory, yet much of their forces have been destroyed. The Iron Dome protection hasn't helped." He pointed at the satellite view showing many impacts. "By the time the invasion starts, Israel will have already lost."

Chapter 79

"I can cook Mexican food tonight, if you'd like," offered Kiki. "I know David likes it. How about you, Daniel?"

"Have not tried but willing to."

"More coffee?" she offered, holding up the pot.

"Coffee very good. Yes, thank you. Very quiet here. Only few boats on lake."

"It is fall. The water cools quickly."

"In Saint Petersburg water is always cold. Do you have boat?" he asked.

David laughed, "Yes, I have a Hobie Cat. It doesn't get used very often. We are in an unseasonably warm period. Would you like to go for a sail?"

"Only hear of Hobie Cat. Fast sports sailboat, yes?"

"It is a lot of fun. After we finish breakfast, you

and I can get it out and rigged."

"Can we take a look at what's happening in the Middle East?" asked Kiki. "I would like to get an idea of what Ron is involved in."

David picked up the remote and thumbed the wide-screen on. The national news channel showed a map of the Golan region on the screen with a retired general narrating.

"After the loss of much of their air force in a disastrous attack on Iran, Israel has directed a tank battalion against Arab forces just out of artillery range in Syria near the Golan Heights. Golan was taken by Israeli forces years ago because they considered it a strategic point crucial to Israel's safety." He drew a circle around the region on the map.

"Normally, air support would soften up the enemy before a ground attack, but Israel doesn't want to risk the loss of any more planes. The Arab forces seem to be moving in random patterns, making the use of ground-to-ground missiles unproductive. These forces have not attacked Golan yet. At present, the Israeli tanks seem to be mired down in a valley under accurate Arab artillery and rocket fire."

"Have the Israelis asked for United States help?" asked the announcer.

The general faced the camera. "Thus far, the Taylor administration has agreed to mediate negotiations for a ceasefire and a peace settlement. Equipment and weapons will be sent, but no troops. At the pace this war is moving, any sent would arrive too late."

"What do you mean by 'too late?'"

"Israel is depleting their weapons to the point that when or if the Arabs do decide to attack, they will swiftly be able to take control."

"You mean Israel could be destroyed?"

"I don't believe the United States will allow that to happen."

"Rumors have circulated for decades that Israel has nuclear weapons. Would they use them?"

"If they have them, something which has never been proven, and use them, Israel would become a pariah. The world would turn against them–including the United States."

"Iran has been trying to develop nuclear weapons for years. Have they succeeded?

"We don't believe they have."

"What's the path out?"

"Israel cannot negotiate from a position of strength at the moment, and delay only weakens them more. A ceasefire needs to be put in place immediately. It is very important to note that no one has claimed responsibility for the strike against Israel's Cyber Center. Israel assumed it was Iran in retaliation for the continuous cyber-attacks Israel has mounted against them. Impulsively, Israel launched an air raid. That force was nearly destroyed mostly over Iranian territory."

"You're saying that after the attack on the Cyber Center, there has been no fighting within Israel's borders? Everything has happened in other countries?"

"That is correct. One would always choose to fight battles elsewhere rather than at home. But in this case, the battle is not for land, it is for world opinion. Aggressively attacking others who have not attacked you cannot be deemed defense. Unless Israel agrees to abide by the terms of negotiation, the US may decide to not use its veto power against United Nations resolutions, something done repeatedly in the past."

David, Katherine, and Daniel were stunned by these reports. "This happened so quickly," said

Kiki.

"It doesn't look like Ron will be back with the commission soon," said David, shaking his head. "We will have to carry on without him. After this prime example of the need for international cyber agreements, we will be pushed to move forward."

"I'll talk to Ron about going ahead with the commission. He'll agree," said Kiki.

"What about investigation?" asked Daniel.

"We'll move ahead with that too," said David. He looked at Daniel. "Have your people had any success in following the money trail?"

"Is complex trail. Accounts in several countries but we are seeing end. What about you?"

"We also are finding evidence of who financed the actions against Russia. I do not want to influence your investigators with ours. When we are done, we will share."

"Da. Let's go sail."

David laughed at the quick change.

Chapter 80

"I understand your problem," said Mohammed al Jar, the Prophet. "The conflict between the tribes in the Middle East had been going on for thousands of years. The problem is they can't let go of the past. Until that can be put aside, there will not be peace."

"How do we get them to do that?" asked Ron. "The cultural traditions require an eye-for-an-eye which becomes eternal."

"I can help with some of that, but more must be done. The push for change must be from outside."

"Are you willing to meet with the parties involved?" asked President Taylor.

"Yes. Set up a meeting for two days from now."

"That's fast. I'm not sure we can put it together that quickly. We need a place that is neutral yet secure."

"You deal with the Israeli Prime Minister," said the Prophet. "I will deal with the Arab forces and get an agreement for a ceasefire today."

* * *

"Mister Prime Minister, Moshe, we can get the Arabs to agree to a ceasefire if you will, but you must withdraw your forces from Syria."

"They will have to let us pull back."

"We also want any meeting to include a more permanent solution."

"Who will attend this meeting?"

"All factions will be represented as a lasting peace can only come when all parties are present."

"We will not sit down with Hamas." There was bitterness in his voice.

"I am not asking," said Ron. "The issues will be resolved. If you do not do this, it would mean you are not interested in peace. The United States will not be able to support you."

"Where will this meeting be held?"

"The United Nations in New York. Mohammed al Jar will mediate."

"He is a Muslim."

"He is a Faithist. He speaks for all religions.

"Who will oversee this ceasefire?"

"We will send in emergency United Nations forces immediately."

"All they do is observe and complain when someone breaks the peace."

"Perhaps not this time. We will arrange for armed response to violators."

"You would have United Nations troops fire on Israelis!"

"Or on Arab forces, but only if they start shooting. Your forces must stand down."

"And if they invade?"

"Mister Prime Minister, it is your forces who have invaded. They will be allowed to pull back to your borders."

"This is very short notice. I will try."

"In the words of a famous sage, 'Try not, do.'"

Ron broke the connection.

"Do you think they will be able to send a delegate with the power to act?" asked the president.

"It's amazing what can be done when the gun is at your head," said the Prophet. "My task may be harder as there are numerous factions. They do have a general in charge, and I will have to meet with him to emphasize the requirement of peace. Unfortunately, factions exist that do not answer to him."

"What were you talking about with armed UN troops?" asked President Taylor.

"Mr. President, I propose observations platforms, both satellite and drone. If anyone fires, we release a Hellfire on their ass."

"That's rather drastic."

"Tough times, tough actions. Personally, I'm tired of these squabbling children dragging the world into conflict. I believe a strong UN presence will be required to maintain peace and see that human rights are followed."

"You are speaking of occupying the region," said the Prophet.

"If that is what it takes, yes."

Chapter 81

"How was sailing?" asked Kiki as David and Daniel entered the kitchen.

"Boat very much fun. Fast, responsive. Must pay attention. I think I will need one when I return to Saint Petersburg."

Kiki laughed.

"Dinner smells good. What are we having?" asked David.

"It's green fare tonight–green chili chilaquiles, guacamole, Spanish rice, green gazpacho. We'll also have green chili chicken and refried beans. Margaritas for beverages."

"Wow! It's a feast. We'll be eating on that for days," exclaimed David. "Calls for Mexican music." He pulled out his phone and within minutes, Linda Ronstadt's *Canciones de Mi Padre* started to play.

Kiki handed them frozen margaritas in frosty salted glasses. She held hers up. "Cheers."

"This very good drink," said Daniel. "What is in it?"

"Lime juice base with lime Cointreau and tequila," she answered. "I make my own Cointreau. Ron had some from our last visit."

Daniel blinked at the mention of tequila. "I never have tequila before. Not common in my country."

"As with many liquors, good tequila is to be savored, like scotch or whiskey," said David.

"Is same for good vodka."

"Go ahead and sit," said Kiki. "Dinner is ready.

Kiki set a small bowl of chopped green chilis on the table. She looked at Daniel. "Not knowing you like spicy food, everything is mild. Add chilis as you desire. Those are medium, but enough will make things hot. David likes hot."

After serving themselves from the dishes, Daniel tasted the chilaquiles. "Nice flavor, not too hot for me." He watched as David and Kiki put a couple of spoonfuls of green chilis on theirs. "Maybe I try a little." He placed a dab on his next bite. "Not bad." His eyes grew wider. "Gets hotter." he reached for his margarita.

Of particular interest was how both Kiki and David would tear off a bite-sized piece of a flour tortilla and spoon the green chili chicken on. He followed suit. "This very good–like spicy stew. Daniel particularly liked the refried beans, putting them on tortilla pieces and eating them. When they could eat no more, David cleared the table.

"I like Mexican food. Think restaurant in Saint Petersburg would be big hit."

Kiki laughed. "Maybe my next big adventure if Ron gets tired of me. Speaking of Ron, it sounds like there's a ceasefire in place in Israel. We'll see how long that holds."

"Much activity in that part of world. Traditions make warring tribes difficult. Russia found out how hard in Afghanistan. America too, I think."

"It has calmed down since the Prophet," said David. "He is remarkable."

"I have heard of him. My parents raised me Orthodox, but I left church."

"If you would like to meet him, perhaps that can be arranged," said David.

"You know this Prophet?"

"I do. I have personally witnessed miracles."
He patted his artificial leg.
"Yes, I like to meet him."
That will be interesting, thought Kiki.

Chapter 82

The delegates representing the countries involved in the conflict with Israel were seated at the conference table in one of the UN rooms. The hastily put together meeting had been driven by the dire consequences of all-out war again in the Middle East. In addition, the Prophet was there.

Ron rose. "Welcome to this meeting." He walked to the door and locked it, putting the key in his pocket. "We will reach an accord, one that will last. The United Nations has changed. It is now a force for peace. I will tell you what will happen. I am not asking." There was murmuring around the table.

"Most of you have children. When your children fight, do you ask them to reach an accord? No. The world is no longer asking. Let's get right to the bottom line. The Palestine state will be formed in the regions outlined in the past. It will not be governed by a Palestinian authority. The UN will govern it." There was a gasp around the table. That government will see that human rights are observed, that business is allowed, that utilities are provided, that housing is available. Israelis living in the area may remain, under the UN government. Property that belonged to Palestinians will again be theirs."

"You cannot do that!" exclaimed Israeli Prime Minister Ayub. "Those settlers built homes and farms. They are citizens."

"They are now citizens of UN Palestine. They can remain, but must buy the property that was confiscated from the previous owners or move out."

"We will never agree to that," shouted Ayub.

"Your agreement is not necessary. UN forces are already on the way."

The Prime Minister looked at the United States President. "Use your veto to this crazy idea."

"No."

"In addition, UN forces will be installed in Israel, Jordan, Syria, Saudi Arabia and Egypt to ensure there are no more attacks. If any occur, they will be met with force."

As one, the delegates rose shouting, fists raised in the air. Ron watched for several minutes before taking a whistle from his pocket. The shrill earsplitting noise quieted the room. "I see no one is happy about this. It must be a good plan. I will let Mohammed al Jar speak."

The Prophet rose from his chair. He was dressed in traditional Arab garb, his flowing white robe seemed to glow as he stood. "Many of you know me both by reputation and personally. I will do two things here. First, I will show you what the next life, Heaven or Paradise, is like. You will feel God. You will understand where life changes. Second, I will show you a future that is coming and you will understand why this fighting will stop."

He raised his arms as a golden glow grew from him until it filled the room. "Close your eyes." He floated in dark space surrounded by the glowing globes of the delegates' minds. They began to move, the lights of stars flashing past. The stars became streaks of light as they accelerated. Ahead, the concentration of stars grew until it became a wall of light with a dark center. The stars were so dense a curtain of light seemed to envelop them.

They plunged into the darkness at the center, the chaos of stars left behind. It was impossible to tell if they were moving or still with no frame of reference. A cloud formed around them like a fog. It seeped into them bringing a sense of peace, of knowledge and understanding. Their sense of self expanded into the cloud like a raindrop falling into the ocean.

"This is Heaven or, if you choose, Paradise. It is Nirvana. This is God. This is Allah. It is where religion says we are to go when we leave our Earthly existence. Let the peace and love fill you. Become a part of it." He paused to let them absorb the radiance around them. "We must return, for there are things to do."

They were back, blinking in the light, frozen in place. Nobody said a word.

"I will now show you the future of the Earth. It is not pleasant. "Close your eyes." They hung in space, the Earth slowly turning below them. Sunlight sparkled from the blue oceans and glared from the clouds. A streak flashed past them and entered the atmosphere. It created a fiery trail until it plunged into the Pacific. Clouds of steam rose and a tsunami raced outward toward the shore. Another followed, this one impacting South America. Another struck the east coast of America. More, too many to count, followed peppering the Earth. Dirty clouds rose covering the land and the sea until nothing of the planet could be seen.

"This will happen. In addition to the death from the strikes, the impact winter will obscure the sunlight for years. Without light, the base of the food chain, plant life, dies. Animal life including humans will follow. You are seeing the extinction of the human race, the death of the Earth. The petty squabbles between peoples is pointless. Instead, you must work to make lives mean something."

Stunned by the immensity of the vision, they were silent. "I will help you convince your people to live peacefully together."

"When you return to your countries, challenge them to look forward and not to the past. It cannot be changed, only the future matters."

Chapter 83

The first violation of the ceasefire occurred when rockets were fired toward Israel. Within seconds, a Hellfire missile obliterated the mobile rocket launcher and the crew operating it. Ron's phone rang. He glanced at General Brown.

"Rockets are striking Israel!" cried Moshe Ayub.

"We know," answered Ron. "Those who launched them are gone."

"I'm being hammered by my people to retaliate," said the Prime Minister.

"It's been taken care of. Do not do anything. Any military action by you will be considered an attack."

"I will tell them to stand down. Even though they are good soldiers, some may not heed my orders."

"Then you must be prepared to suffer casualties. I repeat, do not attack. Those responsible are dead."

As soon as he broke the connection, another call came in. "Mister Carson, there was an attack in my country. We must retaliate."

"Chairman, the attack was directed against a team who fired rockets into Israel. That team has been killed. I warned you about attacks."

"Unfortunately, I do not have the control needed to stop everybody."

"I suggest you find a way to stop them. Further attacks will be dealt with the same way."

"What if Israel attacks us?"

"They will receive the same treatment. I emphasize again to you that attacks will cease." He cut the connection as another call from the Israeli Prime Minister came in.

"I saw your video of those firing the rockets and their destruction. I have given the orders, but I fear that the air base commander will ignore them. He will send planes to attack Hamas."

"Moshe, I am sorry you will suffer being an example of the ceasefire policy. This must stop."

The wide-screen monitor showed a satellite view of the air base. Two fighters were on the tarmac ready to take off. Ron nodded to the general. Within seconds, the jets streaked down the runway, taking off. As their wheels cleared the ground, two incoming streaks destroyed them. His phone rang.

"You destroyed my airplanes!" screamed Moshe.

"We did. I told you not to retaliate. If you put more fighters on the runway, we will strike the headquarters. Have you and your commanders gotten my message?"

"You cannot do this! It is an act of war."

"It's an act to prevent war. We are watching. Any more moves to attack will be met the same way. I want you to know the video of this action is being forwarded to your enemies as an example of the seriousness of violating the ceasefire."

The connection was cut. Ron called the Palestinian chairman. "Did you get my videos?"

"We did. We saw who fired the rockets and their destruction. We also saw your reaction to Israel's attempt to retaliate even though those fighters who fired the rockets were dead. We will attempt to control all factions here." Ron broke the connection.

"Jesus, Ron," said the general, "we'll have everybody pissed at us over this."

"That's the idea. If they're mad at us, they're not fighting each other."

"What happens when they turn on us?"

* * *

Throughout the settlements in the annexed lands UN and Israeli soldiers went to each farm and house. They explained to the inhabitants that the land was being returned to the original owners. Those owners had a choice of reoccupying the land and paying for the improvements, selling the land or leasing it. The Israeli settlers argued that the land had been given to them by the government. They were told that it wasn't the government's to give. They stormed the parliament demanding action but got no satisfaction as UN officials oversaw all transactions.

The state of Palestine was formed. UN loans were made available for those buying land or paying for improvements. Loans were also available for rebuilding much of the infrastructure. The refugee camps began to empty. The borders were opened. Government officials were very dissatisfied to lose their seats of power.

The inevitable strike against the United Nations forces happened with a rocket barrage on their camp followed by Israeli ground forces and tanks. Covering aircraft were quickly shot down, the tanks destroyed as were the rocket launchers. The Israeli military headquarters was leveled.

The call from Prime Minister Moshe Ayub came as expected. "You have attacked us. Have you declared war on Israel?"

"You attacked us, Moshe. If you can't control your forces, you need to step down."

"It's not that simple. What do you suggest?"

"You're right. Surrender. Israeli forces will now be under UN command. Those who cannot follow orders will be removed and imprisoned as traitors. Acknowledge that we are in charge of your security." He heard a moan before the line went dead.

"I never thought I'd see the day when the United States would invade and take over Israel," said General Brown.

"The action is by the United Nations. I said that organization was changing and I intend to see it become a force for peace and equality. Until standing UN forces are fully established, the United States will bear the brunt. With the UN in charge in Israel and Palestine, there is a real chance for peace."

"If we don't get destroyed there and at home.

You haven't been in touch with what's happening here. Demonstrations may turn violent with the announcement that we are invading Israel and Palestine."

"Yeah, lots to worry about. We have to forge ahead."

Chapter 84

Breakfast was fresh fruit and bagels with cream cheese served on David's patio overlooking Lake of the Woods. The coffee was hot and strong. "I've received some word that our team tracking the money has made some progress," said David. "If you want an internet connection to check with your people, I have that."

"I have satellite connection," answered Daniel. "We determine Russian group hit Chinese chip manufacturer with ransomware. They pay two millions of dollars, but Chinese government not like that. Think they hire mercenaries."

"We weren't that far along with our investigation," said David. "The question now is what we do about it?"

"First, we find mercenaries and kill them." said Daniel. "Then we deal with Chinese."

"Any more info on them?" asked Kiki.

"No. Man was Mossad agent who went private. Dead woman still unknown. No lead on other women or on man who got nerve agent. We have people in Mossad who will help us if I ask."

"Wow, Mossad is usually not forthcoming with information about their people."

"Colonel Zoloniski says we will ask forcefully. Don't like that, but at dead end."

"We still have warm weather." David waved his hand at the lake. "Would you like to sail again?"

"Would like to, but need to go to Russian embassy. They will send car to my hotel when I am back."

"We'll close things up here and drive in this afternoon. Is that good enough?"

"Da. Thank you for enjoyment."

* * *

In the lobby of their hotel, Daniel thanked them again for the break. "I will return in two days. Perhaps start again with investigation team."

"I'll send out a memo that we will meet on Tuesday," said Kiki.

Daniel took her hand. "A pleasure to meet you, Ms. Sorvino. Perhaps we will meet again."

"We will see each other in the meetings."

Daniel entered the elevator. David and Kiki went to the coffee shop. Kiki glanced around, but they were seated away from any other people. "He is dangerous to us."

"Yes," agreed David. "What do you propose?"

"I like him, but he's too good. I believe he'll find Ilia, Sasha and Zyra. The Russians may have to break some heads, but that's SOP for them.

"Us too, sometimes. If they question them, it'll lead to Nick and you. Nobody's as good as Nick at interrogations, but eventually they will break someone, and it will involve a lot of pain."

"We have to derail or divert this investigation. We have to give them someone." Kiki looked at David. "Daniel still has to go."

"But not on American soil. That would raise suspicions and cause a lot of diplomatic problems."

"We'll come up with a plan, probably best if you don't know. I'll need a ride to Idaho. Can Ron arrange it? Also, five new IDs for Nick and me, Ilia, Sasha and Zyra. Our plans will involve international travel."

"I'll talk to Ron about his jet and have the docs expressed to Idaho.

Chapter 85

"Your UN troops got into a skirmish with Israeli soldiers doing their job," complained Moshe Ayub.

Ron glanced at General Brown. "With the UN troops there, your soldiers have no job."

"They were serving warrants against terrorist organizations. They had every right."

"Your designation of those aid groups as terrorist organizations had no merit. The UN has ordered you to stop. Besides, the Gaza and the Occupied Lands no longer are under your jurisdiction. They are part of Palestine. Withdraw your troops."

"We will not."

"You want Israel to go to war with the United

Nations? Just because you were able to take over lands that weren't yours does not make them so–especially with your record of human rights violations."

"We only do these things to protect ourselves."

"I believe the Germans used the same arguments in World War II. All wars are justified the same way. The only way to end this continuous fighting is to stop."

"How naive of you. Hamas will send more rockets. Israel will be attacked again. The lives lost will be on your head."

"And if you retaliate, they will retaliate. The only way that ends is with the extermination of them or you. Is that what you want?"

Moshe was silent. "We have lost many lives because of them. Those cannot be forgotten."

"They have lost many because of you. At some point we must begin a new day. The United Nations troops are giving you that opportunity. Take it."

The Israeli Prime Minister hung up.

Ron called the Chairman of Hamas. "Yousaf, Israel is very concerned that more rockets will be launched. Please assure me that isn't so."

"We have many factions not under our direct

control. I am trying very hard to make them see the Zionists will be gone."

"What can we do to help?"

"The removal of Israeli troops from our lands is working, but faster would be better."

"Yousaf, if rockets are fired, we will destroy the launchers and those responsible. If attacks are made, we will destroy the attackers. This peace must hold and cannot be derailed by a few discontents. I may have to call on you for help. It's not always enough to destroy the launchers. Those who set them on that path have to be targets also."

"You would make me a target of my own people. We have many who have lost families, fathers, sons. That cannot be forgotten."

"Nor should it, but seeking revenge would only lead to more death. The Prophet can help if you can put him in touch with your people."

"Yes, our meeting with him was most remarkable. He is celebrated as the Prophet from Allah returned and revered by all Muslims. Perhaps he can calm the hatred."

"He is the envoy from God, everybody's God. He will be visiting the Jews also."

"I pray to Allah this works."

"Thank you, Yousaf"

Ron cut the connection.

"How long before the UN troops are the enemy?" asked General Brown.

"It will happen after the attacks against those refusing to acknowledge the authority of the UN. Another conflict between Israeli soldiers trying to serve warrants where they don't back down or refusing to allow passage of refugees into Palestine which will be met with UN intervention, will be the spark. Or when we destroy another rocket launcher with crew and then the headquarters."

The general frowned. "You are purposely trying make us the bad guys."

"Yup. Eventually they will hate us more than each other. Then it will be time to leave."

His phone rang again. "David, haven't heard from you in a while."

"We were sure your hands were full. We need to start the conference on cybercrime again. That was the spark that ignited the conflict you're in at the moment."

"Yes, but it's been smoldering for decades. You are right about the conference. We have to reach international agreement about how to treat cybercrime. Do you think you could chair?"

"I am involved in the investigation into the terrorist attacks in Russia, but we've made progress. I can fill you in over drinks. By the way, Kiki needs to have your plane fly her to your ranch. She needs to meet with your guests."

Ron paused, the wheels turning as to what was going on. "Sure. I'll call my pilot. When does she need to fly out?"

"Tonight. Perhaps while we're having those drinks."

Chapter 86

The cruise ship docked in Sochi at eleven in the morning. It was crowded with tourists and skiers there for the start of the ski season. Sasha arranged for their gear to be taken to their hotel. Ilia, Sasha, and Zyra had changed their appearances. Sasha had black hair and black-framed glasses, Ilia wore wireframed glasses and a wig, and Zyra had light makeup, dark glasses, and a shawl. She was pushed down the gangway in a wheelchair. Ilia had arranged for their two rooms. Sasha, Ilia, and Zyra had a two-room suite, Nick and Kiki a single king. They met in the suite.

"I've arranged for a passenger van," said Ilia. "It will come tonight with the other equipment we will need. My friends also have eyes on Colonel Zoloniski. His routine is known."

"We will leave early in the morning for

Moscow," said Kiki. She picked up her phone. "Bob, are you on line?"

"I'm here. I've hacked into the communications system for the Cyber Security Command."

"Great. Where are we on the misdirection project?"

"The money trail leads from China to the Gorneski group, Russian mafia specializing in assassinations. I've put files in their database for Sol and Dawn, changing her background, of course. I'm going to put small files in about Ilia, Sasha and Zyra. They are contractors occasionally doing work for the mafia. There will be only fake names and blurry pictures."

"Good work. We'll let you know when we are set up in Moscow."

"Be careful. Once you start, this bell cannot be un-rung. There will be a nationwide manhunt."

"We know."

* * *

The two-day trip had exhausted them, so they took a day to sleep and recover. Meals were room service; nobody left the hotel.

"I had hoped to never return here," said Sasha. "It's so cold, and not just the weather." She was sitting in the room wearing her long black fur coat.

"Maybe need meat on bones," remarked Zyra.

"Ha ha. You're going to find out how cold when you go out."

Zyra looked at the others. "I go now." She wore an ankle-length black leather coat and a black sable hat. A black scarf covered her face.

"Bob, are you ready?"

"Yeah. Zyra, walk in front of the assassins' headquarters. Stop, remove your scarf and glance at the building across the street. I want them to get a look but not a good facial. Cyber Security has an observation room set up there. I'll do some magic with the video, so leave immediately afterward. Take a few turns, climb on a bus before walking back to the hotel."

"Da. I understand."

* * *

Daniel's satellite phone rang. He was instantly awake. "Hello."

"Detective, this is Colonel Zoloniski. One of our surveillance cameras picked up one of the terrorists coming out of the Gorenski headquarters. Either they didn't leave Moscow or they are back. I need you here. You have the most knowledge about them."

"I'll be on a plane tomorrow."

* * *

The group was gathered in the suite watching a video forwarded from Bob. It showed a figure coming out of the Gorenski building dressed in a long black coat with a black sable hat. She removed her scarf and glanced at the sky as if checking the weather. It was Zyra.

"This was forwarded to Colonel Zoloniski who called Detective Novikov," said Bob. "He will be arriving tomorrow morning about seven."

"Any way to monitor him after he's here?"

"I set up his phone like a microphone, but inside the Cyber Center, all signals are blocked. I can monitor internal communications as I hacked into the system."

"Okay, let us know what's being planned."

"Zoloniski is planning an attack on the Gorenski building. He's waiting for Novikov."

"Tomorrow?" asked Kiki.

"Probably. I have no time schedule."

"It'll be a cold night," said Kiki. "Okay, thanks. Keep us informed of any news."

She turned to the group. "I'll set up my hide tonight. Be ready to pick me up. We'll have to clear Moscow before any alerts go out."

* * *

Kiki used the small camera to see over the short wall looking out toward the Gorenski building. The range was three-hundred meters to the steps at the front door. The Dragunov rifle was bedded in sandbags back from the wall so just the tip of the silencer peeked over, crosshairs on the door. Though not familiar with the rifle like her .25-06, there could be no trace this was anything but a Russian operation. She'd leave it behind. She had scattered a few of the cigarette butts and the crumpled package from the terrorist in Arizona. It was a good false trail.

Her hide was an insulated winter cammo blanket covering her and the rifle. It blended in with the patchy snow on the roof. She would only peek above the wall after the targets were visible. It had been a long cold night. The weak sun was at her back, the temperature probably dipped into the low teens. The scarf over her face was frosted by the condensing moisture of her breath.

"He landed fifteen minutes ago. A car picked him up," said Bob. "He'll be there in thirty."

"Thanks. There's activity below," noted Kiki. "A busload of troops have surrounded the building."

"Guess Novikov will meet the perps at the Center for the interrogation," said Ilia. "We may have missed our chance."

"A colonel has gone in with several soldiers. I suspect that's Zoloniski." She waited and watched. *If I take out Zoloniski here, I'll never get a chance at Novikov.* muffled shots came from the building. *Sounds like they're meeting some resistance.* A car pulled up at the curb. A single figure got out and went into the building. *Is that Novikov? It's hard to tell with the hat and scarf.* She put the camera in her pocket and settled in behind the rifle.

Three figures emerged from the building. One was in handcuffs, one was the colonel, and the other was Novikov. They stood at the bottom of the stairs as a car pulled up.

Kiki inhaled and let half the breath out. She

stabilized, locking the rifle on the target. The one in handcuffs was Kiki's first shot, center of mass chest shot. The only sound the others would hear was the snap of the supersonic bullet. Momentarily confused, the two men watched as her target sank to the ground,. Within a second, she moved the crosshairs to the colonel. The rifle bucked against her shoulder with more recoil that her rifle. It was a chest shot.

She didn't know the rifle well enough for head shots, but both hits had been exactly where the cross hairs were. Both shots were killing shots as the heavy 7.62 mm bullet blew up their chests as evidenced by the red gore on the steps and door.

In the second since the colonel fell, Novikov dropped to the ground and scrabbled behind the colonel's body for cover. He peeked over, searching for the source of the shots. She placed the crosshairs on his face as he looked up at the rooftops. There was no panic as he squinted, looking for the shooter. She saw his eyes widen as he realized why he was here. *Sorry Daniel. You were just too good. I never miss.* His face seemed to cave in as the last shot struck. She gasped in horror as a phantom rose from the body and streaked toward her.

Kiki dropped the rifle and sprinted across the roof to the rickety fire escape. She flew down the stairs and jumped into the waiting van. Everyone was there. "Done," she gasped. "Let's get out of here."

Nick glanced at her. "You're pale as a ghost. Are you all right?" Kiki was frozen. "We gottta move."

Nick drove through connecting streets until they were able to get onto M-11 north to Saint Petersburg. It would normally be a seven-hour trip, but traffic made it a little slow today.

"Boy, you stirred up a hornet's nest," said Bob. "They're locking down the city. I think you're beyond the roadblocks, but I'll keep monitoring. They've shut down the train stations and the airport. The military frequency says they've found the rifle and some other evidence. Preliminary assessment is the Gorenski group is responsible. After your shots, the soldiers opened up and killed everyone in the building."

"Thanks, Bob. We'll stay in touch. Let us know of developments," said Ilia.

"I have tickets for us on the ferry to Finland,"

said Ilia. "We must catch the last one tonight."

Kiki appeared to be asleep as Nick and Ilia switched off on the drive. In Saint Petersburg, they drove directly to the dock. With suitcases of clothes and tourist trinkets, they walked onto the ferry, Ilia pushing Zyra in a wheelchair, shawled and hatted with dark glasses. Customs was ready for the day to end and the inspection was quick.

When the agent tried to get a closer look at Zyra, she batted at him with her cane. "Asshole!" she cried in a hoarse and raspy voice.

From the dock in Finland, they took the train to the Helsinki airport. Ilia and Sasha wore their disguises, Zyra remained in the wheelchair, muttering.

"You make a good crotchety old woman," said Nick.

"Fuck off!" responded Zyra. The laughter was a great relief.

Nick had kept Kiki close throughout the trip. She gave only yes or no answers to questions. He was worried.

The flight on SAS to Stockholm wasn't

crowded. Again, they cleared customs without incident, but Zyra was nicer to the Swedish agents. They made connections to Munich, then to London. It was an exhausting series of flights.

David's call directed them to a small jet at Gatwick. "I'll meet you at Orange County Airport." Exhausted, they all slept on the flight.

True to his word, David stood on the grassy strip as they landed.

"Why here?" asked Katherine.

"No eyes or questions. Katherine, you need to stay here to help me with the commissions and the investigation. We can't have you disappear from the sessions.

"K, will you be okay here?" asked Nick, a concerned look on his face. She nodded.

"The rest of you will go to Ron's ranch."

"Is boring there," said Zyra.

"Take up skiing," said Sasha, with a laugh.

David continued. "When the meetings in New York reach a stopping point, Katherine and I will join you. We need to do a major debrief. Nick, do you want to stay or go back to Arizona?"

"I do have a practice where I occasionally work. Arizona."

"We'll get you on a flight from Boise to Tucson."

"What about Ron?" asked Kiki, her first words since Russia.

"He's making some major changes in the role of the United Nations, so he'll be tied up for a while. Maybe he can take a break and meet us in Idaho."

"Major changes?" asked Nick.

It's going to be much more than a place to meet and discuss. Some countries won't like the proposed changes, but many will welcome them."

"That's always the way," said Kiki. "Let's get this investigation closed up."

"David, a word please," said Nick. They moved away from the others.

"Please keep an eye on Kiki. She's had a couple of episodes of PTSD. I'm worried."

"Stay here with us. You two can go together after we make excuses for her departure. I'll get someone else to help with the meetings."

"Thanks. We'll work on treatment as soon as we get back to Tucson. There are new techniques and drugs. I'm confident she'll work this out."

Chapter 87

Ron Carson stared at the text he'd received from David Kennedy. He was closing down the investigation into the attacks in Russia at the request of the Russian government. In the summation, it was explained the Gorenski group, Russian mafia contract assassins, were responsible for the attacks on the cyber community. The appearance of Chinese involvement was not airtight, but the Gorenski group had been eliminated. In the raid, Detective Daniel Novikov and Cyber Security Chief Zoloniski were killed along with almost all of the gang members. One Russian sniper was still being sought.

Why did this feel like the signature of Katherine and the other members of their team? He shrugged. One less thing on his plate, which was full of modifying the charter for the United Nations. His dream of a world government with the power to reduce conflict and ensure human rights was one step closer. There were many steps to go.

He picked up the phone and called David. "I got your text. Please send me a hard copy with any comments you wish to add. Glad to hear the investigation is closed, which brings us back to the cybercrime proposals. How's that going?"

"The Middle East dustup caused a delay, but with the attack on the Israeli Cyber Division being the spark that ignited the conflict, there's a feeling of urgency. I've got one committee working on definitions of cybercrime while another is considering penalties and enforcement. We're paralleling the programs."

"Good work. The United Nations will have to come up with a force of police to administer the laws. Nations won't like foreign soldiers on their shores."

"It's either that or drone strikes like we do with terrorism," said David. "You could get away with that with smaller nations, but I can't see Russia or China putting up with it."

"Western nations either. The threat may be enough to have the problem solved domestically, at least that's the hope."

"Maybe after a few demonstrations. That's

kinda what you're doing in Israel, isn't it?"

"The UN used peace keepers before. These forces are more aggressive."

"Before that's over, they'll have to be a lot more aggressive, as in occupying. You do realize massive demonstrations are being planned by the pro-Israel factions."

"Yeah, the pro-Arab factions also. If nobody's happy, I know we're on the right track."

"You want them fighting the UN and forget about each other, don't ya? UN troops won't be happy about that."

"It's either that or pull out and let them battle to the death. If we threw up a blockade so arms couldn't flow in, that wouldn't take long."

"They'd resort to simitars and lances. These conflicts have been going on for centuries. I don't believe there will ever be peace."

"If the Prophet is right about the future, peace will reign because everybody will be dead."

"Any idea of the time frame for this catastrophe?"

Ron paused to think. "I'm pretty sure it won't be in our lifetimes." *Maybe.*

David sighed. "I'm going fishing. Let the kids

handle it."

"Speaking of the kids, how are they doing?"

"Katherine and Nick are here in New York with me. Zyra, Sasha, and Ilia are at your place in Idaho but getting restless."

"Them restless? That's not good."

"With the terrorists dead in Russia, I think they can return to Israel."

"What do you mean?" asked Ron.

"Through some crazy misidentification, they were suspects in the terrorist attacks. Now that it's solved, maybe they can travel."

"You owe me an explanation."

"I can spin a tale, if you want. Or I can give you the truth. Which is it?"

"Shit. I knew they were mixed up in this. And that sharp detective Novikov?"

David said nothing.

"At this stage, it's best if I don't know, but I want a full accounting written up and locked away. Someday I may want some bedtime reading."

"Yes, sir, but I don't think it will put you to sleep."

Robert Clayton

Long-time Tucson resident R. L. Clayton's career as an author began in earnest when he published his first book in 2012. "I wanted to write a story about human evolution going forward, the theme in the *Evolution River Series*. *Sea Species* is the unrecognized next step occurring now. The true scope of the age of genetics is beyond our understanding." Clayton's science fiction trilogy, *The Evolution River Series* takes a fanciful path from humans today to the eventual end of evolution.

Clayton's next endeavor, *Wings of the WASP* was a departure from science fiction. "My mother was a pilot in WWII, a member of the Women Airforce Service Pilots. I wanted to write a story about them, but not another documentary." This historical novel is based on an incident that happened to his mother, and though fiction, it portrays many of the issues those women faced and illustrates the spirit of the WASP.

In yet another genre, Clayton published *Dead & Dead For Real* in 2016, the first book in his "Dead" series of techno-thrillers. This fast-paced series explores chilling all-too-real scenarios, some taking place today.

All of Clayton's books take place in Arizona and the Tucson area. "I have self-published my books because I'm impatient." His books are available at local bookstore, Mostly Books. Print books are available directly from his website, www.rlclaytonbooks.com. Both print and e-books are available online. "I enjoy hearing from readers and entering into discussions about my stories. Email me at rlclayton10@gmail.com." Facebook:www.facebook.com/RLClayton-492878487412902, www.facebook.com/people/Robert-Clayton/100011735257224,

Twitter; twitter.com/rlclaytonwriter

www.ingramcontent.com/pod-product-compliance
Lightning Source LLC
Chambersburg PA
CBHW061611210726
48287CB00001B/88